by Robert Weinberg

Book I
THE ROAD TO HELL

a World of
Darkness
Trilogy

THE ROAD TO HELL is
a product of White Wolf Publishing.

Cover Illustration: Jason Felix
Cover Design: Michelle Prahler

White Wolf Publishing
 780 Park North Boulevard, Suite 100
Clarkston, GA 30021
World Wide Web page: www.white-wolf.com

PRINTED IN CANADA

AUTHOR'S NOTE:

While the locations and history of this world may seem familiar, it is not our reality. The setting for *The Horizon War* is a harsher, crueler version of our own universe. It is a stark, desolate landscape where nothing is what it seems to be on the surface. It is truly a World of Darkness.

Certain concepts and characters have been inspired by those originally created by Bill Bridges, Steven C. Brown, Phil Brucato, Elizabeth Fischi, Chris Hind, James E. Moore, Micky Rea and Stewart Wieck.

"For it is not the least of its terrors that this evil thing is rooted deep in all good..."
— from *Dracula*
by Bram Stoker

Prologue

hadow of the Dawn was just finishing an
exercise with her twin swords, a complex
series of maneuvers known as the Serpent's
Teeth, when she spotted a stranger watching her
from the trees. Somehow, the man had traversed
the surrounding wilderness without her becoming
aware of his presence. Attuned as she was to the
essence of the land, Shadow had thought such an
act impossible. Though she continued her exercise
without pause, she kept her eyes focused on the
outsider.

Moving with the grace and beauty of a stalking
jungle cat, Shadow refused to allow the stranger to
disrupt her concentration. With incredible skill,
she wove Scream and Whisper around her body in
a *Do* tapestry. The two swords were no longer
separate forms, but extensions of her limbs, and the
air quivered with the force of her blows. Though

many sword masters liked to shout as they fought, Shadow worked soundlessly; her blades alone would speak for her.

Tall and slender, she had saffron-colored skin and long black hair, which she wove into a simple braid tied off with a round wooden dowel. Few knew that two spring-driven steel blades were concealed within the decorative accessory. When necessary, even her hair piece served as a weapon.

She wore a loose-fitting blue jacket and comfortable pants. Her oval shaped face bore a small nose, thin lips and bright green catlike eyes with long black lashes. While she was not considered beautiful in the standard sense of the word, Shadow possessed *interesting* features. With a sly, enigmatic smile, she had intrigued more than a few men in the short span of her adult years.

A twist, a turn, and two quick thrusts completed the pattern. Only then did Shadow lower her swords and allow herself to examine her unexpected visitor.

Tall and golden skinned, the stranger was broad-shouldered with a trim, tapered figure. His muscular arms were folded across his chest, and Shadow noted that both of the man's long, delicate-fingered hands were covered with tattoos, though she could not make out the markings. He had a strong, powerful face with square jaw and short, closely trimmed dark beard, and long thick hair that curled in a ponytail down his back. A bold hook nose gave his features a slightly Semitic look, and a tiny diamond chip in his right ear glistened in the morning sun. His large, dark eyes smoldered with an inner fire.

The stranger wore a pair of blue jeans, a heavy wool parka, black leather boots, and a fur cap. He looked to be about forty years old, but Shadow knew that appearances could be deceiving.

"Greetings, Shadow of the Dawn," said the man, his deep voice resonating through the clearing. He remained stationary, the slightest smile curling his lips. "I wish you well on your twenty-fifth birthday."

"My thanks," said Shadow, her swords held at the ready, crossed in front of her body. The young woman trusted no one. Though she was certain she had never encountered this man before, he knew her name. She did not like what that implied. Still, as her mentors in the Akashic Brotherhood had taught her, she remained polite. "Who are you, distinguished sir, and why are you here?"

"Your skill with the swords is extraordinary," said the man, ignoring her question. He spoke with quiet dignity and supreme confidence. "I've seen many great fighters in my long life, but you are without question the finest."

Shadow bowed her head slightly, never taking her gaze off the stranger. She disliked mysteries. "Again, my thanks for your compliment," she said. "However, I must inquire a second time. Who are you and why are you here?"

"My identity is unimportant," he replied. Lowering his arms, he took a step forward. The twin blades in the young woman's hands did not seem to concern him. "Think of me as a weary, lonesome traveler, striding out of history to find you."

His eyes blazed with energy. "The wheel of Drahma has turned another cycle, Shadow of the Dawn. Serious events are soon to occur. The time for waiting is over; the moment you have been expecting all of your life is at hand. Your destiny calls."

The young woman laughed, a soft, tinkling sound like water cascading over stone. "Am I a naive child to believe the words of a stranger without a name who comes upon me like a snake in the woods? You must think me a stupid Tokyo city girl. Or a fool, beguiled by the mysterious prophecies of a bearded man."

"I know you are neither," said her visitor. He took another step closer to Shadow, his features suddenly grave, his voice turned cold and distant. "As a student of the ways of the Akashic Brotherhood in the Fukuoka Chantry House, you took the name, Questing Child. The title described you well, for you hungered for knowledge and enlightenment. After seven years, you found you had learned everything the school could offer. Seeking inner wisdom, you came here, to the slopes of Mt. Kuromasa, a holy place where the greatest warriors of the Brotherhood have trained in solitude for centuries. Traces of their presence still haunt the mountain. Because you rose each morning with the sun, you changed your name to Shadow of the Dawn."

Shadow's eyes narrowed with suspicion. The stranger knew more about her than she thought possible. She lived alone in a small hut at the edge of the great forest that surrounded the mystic peak—alone except for the beasts that inhabited the great forest. The intense solitude and tranquility suited her meditations. It disturbed her to realize that her actions had been monitored, unbeknownst to her, by unseen watchers.

"You are evading my questions," said Shadow.

"Strange and horrifying events are brewing throughout the Tellurian," said the stranger. "The fabric of the Tapestry of All Things is going to be ripped and torn asunder, twisting reality in a manner unseen for five hundred years. Unless this is stopped, there will be a frightful war in Heaven. And possibly, hell on Earth."

Despite her suspicions, Shadow shivered. Her *Do* training enabled her to detect lies as they were spoken. The stranger was telling the truth. Or at least he was saying what he believed to be the truth. The young woman was not foolish enough to accept mere words, no matter how convincing, as proof; the bearded man could be a Marauder, one of the insane magick makers who believed only in chaos. Truth was a coat of many colors and hues, not all of them visible to the naked eye.

The stranger seemed to sense her doubts. Chuckling, he shook his head. "I did not expect you to believe me. Why should you? That was why I revealed my knowledge of your past."

Pointing to her two swords, he continued. "Like many mages, you channel your magick and direct your will through specific objects. Your two blades came off the wall of the armory at Fukuoka. You picked them yourself. Though you were unaware of their history, they had been waiting for you for nearly half a millennia."

His gaze turned to her long sword. "You call your katana Whisper." Moving his head slightly, he focused on the matching shorter blade. "The wakizashi, you name Scream. Appropriate titles for such deadly weapons. They glow with mystic energy."

With the slightest shrug of his shoulders, the bearded man slipped out of his jacket and tossed it to the ground a half-dozen steps away. His hat followed. A thin, royal purple silk shirt covered his chest. His whipcord-lean muscles rippled beneath the material.

"Warriors throughout the world consider a katana the finest sword ever made," declared the stranger, flexing his arms and taking a few deep breaths. "The blade, with its sharp, triangular point, is designed for slashing and slicing. The metal has been folded and refolded hundreds and hundreds of times to strengthen the steel of the weapon. It can be held with one or two hands. I know you are mistress of both such fighting styles."

Shadow said nothing. Senses alert, she scanned the clearing, checking for other intruders. She saw no one. They were alone. Whatever the outsider planned, he meant to do it alone.

"You are an Akashic Dragon Scale, a swords mistress of tremendous strength," the bearded man declared, his dark eyes glittering. "There is magic in your twin blades, Whisper and Scream. No warrior can stand before your skill. You have never been beaten in a duel. Yet, I am not afraid. I challenge your might, Shadow of the Dawn. *Strike me if you can.*"

Shadow's eyes widened in amazement. She was not easily surprised, but the stranger's request was entirely unexpected. It was an invitation to murder. And, despite the outsider's seeming lack of fear, she hesitated to cut down an unarmed man.

"Strike," repeated the bearded man, chuckling. He sounded smug and self-confident. "My life is my own to risk. Accept my challenge. I know what I am doing."

"That I strongly doubt," muttered Shadow. With a smooth motion, she sheathed Scream in the scabbard hanging from her belt, and wrapped both hands around Whisper's hilt. The double grip gave her more precise control over the blade. She could peel an orange using its razor sharpness. "But we shall soon see."

Drawing a deep breath, the young woman let the internal magick of a *Do* practitioner fill her thoughts. Moving faster than sight, she lashed out with Whisper, aiming for the stranger's shoulder. Such was Shadow's total control of the katana that she intended only to nick the man's arrogance. But, she soon discovered that the bearded stranger had good reason for his insolence.

With a slight twist of his torso, he turned slightly to the side, avoiding the blow by scant inches. "Miss," he declared with a dry chuckle. "Try again?"

Needing no urging, Shadow whipped the sword up and then down in a lightning-fast strike at the man's other shoulder. Again, with a barest change of position, he moved out of the blade's path. There was no fear in his expression, only amusement.

This time, however, Shadow was prepared for the motion. Flicking her wrists, she sliced upward and across, aiming to slice the bearded man across the chest. Seemingly without effort, the stranger dropped to his knees. Whisper cut harmlessly through the air above his dark hair.

"Missed again," he declared. "You must try harder. I am unarmed and yet untouched."

Frowning, Shadow pulled her sword back and assumed attack position, her hands waist high in front of her body, the katana held skyward. She couldn't understand how the stranger escaped her blows. Even a mind reader could not anticipate the sudden, random attack of a *Do* sword fighter. Besides, Shadow sensed that the man was not using any type of magick for protection. More determined than ever, she resumed her attack.

The results were the same. Somehow, the stranger seemed to know where she was going to strike an instant before her blade moved. He twisted and turned and ducked and jumped with an annoying lack of concern. Once, he rapped his knuckles against Whisper's side as the blade slashed inches away from his fingers. Shadow used the Serpent's Teeth, the Creeping Mongoose, and the Cunning Hawk techniques, all without success.

Changing tactics, Shadow released her right hand from the sword. Using her left to guide the sword lessened the impact of her blows but heightened the speed with which she wielded the blade. The katana spun in a glittering net in the bright sunshine. Yet, nothing she did caught the stranger by surprise. Even a sudden switch of the blade from her left to right hand didn't work. He was always a step ahead of her.

After fifteen minutes of futility, Shadow stepped back and away from her enigmatic opponent. Though his face was flushed from exertion, the man was otherwise unharmed. Not once had he been touched by the steel.

Calmly, Shadow slid her katana into its sheath across her back. A true *Do* disciple never lost her temper. Faithful to her Tradition, Shadow felt no anger, only intense curiosity. She bowed her head to the stranger, careful not to let him out of her sight.

"I salute your skill," she declared. "Never before have I fought the wayward wind. I freely admit that I cannot harm you with my blade. It has been an important lesson in humility."

"If I came here to kill you," said the bearded man, his voice pleasant and slightly amused, "I could do so with equal ease. Your life is in my hands."

"Perhaps," replied Shadow. "I would not perish easily."

The man chuckled. "No, you would not. Still, you would perish. For not even a Dragon Scale warrior can defend herself against that which has already come."

Shadow's lips tightened as she pondered the meaning of the stranger's odd words. Members of the Akashic Brotherhood were rigorously tutored to think logically. Combining the stranger's actions with his pronouncements, Shadow swiftly extrapolated the most probable explanation of the man's talent.

"You can see the future?" she half-asked, half-declared. "That is how you defeated me."

"Of course," said the stranger. "I have followed your life since the day you were born. For the past ten years, I carefully studied your every movement in our duel today. Knowing in advance where you would strike, I was able to train myself to avoid each blow as it happened."

Shadow shook her head. She didn't like what she was hearing. "Then that which is to come is already set and we can do nothing to change it? Our feet walk on a path already chosen?"

"Nonsense," said the stranger. "The future is not static. I can see *possibilities*, not *certainties*. Destiny is not *what is*, but *what may be*. If I had chosen not to confront you this morning, our meeting would never have taken place. This conversation would not be spoken. And all of my preparations over the past decade would have been for naught."

"You see through the door to the future?" said Shadow.

"I do," admitted the bearded man. "Some call me a Time Master, though I prefer merely to be thought a seeker of wisdom. This brief demonstration was the quickest method of convincing you of my powers. I need your assistance. What I said earlier is true: a major conflict is about to shake the Tellurian to its foundations. After centuries, a great circle is finally closing, and a disaster beyond mortal comprehension brews. Will you accept your fate, Shadow of the Dawn? With your aid, I may be able to prevent what otherwise seems inevitable. Working alone, I cannot."

"You have seen the results of this battle?" asked Shadow.

"The repercussions have haunted my dreams for hundreds of years," said the bearded man. Shadow accepted the stranger's incredible life span without question. Time Masters possessed the power to halt or even reverse the aging process. They were virtually immortal. "At best—at the least—if this fight is lost, it will signal the destruction of the Nine Traditions. More than that I cannot reveal."

"At best?" repeated Shadow. Though she had been trained to conceal her emotions, she could not repress a shudder of fear. Features drawn, she turned horrified eyes upon the bearded man. "Who are you, stranger, that you bring with you such monstrous tidings?"

The stranger told her his name and his title. It was this revelation that convinced Shadow that the man before her spoke the truth. He was a traveler of history and legend. On this day, in this hour, the young woman finally understood her destiny.

"I accept my fate," declared Shadow solemnly. "As a Dragon Scale of the Akashic Brotherhood, I can do no less. Where you lead, I will follow."

The seer nodded, his features grim. His eyes were cloudy, as if they were studying things that were not visible. His voice sounded near and yet very distant. "I expected no less. Together we shall climb the stairs to heaven. And descend the road to hell."

Chapter One

A woman's voice, soft and urgent, woke him from a deep, dreamless sleep. "Number Seventeen," she whispered. "Number Seventeen. Get up, get up. There's not much time."

His eyes opened. Carefully, he surveyed the small cell in which he was imprisoned. Nothing had changed during the hours he had been sleeping. Not that he had expected anything different. The chamber held a small table and chair, his cot, and toilet facilities. He had neither a window, nor decorations of any sort. It was a stark, utilitarian room, a perfect example of the sterile environment his captors favored. In truth, the only difference between his cell and the offices of the scientists who maintained this facility was that his door consisted of primium steel bars while theirs were made of duralloy plastic.

"Seventeen," came the whisper again. The

woman sounded concerned, and with good reason. Talking between cells was not permitted. If she was caught speaking, her vocals chords would be severed. "Are you all right?"

"Yes," the man addressed as Seventeen replied. He had a deep, powerful voice. Rising off the narrow cot in the rear of the cell, he padded on bare feet to the reinforced metal bars that fronted the room. "I'm fine, Fourteen. What do you want?"

Though darkness shrouded the hall, he could see nearly as well as when the lights were on. His eyes adjusted without effort to the lack of light. Gripping the steel bars with both hands, he stared across the twelve-foot hall at the woman in the cell directly across from his. She would not have risked calling to him unless the matter was urgent.

"Tonight is the night," she declared, her voice taut with excitement. "Everything has come together in the past hour. All of the necessary elements are in place, and the probability curves are at their peak. Your chances of escape are at maximum. There won't be another opportunity like this for months. And by then, it will be too late."

"Tonight?" repeated Seventeen. Though he had been expecting the message for weeks, ever since they had begun planning the escape, he was still unprepared for the news. "You're sure?"

"I'm positive," whispered the woman. There was no hint of doubt in her voice. Tall and slender, with dark brown hair and matching eyes, she appeared to be in her mid-thirties. Like all of the captives imprisoned in the center known as the Gray Collective, she was one of the Awakened. Fourteen was an expert at reading and reshaping probability curves. Though the tall woman could not make the impossible happen, she could make the unlikely possible. "In a few minutes, the chances for your success will be at their highest possible probability levels. Unfortunately, the odds remain abysmally low. I suspect that they won't get any better."

She hesitated. "Are you still sure you want to try?"

For a moment, Seventeen didn't answer. He stood still, silently contemplating his mission. A shade under six feet, three inches tall, with broad shoulders, barrel chest, and narrow waist, he was a near perfect physical specimen. Muscles like steel ropes rippled beneath the flesh of his arms and legs. His body looked at is if were carved from granite.

Blunt, thick fingers capped huge hands capable of amazing feats of strength. His face was harsh and angular and totally without hair. Like all the other prisoners, he wore the stark gray uniform that served as their only clothing. More than once, Fourteen had made it clear in their conversations that he was the most imposing figure she had ever seen.

"I don't have any real choice," he finally replied, his thoughts crystallizing into words. "I'm not afraid. Once they close down this project, everyone's going to die anyway. We know much too much to be let free. Better I try to do something than be slaughtered without a fight."

"Remember," said Fourteen. "If you gain your freedom, you must locate my brother, Alvin Reynolds. He's a computer hacker and a willworker. We've always been close. I feel certain that Alvin's been searching for me. Find him and he'll come for me, no matter what the odds. The Gray Collective, tell him. The Gray Collective."

"If I survive, I'll find him," said the man called Seventeen. "When will the time be right?"

"In approximately three minutes. You should get ready. Once the shift changes in the laboratory, it will be time to start. You will have fifteen minutes to make your escape."

Seventeen put the plastic sandals that served as shoes for the prisoners into his trouser pockets. The first part of their plan required him to walk across the floor barefoot.

One last time, he scanned the contents of the small cell. There was nothing there that would help in his escape attempt. He had no personal property; none of the prisoners did. Their captors considered possessions to be mere emotional foolishness. Their world was a stark, antiseptic place of grays and blacks, of remorseless, unfeeling logic. And, if they succeeded in their work, it would become the future of humanity.

He positioned himself by the electronic lock on the cell bars. In theory, the door could only be opened by one of his captors, using an oscillating vibronic key set at the exact frequency of the lock. The locks were completely independent of the main computer system and thus continued to work even if the mainframe went down. However, like most mechanisms in this complex, the devices functioned partially through magick. A wizard possessing phenomenal powers over the flow of electrons could mentally spring the lock just by strength of will. The woman known as Prisoner Fourteen controlled such talent. And as long as she was alone in the cell block, she could use her power.

This prison block had been designed to hold mages captive. All of the equipment in the area functioned using both magick energy and electrical power. Supposedly, one source worked as a backup for the other. In truth, neither system was proof against a willworker who could effectively manipulate reality without causing noticeable changes. Despite their seeming differences, technological magick and supernatural magick were essentially the same force. The difference lay only in the perceptions of the users.

Four video cameras, constructed of near-indestructible carbonized polymers, were placed strategically on the ceiling to monitor every inch of the corridor. The cameras linked to a computer that immediately detected any motion on the floor. No one could enter the hall without being seen. The Technomancer wardens of the cellblock considered the machines infallible guardians, always alert and immune to inattention or weariness.

Heat detectors in the floor, switched on after human guards made their evening rounds, sounded alarms throughout the complex at the slightest variation of temperature upon their surface. It was impossible for anyone to walk across the corridor without setting them off.

A random number generator, part of the citadel's mainframe computer, controlled the combination of the heavy steel door that blocked exit from the room. Constructed of six-inch sheets of inert titanium, the barrier was proof against any physical assault. A bazooka shell wouldn't even scratch its surface.

Similar doors were scattered throughout the citadel, making traveling between sections of the compound impossible for all but an elite few who held one of the micro-computers directly linked to the complex's mainframe. Each area of the gigantic building was dedicated to a single objective and fraternizing between mages was discouraged.

No one had ever escaped from the confines of the Gray Collective. Few even tried. The penalty for failure was dire.

Four months earlier, one of the prisoners in their

cell block, Number Twenty-Seven, had built a hand-held teleportation device using tiny scraps of metal and string from his bedding. Serving as a focal point for Twenty-Seven's mage powers, the unit was only capable of moving him short distances. Still, the wizard, a short, cheerful fellow of unbounded enthusiasm, was convinced it would be enough.

Late one night, Twenty-Seven bade the others in the cell block goodbye and switched on his impossible machine. His first jump took him from his cell to the floor of the corridor. The second leap, with alarm bells shrilly ringing, transported him beyond the steel door. He never had a chance to attempt a third. The alarms ceased instants after he vanished into the next room.

Early the following morning, several guards, their stoic features an unnatural shade of green, entered the corridor carrying several large plastic sacks. They emptied the contents of the bags on the floor of the cell block and then left without saying a word. The grisly remains of Twenty-Seven spoke volumes. His body had been torn into a dozen pieces—hands, feet, arms, legs, parts of torso and head. Though much of the body was brutally mutilated, the man's facial features had not been touched. His horrified expression haunted the prisoners' sleep for days afterward. No one had attempted an escape since. Until tonight.

"Alvin Reynolds," whispered Fourteen, one last

time. "Tell him his sister, Cindy, is waiting. I'm here in the Gray Collective."

"I won't forget you," said Seventeen. Across the hall, the woman's face seemed to glow, as she summoned a small measure of the force of her will. The apex probability point was approaching. In a few seconds, the moment would be right. "I plan to be back."

Fourteen nodded. "Now," she whispered, closing her eyes in concentration. "Fifteen minutes are all you have between shifts. Do not waste a second."

Reality shifted on a microscopic scale. A quartet of circuits failed at the same instant. The outage caused the current image on the lens of the four overhead cameras to freeze. The picture transmitted to the main computer was static and unchanging. However, where a human operator might have questioned the fixed nature of the image, a machine did not. It was programmed only to note changes, not lack of changes.

The slightest click in the cell door lock indicated that Fourteen had successfully jumbled the electronic code of the mechanism. Muscles bulging beneath his shirt, prisoner Seventeen pulled at the steel bars with all of his strength. For an instant, the door hesitated, as if in protest to this sudden attack, and then, without a sound, it slid open on well-oiled tracks.

Hurriedly, the big man stepped out of the cell. Closing the door from the outside was easier than opening it from the inside. With no human guards patrolling the corridor at night, his disappearance wouldn't be noticed until morning.

The floor segments were keyed to report immediately any changes in temperature. Yet, as Seventeen walked across the sensors, no alarms sounded. He felt confident none would. In some manner he could not explain, the prisoner instinctively controlled every aspect of his internal chemistry. The soles of his feet adjusted to temperature of the floor tiles. There was no temperature shift to trigger the alarms.

Seventeen walked swiftly down the corridor, heading for the vaultlike steel door that separated the prison block from the laboratory. Inside the locked cells, the other prisoners watched quietly. Though few of them knew any of the others—each was subject to separate and equally grisly experiments—they shared a common hatred of their jailers. The captives could do nothing to help Seventeen, but they would do nothing to stop him.

Reaching the door, Seventeen stretched out his short, blunt fingers and pressed them onto the front of the huge metal slab. Unlike Fourteen, he needed actual physical contact to use his magick. His lips curled into a smile of satisfaction as he sensed the flow of encoded bits of information from the mainframe computer to the door's memory bank. Seventeen nodded, blending his thoughts with the data. Effortlessly, he inserted his own string of numbers into the pattern. In a microsecond, the new code replaced the current lock listing.

Raising his hands off the metal, Seventeen placed his fingers on the entry box and typed in the replacement information. With a satisfied hum, the steel door swung open, and Seventeen slid out of the prison complex and into the laboratory. Pausing for an instant, he slipped on his shoes; there were no heat detection units in the development center. Seconds later, the portal behind him sealed itself, and the lock reset with a new combination.

Anxiously, he looked around the huge research facility. No one was about; the entire place was deserted. The second shift had ended just minutes ago. Normally, men and women would already be filing into the laboratory to begin the next work cycle. A random security check of all personnel, however, had delayed them. In the paranoid atmosphere of the citadel, such protective measures were common. Tonight, coincidence had been twisted slightly to assure Seventeen precious minutes alone.

There were sensors everywhere. An ordinary man would have set off dozens of alarms, started automatic laser guns firing, and summoned the night patrol. But Seventeen was not ordinary. During his brief electronic conversation with the citadel mainframe, he had instructed the computer to ignore all future evidence of his existence. Thus, Seventeen no longer registered on any detection device in the building. He was a blind spot on the computer grid. Video monitors scanning his physical appearance immediately listed the space where he stood as empty: He was effectively an invisible man.

He walked at a brisk pace across the floor. There were too many tables set up at odd locations, too many fragile devices of unknown purpose scattered throughout the aisles, for him to run. The entrance to the shipping depot was directly across from the prison block. The loading dock was Seventeen's final destination. It was his only possible exit from the citadel.

He had been in the laboratory many times before. The technicians had run numerous tests on him in this chamber—one of several in the gigantic research center. By far, this lab was the largest and most important in the building. A square room a hundred feet on a side, with twenty-foot-high ceilings, it was filled with all sorts of scientific and magickal equipment. Computers and calculators rested side by side with well-worn slide-rules and mysterious gray powders.

In the exact center of the lab, dominating the room, was a sunken circular section of the floor fifteen feet in diameter, surrounded by a four-foot-high steel fence. Computer workstations were located at ten-foot intervals around the metal barrier. In the middle of the shallow pit stood a huge transparent Progenitor growth tube that stretched from floor to ceiling. Four feet wide, it was filled with a clear amber solution that was not water. Floating in the container, connected to it top and bottom by black umbilical cables that merged right into its flesh, was a humanoid figure. The being's eyes were closed and its chest did not move. But, somehow, the figure did not appear to be dead. Neither was it alive. To Seventeen, the thing in the gigantic test tube was merely waiting.

The floating being was sexless. It had neither male nor female sex organs. Still, it appeared completely natural. The rest of its body was perfectly formed: arms and legs were exactly symmetrical; muscles were clearly defined. It had the longest fingers Seventeen had ever seen. Nearly seven feet tall, the being had broad shoulders and a narrow waist. Its features were strong, dignified, even majestic. The pattern-clone appeared to be in perfect repose.

Seventeen knew nothing about the strange form in the tank, and yet, staring at it he felt a chill of apprehension sweep through him. From his visits to the lab, he understood that all of the energies of the Gray Collective were focused on bringing life to this artificial creation. It was linked in some unknown way with the prisoners in the cell block. From brief snatches of conversation overheard through the course of his captivity, Seventeen deduced that the being was the most advanced clone ever created by the Technocracy.

Banishing his fears, Seventeen padded past the

last few rows of workbenches to the doorway to the tunnel. He had never actually entered the loading area and didn't know what to expect. His eyes narrowed. The muscles in his arms and chest tightened. Neither Fourteen nor any of the other prisoners in the cell block had any knowledge of what lay beyond this doorway. From now on, he was entirely on his own. The only sure fact was that he had eight minutes left before his time ran out.

The crunch of broken glass saved his life. Seventeen dropped to the floor, spinning in place as he did so. Hurtling toward him at inhuman speed from across the laboratory was a nightmarish creation. In the fury of its attack, the monster had knocked a lab beaker off a counter. Otherwise, it moved without a sound. A horrid combination of man and reptile, it glared at Seventeen with black, unblinking eyes. Huge jaws filled with needle-sharp teeth gaped open like a bear-trap. Clawlike hands outstretched to rend and tear, the creature leapt into the air a dozen feet from the shocked prisoner. Here was the thing that had ripped Prisoner Twenty-Seven to shreds.

Reflexes Seventeen did not know he possessed saved him. Instinctively, he rolled to his left, his arms and legs tucked into a ball. The monster effortlessly hurtled the spot where he had been an instant before. With a crunch, the creature bounced into the heavy metal door leading to the service tunnel. The impact against the steel panel stunned it for a moment. Then, with a snakelike hiss, the lizard man whirled about, its hellish black orbs searching for Seventeen.

He wasn't difficult to find. With a thunk of flesh hitting flesh, the big prisoner slammed into the monster's midsection and grabbed it in a powerful hold, trapping its arms at its sides. The thing was cold and clammy, covered with sleek green scales. Legs pumping like trip hammers, Seventeen slammed the monstrous crossbreed with all of his strength into the metal door.

Sauroid. The word welled up from the depths of his memory as the reptilian creature tried to bend its head forward far enough to sink its huge teeth into Seventeen's back or shoulders, its fangs dripping with deadly poison. The sauroid, a savage killer of limited intelligence, was a product of the genetic growth tanks.

Desperately, Seventeen smashed the sauroid into the steel again. He was running out of time: In just a few minutes, the new shift of Technocrats would be entering the lab. If he was going to escape, he had to kill the monster, and kill it fast.

Hissing like a steam shovel, the sauroid planted its feet against the rear wall and lunged forward. Unprepared, Seventeen dropped back, his arms still wrapped around the monster. They tumbled to the floor. The sauroid's teeth snapped ferociously at air as it strove without success to rip Seventeen to shreds. Hanging on for his life, the prisoner kept his head pressed into the monster's chest and continued to squeeze.

Again, fighting skills he did not know he possessed came to Seventeen's aide. Arms still locked about the monster, Seventeen thrust himself forward until his hairless head jammed into the monster's lower jaw. Suddenly, the sauroid was unable to open its immense mouth. The creature grunted in unexpected pain. Seventeen, acting entirely on instinct, pushed up harder, wedging his head into the soft flesh beneath the sauroid's skull.

Its mouth clamped shut from the pressure beneath, the monster stopped hissing. Though it flailed wildly back and forth on the concrete floor, Seventeen's grip was unbreakable: The big prisoner possessed astonishing strength, and he refused to let go. The monster's struggles grew more and more desperate, as its head was forced further and further back. Digging his feet into the floor, Seventeen used the additional leverage to push harder. And yet harder.

Something had to give. With a crack that echoed through the silent laboratory, the sauroid's spine snapped. It collapsed like a rag doll in Seventeen's arms. Dead.

The prisoner rose swiftly to his feet. Normally, the sauroids roamed in packs of three or four. Fortunately, it seemed that this one had been alone. Still, he couldn't leave its corpse on the floor to be found by the incoming Technomancers; the resulting hue and cry would surely put a quick end to his escape attempt.

Seventeen scanned the lab for a place to hide the body. Precious seconds ticked away before he finally located a supply closet a dozen yards away. Arms aching, he hoisted the sauroid's body over his shoulder and carried it across the room. Luck was with him. While the shelves were filled, the bottom third of the closet was empty. He jammed the creature into the space. It would be discovered sooner or later, but hopefully not until after he had long departed from the complex.

Slamming the door, Seventeen rushed through the lab to the far door. The window of opportunity was rapidly narrowing. Any moment now, people would be hurrying to their posts. There was no time left for caution; he needed to be out of the chamber and onto the loading dock immediately. Grabbing the handle of the heavy steel door, he wrenched it open and barreled into the hallway connecting the lab to the delivery zone.

The short, cement block corridor ended in a long flight of metal steps. Gasping for breath, Seventeen bolted down the stairway. Fourteen had assured him that the loading dock would be deserted for fourteen minutes between shifts. By his reckoning, he had little more than sixty seconds left before the drivers arrived.

Abandoning all thoughts of caution, he burst through the door at the bottom of the stairwell, and found himself standing at the rear of a large dock filled with wooden shipping crates. He had no idea what was inside the boxes, nor did he care. He noted, however, that most of the containers were destined for "Everwell Chemicals, Rochester, New York." Oddly, the name struck him as important, though he had no idea why.

As Fourteen predicted, the place was deserted; but he knew that the drivers would be arriving any second, ready to depart the citadel with their cargo. All of the trucks were filled to near overflowing with the oversized crates. He squeezed into the least crowded trailer, and after some maneuvering, managed to hide himself behind several of the largest boxes. The space was cramped and confining, but comfort was the least of his concerns.

Thirty seconds after he had settled into place, the sound of men's voices drifted through a crack in the wall of boxes. Seventeen couldn't make out what the drivers were saying, but he could tell from the tone that they were calm and relaxed. Apparently no alarms had been sounded to signal the discovery of the sauroid's body.

A second later, the grooved metal door on the rear of the trailer slammed shut, leaving him in total darkness. A minute afterward, the truck's vast motor roared to life, gears shifted and the gigantic vehicle rolled forward. The air in the transport seemed to bend and twist as if for an instant, reality shifted. Seventeen knew for certain they had left the citadel behind.

The prisoner breathed a deep sigh of relief. Though he had no idea what his final destination would be, he knew that he was, at least, headed for freedom. He had completed the first step in his escape. Now outside the confines of the Gray Collective, he was no longer a prisoner of the Technocracy.

Still, in time, he intended to return to the complex. He had promised Prisoner Fourteen he would come back for her, and he never broke his word. But he also had a second agenda, equally urgent in his mind: the strange form floating in the growth tank. Seventeen shuddered as a wave of revulsion swept through him. Whatever that thing was, he knew without question that it had to be destroyed. No matter what the cost, the mysterious being could not be allowed to awaken.

Chapter Two

Comptroller Klair's dream always began the same way. He was in a huge, dark room, so vast that he could not make out the ceiling. The floor was the color of burnished copper and felt warm to his flesh. He was entirely without clothing. Nor did any of the biomechanisms with which he had enhanced his form, including his replacement hand and artificial eye, exist here: He was mere flesh and blood. The Comptroller felt certain that his nakedness served to emphasize the fact that he was not a being of wire and steel. *The Computer* liked to convey its messages in such a subtle fashion.

He stood before a vast Artificial Intelligence. The machine, stretching hundreds of feet high and hundreds of feet wide, was nearly the size of a large department store. The number of linkages in the computer numbered in the billions, and it contained enough wire to circle the Earth a dozen times. Visible in its walls were millions of lights, diodes, switches, circuit boards, and video monitors, but none of this meant anything; it was all for show. Micro-circuitry had long ago made such devices unnecessary. But, *The Computer* existed in symbolic as well as material form. Its appearance was dictated by what it had been as well as what it was.

In the past few decades, the titanic machine had expanded by a thousandfold as humanity's fascination with thinking machines grew. In a sense, *The Computer* was the center of an entirely new branch of mythology. It was the largest such artifact in the universe. To Comptroller Klair, and the other leaders of Iteration X—those Technomancers who believe that only through the combined efforts of man and machinery can humanity progress to Ascension—this machine was *The Computer*. It needed no other name.

As a child, Charles Klair had been fascinated by the movie *Forbidden Planet* and the Krell factory that stretched for miles and miles beneath the surface of the world. The gigantic machinery had captured his imagination and set him upon the road that led to Iteration X. In Comptroller Klair's thoughts, *The Computer* belonged in the Krell universe.

Lurking in the background of the chamber, almost but not completely out of sight, stood a legion of ten-foot-tall robotic figures. They were humanoid in design, with slender, whipcordlike legs and arms ending in razor-edged mandibles. Each mechanoid had a gleaming, silver, barrel-shaped torso and a squat soda-bottle head with one huge unblinking red eye directly in the center. Though the robots never moved during the Comptroller's dream, he feared them. Their purpose was clear: They acted as *The Computer*'s guards—and when necessary, they served as its hunters.

Few, if any, of the Technocrats had actually gazed upon the Artificial Intelligence that ruled their order. Klair had yet to meet one who admitted to having seen the cybernetic giant with his own eyes. *The Computer* communicated with its loyal followers through dreams like this one. In such manner, the AI kept its exact location a secret. What no one knew, no one could tell.

The Comptroller suspected, though he had no evidence other than his own deductive reasoning, that the gigantic machine existed in the center of the Pattern realm known as Autocthonia. Only in such a place, where the very nature of reality was fluid and shaped by willpower alone, could a structure the size and density of the gigantic machine exist. Klair was wise enough not to mention his deductions to his fellow Technocrats or *The Computer*. Too much knowledge could get you killed.

Though *The Computer* possessed mental powers beyond mortal comprehension, the machine was not all powerful. Often, what it did not say was just as important as what it did. By paying close attention to every word the Artificial Intelligence had spoken to him over the years, the Comptroller had deduced that the gigantic electronic brain feared certain unnamed beings who haunted the Deep Universe. Klair sometimes found himself wondering what horrors could be so grotesque as to frighten the most powerful thinking machine ever invented—he was not sure that he wanted to know the answer.

"Comptroller Klair," said *The Computer*. Its voice came from a hundred different speakers scattered throughout the body of the machine. Until recently, the machine had spoken in a raspy monotone, with a constant electrical crackle and hiss in the background. It had finally upgraded its speech capacities, fueled in part by the popularity of several science fiction television shows featuring computers with well-modulated voices. Now, the mechanical brain spoke with the bland, suave tones of an insurance salesman. "Step forward to begin identification processing."

These dreams always followed the same pattern. Klair felt certain that the machine used a basic subroutine to summon his sleeping mind to its headquarters, as the procedure and dialogue never varied. While *The Computer* might have achieved sentience, it still lacked creativity.

The Comptroller walked forward to the correct spot, then took his place in a high-backed steel chair without any sort of padding. Bright white lights shone in his face, nearly blinding him. Though it was only a dream, he felt uncomfortable sitting in the metal frame. He shifted about nervously. An unexpected surge of electrical power through the seat would fry his naked flesh to a crisp. If his mind perished in this dream, his body on Earth would remain an empty husk, devoid of intelligence, waiting futilely for his return.

A three-dimensional holographic face hovered inches away from Klair's own, a composite of a thousand images in the machine's memory bank. To the Comptroller it looked unnatural and inhuman. "State your identification number and position with Iteration X," said the computer-generated voice, the lips moving in perfect timing with the words. "Please be concise but complete in your reply."

"I am the human identified as GH23765," said the Comptroller, forming his numbers carefully. A misstated syllable could result in disaster. He did not take unnecessary chances. If the Artificial Intelligence doubted his identity, his life would be over. *The Computer* considered no human to be essential to its plans; not even Klair, who was in charge of the most important scheme the machine had ever attempted. Logic, not sentiment or loyalty, guided its every action. "At the moment, to ease communication with Technocrats not of our Order, I am using the title, Comptroller Klair. I am a loyal member of Iteration X. In service to Unity, I work as the coordinator of computer research and development for the AW project in the Gray Collective."

"Scanning your code now for verification," said the same bland voice, the eyes of the hologram staring directly into his.

Though only seconds passed, it felt like an eternity to the Comptroller, as he waited nervously. This obsession with identity checks was another sign to him that *The Computer* feared intruders. Why query someone who had been brought into your domain unless the possibility of infiltration existed? Klair did not like the implications of an enemy that strong. Or that clever.

"Your identity is confirmed," said the holographic face. "Retinal patterns, brain waves, and fingerprints match. No evidence of cloning is detected. You are the human, GH23765, now using the designation, Comptroller Klair. Report to me your progress on the AW project."

"The work proceeds as swiftly as can be hoped," said Klair. "As I explained in my last debriefing, Sharon Reed, the leader of the Progenitor faction in the compound, continues to be a major stumbling block in finishing the project to our satisfaction. No doubt she feels the same about me. Each of us has a personal vested interest in the success of the AW undertaking. She cannot complete the venture without our cooperation; however, we are equally dependent upon her assistance. Our teams of experts clash frequently over methods and techniques. Although the efforts of the Method Specialist, Terrence Shade, have prevented any actual violence, several times the situation has been tense."

"Their goal of achieving oneness with the universe is hopeless," declared the hologram. "Sooner or later, the Progenitors will see their error and join us. Iteration X offers the only logical course to Unity."

Klair nodded. Loyal to his order, he yearned for the day when all of the Enlightened would recognize the truth and become one with technology.

"Maybe," he said. "I am not counting on Sharon Reed's adopting of our viewpoint any time in the near future. Nor, for that matter, do I foresee that Terrence Shade will ever be persuaded. I feel certain that the Method Specialist reports on our activities to the Inner Circle of the Technocracy. The man acts as little more than a spy for the Union."

"Such behavior clarification for those two does seem remote," said the hologram. "Would removal of the female Progenitor speed up the completion of the project?"

"Unfortunately not," admitted Charles, though he hated defending Reed. "The woman is a brilliant genetic engineer and Technomancer. She does get things accomplished. Killing her would throw a random variable into our calculations: Her replacement could be immeasurably worse. At best, our timetable would be thrown back a week. At worst, it could mean delays of a month or more."

"Such postponements are unacceptable," declared the hologram. "Certain events in the Deep Universe require extra attention. The AW pattern-clone must be finished within the next ten days. You must cooperate with the woman until the job is completed. Afterward, her termination is required, as is the case with all of the inhabitants of the Gray Collective. The success of the project demands absolute and total secrecy."

"The necessary HIT Mark warriors stand ready to attack the moment the mission is brought to a close," said the Comptroller. He smiled briefly. The tracer bullets from the HIT Marks caused incredible damage. In his mind's eye, he envisioned Sharon Reed's head exploding like a ripe tomato. She had laughed at him once, mocking his biomechanical hand and eye as *tinkertoys*. Klair believed in repaying his debts. "I personally supervised their programming. No one involved with the AW development other than members of our Convention will survive the attack."

"You misunderstand my directive," said the hologram. The face twisted into something only vaguely human. "The elimination of *all* inhabitants of the complex is required. Only those of Comptroller rank are excluded."

Klair's eyes widened. "But, I'm the only Comptroller involved with this scenario. All the rest of the mages from Iteration X are Programmers or Armatures that I recruited from other collectives. They are dependable, loyal followers of our Convention. Several, including my assistant, Ernest Nelson, have served Iteration X for years."

"They are expendable," said the hologram. "As are the HIT Marks who will destroy them. Once the extermination is completed, you will supervise the deactivation and disassembly of the biomech assassins as well. Do you understand?"

The Comptroller didn't answer for a moment. He had just been ordered to kill everyone remotely connected with the AW project. Though cold and remorseless, he was neither vindictive nor cruel. Many of these people were long-time associates and friends. His actions were governed by his belief that what he did was in the best interest of humanity. Destroying members of his own Convention without reason was incomprehensible.

As if sensing Klair's thoughts, the hologram

added, "The ends in this situation justify the means. Are you prepared to carry out your assignment? Or should the responsibility be transferred to another Comptroller?"

"No, no," said Klair quickly. He knew that reassignment meant death. Either he cooperated with *The Computer*'s plans or he would be terminated. In basic technological terms, the prime directive guiding the Comptroller's life was survival. "I will reprogram the HIT Marks for total annihilation. The mission will proceed according to your wishes."

"Good," said the holographic face. For an instant, Klair thought he detected a note of satisfaction in the machine's artificial voice. That was, of course, impossible. "This project is an important step in our plan for achieving total domination of the Technocracy, and thus, all mankind. Failure could mean a delay of years in our assuming control."

The Comptroller recognized a threat when he heard one. "I will not fail. The AW undertaking will be completed to your satisfaction in the allocated time period." Klair paused. "Assuming there are no further modifications necessary to the pattern-clone."

"Only one minor modification," said the hologram. "Implementing the changes should not be difficult."

Grimacing, Charles looked down at the circuit

diagram that rested on his lap. It had not been there an instant ago. The problem with a dream was that the impossible was commonplace. *The Computer* operated at the speed of thought. Its word was all that was necessary for things to appear.

He examined the document closely. When he awoke, the schematic would be burned into his brain. Though often he found he could not remember many of the small details of his dream sessions with the Artificial Intelligence, the diagrams he studied in limbo remained imprinted in his brain. It was just another example of the machine's astonishing powers.

The frown on the Comptroller's face deepened as he studied the diagrams. "These revisions to the nervous system demand the impression of yet another set of molecular implants. The amount of work involved in such a task is considerable. Sharon Reed will not be pleased."

"The necessary alterations can be completed in sixteen hours," said the hologram, "if she allows the compound's mainframe to guide her nanotech drivers. It is your job to convince her of the importance of the improvements."

Klair looked down again at the representation. He shook his head in bewilderment. "The pattern-clone is already powerful enough to break into any data slipstream and substitute information and data. If I am reading these command signals correctly, this new subroutine will give him the ability to override the operating system of the computer and take charge of the central processing unit."

"That is essentially a correct if incomplete evaluation of the procedure," said the hologram.

Nervously, Klair bit his lower lip. It was a bad habit from his childhood, one that he had long ago suppressed, but which had returned since he had begun his work on the AW assignment. "Such a talent will give the AW pattern-clone absolute mastery over any computer he touches," he declared.

"Exactly," said the hologram. The three-dimensional image smiled, the first time the Comptroller had ever seen the representation express any emotion. "That will make it the most powerful being on Earth."

Chapter Three

The fax machine in Sharon Reed's bedroom beeped. Groggily, she raised her head from the pillow and cursed. "Son-of-a-bitch. It's the middle of the night."

Groaning, she threw off the blankets and sat up. Except for the glow of a small night light, the room was pitch black: After working in the bright lights of the laboratory for long periods of time, Sharon preferred absolute darkness when she rested. With a heavy sigh, she swung her long legs over the side of the bed and stood up. She sucked in a deep breath and padded over to the fax on bare feet.

Sharon Reed slept in the nude. She hated pajamas and rarely wore them. As the Progenitor Research Director on the AW project, she merited her own apartment in the Gray Collective, and kept the suite's temperature at a steady eighty degrees. Originally from southern California, she appreciated the warmth. The carpet, a biological creation from the labs, adjusted its temperature to that of the soles of her feet, and thousands of tiny hairlike bristles massaged her toes and heels as she walked across them. The floor covering was pleasantly warm to her touch, like the sand on a beach. In her isolated little world, clothes were not a necessity.

A tall, slender woman with short clipped brown hair that clung to her face like a helmet, Sharon looked too grim to be considered attractive. Her strong, gaunt features were always twisted into a grimace of annoyance. The trim fitness of her body suggested that she was in her late twenties or early thirties, when actually, she was close to eighty years old. An intense program of daily exercise combined with magickal drugs from the Pharmatologist branch of her Convention kept her looking and feeling young.

Sharon dropped down into the chair at the workstation in her bedroom and snapped on the overhead light. A single page rested in the out bin of her fax machine. As usual, there was no return station listed. This meant that the orders came from the secret administrators of the Progenitors.

The page held a single paragraph of instructions, printed in a complex code based on the structure of a specific DNA molecule that changed every day.

Sharon had no problem translating it, although it would be meaningless garbage to anyone else in the citadel. And the words were not unexpected.

Finish AW synthesis with all possible speed. Upon successful completion, obtain necessary tissue samples for cloning labs. Use sauroids to destroy prototype and eliminate all participants involved. Return cells to EcoR Horizon Realm.

"Short and sweet," murmured Sharon, smiling with satisfaction. She was pleased to have at last received the instructions she had been anticipating for weeks. They confirmed her own feelings about the AW project: It was much too important a venture to be shared with any other Convention—especially the fools from Iteration X and that demented metalhead, Comptroller Klair.

Carefully, Sharon ripped the fax paper into shreds and sprinkled it on the carpet. The tiny bristles whipped around the fragments hungrily, secreting minute streams of acid to dissolve the paper. In seconds, nothing remained. Sharon ran her tongue over her upper lip, wondering how long it would take to feed the Comptroller to her pet. She suspected it would take too much effort to slice him into pieces of the right size. Still, the thought amused her. It was worth serious consideration.

Sharon had been involved in the AW project since its inception, nearly a year ago. Most of the technicians working in the Gray Collective had been staff members at her research laboratory based in Minneapolis in the real world. New members had joined the team as required. There were approximately a dozen Progenitor investigators and associates living in the complex at the moment, and an equal number of Iteration X programmers and armatures also stationed in the building. While other research was conducted in the smaller labs, the main focus of attention was on the AW enterprise.

Sharon knew from personal experience that the Progenitor administrators juggled twenty or more important projects during the year. More than once, she had been transferred from one to another to handle a major problem that could not be solved by the team on site. However, never before had she been associated with so secretive a mission. Technocrats assigned to the Gray Collective were never transferred out. No details of their work were shared with other work groups. Communication with the outside world was strictly forbidden. It was quite unsettling.

Reaching across the fax machine, Sharon picked up the telephone and punched the button for her personal assistant's room. On the second ring, a woman's smooth, sultry voice answered. "Yes, director?"

"Velma," said Sharon. "Please join me for a game of cards. I have insomnia and can't sleep."

"Of course, director," said Velma. No matter when Sharon called, her assistant never sounded surprised or tired. She never questioned any request. "I'll be there in a minute."

Sharon replaced the receiver and rose to her feet. She knew better than to trust the phone lines with any message of importance. No amount of scrambling could keep secrets from the tech wizards of Iteration X. She felt equally certain that her quarters were monitored by Terrence Shade, the on-site representative of the New World Order. Deceit was his stock and trade.

By the time she had shrugged into a blue dressing robe, there was a knock on the door to her chambers. As the most important member of the Progenitor contingent at the Gray Collective, Sharon had the privilege of wearing colored clothing if she desired. She only did so in her private quarters. When working with her team, she dressed in the dull gray uniforms of her lesser assistants. Separating herself from the crowd did not create unity of spirit. Sharon had enough problems without having to deal with petty jealousy.

She pulled open the door to admit Velma. Her assistant was a short, petite woman, standing only a fraction over five feet tall and weighing less than a hundred pounds. This week, she had curly jet black hair that fell in ringlets to her shoulders, green catlike eyes, ruby-red lips, and skin as white as paper. Velma was an expert shapeshifter, and was constantly experimenting with her appearance.

Two factors about her never changed, however: She remained obsessively loyal to her mentor, Sharon Reed; and she possessed no moral or ethical code.

"I brought two decks of playing cards," said Velma, as she walked into the front room. Casually, she dropped the twin boxes onto the all-purpose table. "Did you want to continue our gin rummy game from last week? I saved the score sheet."

"That sounds fine," said Sharon. "Would you care for something to eat? Or perhaps a drink?"

"No thank you, director," said Velma, sitting down in her usual chair. "Please have whatever you like. I'll deal out the cards."

In their years working together, Sharon and her assistant had meticulously constructed a complex code system that involved a number of commonplace questions and answers. Each response triggered a signal to the other's enhanced memory until they had settled on a specific numerical sequence involving the cards in the playing decks. It was a technique available only to the gene masters of the Progenitors, thus ensuring that they could communicate without fear of their rivals learning any of their secrets.

"I hope I play a better game than I did last time," said Sharon, as she pulled a half-empty bottle of orange juice from her refrigerator. "You slaughtered me. I'm having some juice. Are you sure you don't want any?"

"I'm not thirsty, director," said Velma, clueing in

the final response line to the code. In all of their years together, Sharon had never seen her assistant eat or drink. The shapeshifter always dined alone. The director had her suspicions about Velma's metabolism, but kept them to herself; the woman's quirky behavior did not concern her. Velma was intelligent, trustworthy and clever, and with her quick wits, she could solve the most difficult problems with ease. She was much too valuable to abandon because of a minor mental aberration.

"According to my notes," said the dark-haired woman, passing a deck of cards to Sharon, "it was your deal."

Nodding, the director shuffled the playing cards carefully. Using their code required time and patience. Sharon had both.

Before they could complete a single hand, the door to the suite clattered with a loud, insistent pounding, as if someone were hitting the steel with a small jackhammer. Sharon shook her head in disgust. It was turning into one of those nights, where nothing went as planned. She had not been able to transmit even a line of the new orders to Velma. Obviously, they would have to wait. There was no mistaking the distinctive summons of one of the sauroids.

Velma, moving with pantherish speed, was up from her chair and at the door before Sharon could move. As expected, it was Sh-reeth-Sh, the commander of the snake men who served as security guards for the citadel. Covered with silver scales and standing nearly six feet tall, Sh-reeth-Sh possessed near human intelligence.

Seeing Velma, the creature hissed out its story in swift detail. Along with her many other talents, the dark-haired woman understood the language of the sauroids. The expression on Velma's face made it quite clear that the snake-man did not bring good news.

Snarling with anger, Velma hissed a series of commands to Sh-reeth-Sh. The creature nodded.

"What's happened?" asked Sharon.

"One of the night watch was found murdered in Laboratory One a few minutes ago," said Velma, her voice icy calm.

"Seal the building immediately," Sharon responded without pause. "We're probably too late, but we must go through the motions. How was the guard killed?"

"Its spine was snapped," said Velma.

"Damn! That can only mean one of the experimental subjects. They're the only ones with that kind of strength." Sharon hurried over to the phone. "I've got to call that fool, Klair. Then inform Shade. In the meantime, have Sh-reeth-Sh and his crew search the cell block. I want to know which of our subjects is missing and how he broke out. No delays."

Velma hissed the message to Sh-reeth-Sh as Sharon punched in the number for the Iteration X chief. When she looked up, the sauroid was gone. Velma stood nearby, waiting for further orders.

It took ten rings before Klair picked up the phone. The Comptroller must have been in a deep sleep. Sharon knew he couldn't be with female company. Klair had no sex drive, no desires other than to serve the machines. He was the coldest man she had ever met. In a way, they were very similar. She grinned at his groggy voice. Tormenting Klair was one of her greatest pleasures.

"Comptroller Klair here," he declared. "Who is this and what do you want?"

"Sharon Reed, Comptroller Klair," she said, maintaining a strictly neutral tone. She knew it was possible, even likely, that this conversation was being recorded. "One of the sauroids patrolling the Collective halls has been found murdered in Laboratory One. I thought you needed to be informed immediately. Of course, you understand that it can mean only one thing: A prisoner has escaped."

"*Fuck*," said Klair, no longer sounding sleepy. "I thought those beasts of yours were difficult to kill?"

"They are," said Sharon. "That's what worries me."

"It has to be one of the experimental subjects," said Klair, his thoughts duplicating hers. "We'd better close access from the Collective to the outside world. Then learn who's not in their cell. Search the entire complex. Damn, I thought after that last attempt our precautions had ensured that escape from that section was impossible."

"So you said," declared Sharon, inserting the needle. If Terrence Shade was listening, she wanted to make clear who to blame for the disaster. "I already issued the necessary commands. Nobody's leaving now. Though I suspect we're too late."

"I'll meet you at the cell block in five minutes," said Klair. "We can inform Mr. Shade of the situation after we've talked. No reason to involve him until we have all the facts. Maybe it isn't as bad as we think."

Klair was right in a sense. The situation was worse. Sharon stared at the empty cell in disgust. Velma stood a step behind her. The Comptroller's face was a mask of rage. A tall, gangly man, nearly bald with thin tuffs of brown hair above his ears, his unblinking mechanical eye was fixed on Sharon as if taking her photograph. "Prisoner Seventeen," he declared, his voice shrill with anger. "I warned you that he should be destroyed."

"I checked the records for the night," said X344, Klair's chief flunky. A short man with massive shoulders and brutal features, he had steel claws for hands and tank treads for feet. Mostly because it infuriated him, Sharon insisted upon calling him Ernest Nelson, his name before he had become one of the Enlightened. "No heat trace at all registered on the floorboards. Nor is there any record on the video tapes of his departure."

"Of course not," said Klair, sarcasm dripping from his voice. "Ms. Reed's experiments with blood and body modifications on Prisoner Seventeen gave him subconscious control over powers we had yet to completely catalog. He was a wild card and should have been destroyed immediately after our initial reconstruction was completed. But she refused to authorize his termination."

"Waste not, want not," snapped Sharon, her temper rising. At the moment, she would have gladly rolled Comptroller Klair in her living carpet and let the organism spend weeks devouring him. "Until the AW pattern-clone was fully functional, I felt we needed Seventeen alive for possible transfusions. If I remember correctly, you agreed with my conclusion."

Klair scowled. "It seemed the logical course of action at the time. I had no idea he was capable of escaping the cell block. How did he get past the vault door?"

"You insisted on placing neural links in his fingertips that led directly to his cortex," said Sharon viciously. "He probably hooked up with the mainframe and told the computer that he wanted out. The stupid machine opened the door for him."

"It's possible," muttered Nelson. "His interface procedures combined with the implants give him tremendous bypass controls. There are few computers that could resist direct override instructions."

"At least that makes it clear who's to blame for this disaster," said Sharon, sneering.

"Who assured me that the sauroids patrolling the corridors were a match for any escapees?" retorted Klair, his voice cold. "Why don't we talk about the dead body in the lab?"

"Enough bickering," said Velma unexpectedly. "Fault-finding isn't going to solve our problem. The important thing is to terminate Prisoner Seventeen before he becomes a major embarrassment to all of us. We've scoured the entire complex. He's gone. Vanished."

"A fleet of transports departed the Collective five minutes before we sealed the gateway between the Horizon Realm and Earth," said Nelson. "It seems unlikely that their departure and the prisoner's escape were coincidental."

"Undoubtedly he received aid and advice from others in this detention ward," said Klair. The Comptroller shrugged. "That they could plan an escape is no surprise. Such resistance was expected. We can discuss the appropriate punishment for the remaining prisoners later. First, as your assistant suggested, we must eliminate the escapee."

"He's on trucks bound for the Everwell Chemical factory in New York State," said Nelson. "Considering the locked doors and the speed at which the trucks travel, it's doubtful he would try to escape until they reach their destination. That won't be for several hours. We could contact the plant manager and..."

"Out of the question," declared Sharon, her voice sharp with concern. "Everwell Corporation supplies us with chemical supplies in return for special biotech projects. We do not want to reveal any of our secrets to them."

"We can stop the convoy en route," said Klair. "There is an Iteration X Institute in Syracuse. It's not far from the factory. Several HIT Marks can be instructed to rendezvous with the trucks before they enter Everwell grounds. It won't take the HIT Marks more than a few minutes to locate and destroy the escapee. The convoy can then proceed to make their delivery with no one the wiser."

"That sounds acceptable," said Sharon, much as she disliked agreeing with Klair. "You're positive those robotic killers of yours won't experience difficulties eliminating Seventeen? He's already demonstrated he's no ordinary target."

"Unlike your sauroids," declared Klair smugly, "the HIT Marks possess true human intelligence. They are not animals. Nor can their thoughts be overridden by a neural link. The machine men combine a mortal's brain with a near-invincible mechanical body. Arming them with the most advanced weapons available creates the finest killer elite in the world. They will not fail. Prisoner Seventeen is as good as dead."

"I hope you're right," said Sharon. Somehow, she had a feeling deep inside herself that she would encounter the escapee again. And she was certain the confrontation would not be pleasant.

Chapter Four

S t. Mark's Square stands in the center of Venice, Italy. The vast plaza is anchored at its eastern end by one of the city's most famous structures, St. Mark's Cathedral, a huge, thousand-year-old church. Nearby is the Doge's Palace, originally built in 1814, destroyed by fire four times, and rebuilt more opulently after each blaze. At the rear of the palace is the famous Bridge of Sighs. Beyond that noted historic landmark stands an immense, black skyscraper made entirely of glass and steel. Forty stories high, the imposing structure exudes menace. A wide courtyard surrounded by a twelve-foot-tall wall protects the building's privacy. Except for a street address, the edifice has no name. None is needed. Whispers throughout Venice call it The Mausoleum.

Robert Weinberg

Huge panes of darkened glass surround the top floor of the building. An office on that level would provide a commanding view of the entire city. Lines of sight extend for miles in all directions. In such a location, a king might survey his kingdom, an emperor his domain.

Peering out across the metropolis, Pietro Giovanni, the master of the Mausoleum, considered the comparison quite fitting. A tall figure with dark hair streaked with lines of silver, he had the face of an aristocrat. His skin was pale, his eyes a piercing gray. He wore a perfectly tailored dark blue three-piece-suit, a white shirt and a plain blue tie. A magnificent, oversized crimson rose decorated the upper buttonhole of his jacket. Pietro was an obsessive gardener, and not even his transformation into a vampire centuries ago had destroyed his passion for cultivating rare blooms. He called this latest creation a "Blood Rose." It had taken him nearly a hundred years to develop a unique strain of flower that lived on human vitae, and he displayed it on his collar proudly.

Smiling, the ancient Cainite turned his back on the city lights and returned to the comfort of the black leather chair behind his ebony desk. Except for an intercom and a telephone, the top of the desk was clear. Others in the Mausoleum handled the normal night-to-night operation of the building. Pietro dealt only with problems that did not require paperwork. As one of the most powerful

Kindred in the world, he did not concern himself with trivial matters.

The ornate grandfather's clock standing against the inner wall of Pietro's office struck midnight. One of only seven such instruments designed and built by the master craftsman August LeClair in the late 19th century, the clock had been given to him by Charles de Gaulle shortly after the conclusion of World War II, a gift for favors extended. Pietro considered it one of his most prized possessions. Though it was over a century old, the mechanism, an engineering marvel, had never lost a second. Now as the clock struck, the deep, rich chimes echoing through the immense room, Pietro turned toward the door a few feet away. As expected, the portal opened as the last notes sounded. Madeleine was never late.

Two figures entered the chamber. In the lead was a slender, attractive young woman with chalk-white skin. She had flashing eyes, dark hair and lips as crimson as Pietro's rose. Her outfit consisted of a simple black tank dress extending half-way down her thighs, black stockings, and low heels. Around her neck she wore a silver necklace decorated with the Giovanni family crest.

Her name was Madeleine Giovanni. She was Pietro's granddaughter. Among the Kindred, she was known as the Dagger of the Giovanni—and she had earned her title in blood.

Accompanying her into the chamber was her

cousin, Montifloro. A short, frail-looking man, he appeared to be in his mid-thirties. His eyes were dark and his thick hair was jet black without a streak of gray. Impeccably dressed in an Armani suit and Tuscany shoes, Montifloro looked like a typical midlevel management executive. Only his too-white skin and drawn features gave any indication that he was a member of the Kindred.

Montifloro and his brother, Cesare, normally worked together as a team on clan business. Cesare was a feared knife-fighter. Montifloro knew how to kill as well, but was noted more for his devious mind than his assassin's skills. He was an expert at manipulation and intrigue. The standard joke among Giovanni elders was "after shaking hands with Montifloro, be sure to count your fingers."

"Madeleine, my childe," said Pietro, half-rising from his chair in acknowledgment. "It is good to see you after these months. You are on time as usual."

"We have been in the building for hours, sire," said Madeleine, her tone polite. "Montifloro has not been here since before the latest round of remodeling. I was showing him around. I calculated our tour so that it brought us here at the stroke of twelve."

"You are as precise as my clock," said Pietro. He turned to Madeleine's companion. "Montifloro, you look as dapper as ever. Someday I must get the name of your tailor. How goes the work in Paris?"

"As good as can be expected," said Montifloro. He was by nature a pessimist. It made him suspicious of everything, a valuable trait for a Cainite. "The French continue to battle the European Union which we support. Cesare and I struggle constantly to maintain the family influence in such unstable times."

"Sit down," said Pietro. "I have much to discuss with the two of you tonight."

Montifloro settled into an armchair directly facing Pietro. Madeleine, who burned with energy and disliked any sort of confinement, perched on the arm of a second chair close by.

"Your efforts in France are appreciated," said Pietro politely. "The reward hopefully will be worth the long years of toil."

Shifting slightly in his chair, Pietro focused his attention on his granddaughter. "What news of the Mafia?"

"The destruction of Don Caravelli has initiated a savage power struggle among the many factions of the organization," said Madeleine, with the merest hint of a smile. She made no reference to the fact that she was directly responsible for the chaos, having destroyed the Capo de Capo in a duel ten months earlier. Madeleine was not a braggart. "Alliances are made and broken in a single night. Suppressed rivalries rise to the surface, shattering long-held truces. It is amusing to observe."

"Your hand remains unseen in the conflict?"

asked Pietro, knowing the answer before he asked the question.

"I use force sparingly," replied Madeleine. "Few among the possible successors to Don Caravelli are cause for worry. Those I eliminate, shifting the blame to gang warfare. Otherwise, I merely watch and wait. Whoever finally achieves mastery of the Mafia, I can assure you he will not be a threat to our clan."

"Splendid," said Pietro. "But, I expected no less from the Dagger of the Giovanni."

Pushing his chair back, the master of the Mausoleum rose to his feet and strode to the window. "I know you are both wondering why I summoned you here this evening. Recent developments are causing me great concern. While the matters you mention are important, I need for each of you to take a new assignment."

"What?" said Montifloro, scowling. "Cesare…"

"Your brother can handle the events in Paris without your aid," said Pietro, his brusque tone signaling that he was not prepared for an argument. "If there is a problem with the negotiations, Lisandro has recently returned from Mexico City. He can assist Cesare. I need your cunning elsewhere."

Madeleine, as usual, said nothing. The ultimate weapon, she accepted each assignment without question. Of all the Giovanni, she was by far the most deadly.

The Road to Hell

"During the past few decades," continued Pietro, "a number of extremely important clan intrigues involving the volatile fuel market turned sour. These were long-range plans, some dating as far back as the end of the Second World War. In all cases, a globe-spanning energy conglomerate named Endron International was behind the failures. The clan elders were not pleased. They wanted explanations.

"Acting on *my* advice, they turned to Enzo Giovanni, the leader of our family in England. He was, in my opinion, the logical choice for the job. As chairman of Irish Eyes Enterprises, Enzo controlled numerous newspapers, TV and radio stations. He had the necessary resources to investigate Endron. It did not take him long to discover that the conglomerate had ambitious plans to dominate the world economy by manipulating the major sources of oil. There were even vague suggestions that Endron was part of a larger, more dangerous conspiracy."

"I've heard of Endron International," said Montifloro. "They are very slick. Too slick, in my opinion, to be merely an oil company."

"Once or twice I encountered agents for the corporation," added Madeleine. "I found them *distasteful*."

"They employ scum," said Pietro, raising a hand for silence. "The organization is without honor. Needless to say, the elders instructed Enzo to take control of the corporation. In 1993, several members of the Board of Directors of Endron International were killed in an eco-terrorist attack. Using all of his considerable business acumen, Enzo succeeded in gaining a chair on the Board. He has been a member of the group ever since."

Montifloro nodded. "Typical of the way our cousin operates. I worked with Enzo years ago when he first started Irish Eyes. He is a brilliant tactician." He laughed. "Eco-terrorists? I expect that Endron International will soon be ours?"

"No," said Pietro Giovanni, his voice harsh and filled with anger. "Not at all. That is why you are here, Montifloro."

Walking back to his desk, Pietro sat down in his black leather chair. Opening a drawer, he pulled out a manila file and dropped it on the desk, his eyes burning with rage. He flipped open the envelope. There was nothing inside.

"Here is the sum and substance of our reports from Enzo about the inner workings of Endron International. We receive sporadic messages from him, referring to unspecified problems and numerous delays. Facts and figures are never supplied. We know no more about the energy giant and those who stand behind it than we did when Enzo first joined their ranks. There is growing talk of treachery."

"Betrayal?" asked Madeleine, her gaze fixed on the empty file. "Surely you are not suggesting that

Enzo has turned his back on our family, grandfather?"

"Over the past three years, Vesuvius Inc., a publishing giant closely linked to Endron International, has acquired through secret market transactions a majority of stock in Irish Eyes Enterprises," said Pietro slowly. "Enzo's former company."

Fury smoldered in his voice as he spoke. "Clan Giovanni no longer owns that corporation or its numerous media outlets. Its loss has been a major setback in our plan for Great Britain. Without Enzo's complete cooperation, such a takeover would have been impossible. For some, that loss is evidence enough."

"I don't understand," said Montifloro. He sounded bewildered. "There must be another answer. Enzo has always been loyal. He and Cesare and I spent many long hours together. He is Giovanni. Why would he suddenly become a turncoat?"

Pietro leaned forward, his arms resting on the ebony desk, his eyes fixed on Montifloro. "That is what I want you to learn, Montifloro. You were selected by the clan elders as the one most capable of discovering the truth about Enzo. Has he turned against his family and clan? Or are there other circumstances of which we are not aware? Go to America. Investigate our dear relative, without raising his suspicions. Learn his secrets. Then report back to me personally."

"As you command," said Montifloro. Though he looked less than pleased, he sounded resigned to his new assignment. "I will make arrangements for my departure immediately."

"Tomorrow night will be early enough," said Pietro, with a wave of a hand. "Your transportation has already been arranged. Enzo has recently relocated his center of operations to an old factory in New York state. I believe the name of the city is Rochester."

"I will return with the truth," said Montifloro, his expression grim. "Enzo knows and trusts me. We are old comrades. Deceiving him about my mission will not be difficult."

"Be wary, Montifloro," said Pietro. "You're not the first who has tried to investigate Enzo. Others have been sent to monitor his activities over the past few years. None have returned. They vanish without a trace. The full resources of our family are at your disposal. Do whatever you must. But, find me the answer."

"Honor over death," declared Montifloro, rising from his chair. It was evident from Pietro's tone that the conversation was at an end.

"Honor over death," said Pietro, repeating one of the basic tenants of Clan Giovanni. "Now, leave us. I wish to speak with Madeleine alone."

Montifloro bowed his head slightly to Pietro and

then to Madeleine. Without another word, he exited through the same door they had entered. The antique grandfather's clock chimed the half-hour with his departure.

"Very dramatic, grandfather," said Madeleine, once the sound of the descending elevator indicated that Montifloro was gone. "Do you have a similar job for me? Studying the love life of the prince of Paris, perhaps? Or learning the whereabouts of Caine?"

Pietro smiled. "You mock me, childe. Is that how you show respect to your sire?"

Madeleine laughed. "I am a dutiful servant of my clan and my sire," she declared. "However, you frightened poor Montifloro into thinking he was stepping through the jaws of hell. Was that really necessary?"

"I truly suspect that Montifloro may be entering Infernal Regions," said Pietro, his expression sobering. "If so, at least he is persuasive enough to convince Lucifer he is only a tourist."

Leaving his chair, Pietro strolled across the room to the antique clock and rested one hand on the delicate instrument. Madeleine swung around on the arm of her chair to keep him in sight. Pietro smiled. His childe didn't like to have anyone behind her. He appreciated her caution.

"Our family controls great power, Madeleine," he said, weighing his words carefully. "Sometimes we forget that there are others who are equally dangerous. In the past year, you dealt with several such individuals."

Madeleine shrugged. "You think mages are involved with Enzo?"

"When the Red Death threatened to gain control of the Kindred," said Pietro, "it was Dire McCann, a willworker, who thwarted him."

"McCann was no ordinary wizard," said Madeleine.

"Nor was Rambam and his pupil, the young man Elisha who accompanied you on much of the adventure," said Pietro. His eyes narrowed as he watched Madeleine for any reaction to his words. "Have you been in contact with the apprentice spellcaster since those days?"

"Not recently," said Madeleine, her voice level and unconcerned. "I believe Rambam sent him to Switzerland to study with a noted sorcerer. Our last conversation was months ago."

"Too bad," said Pietro. "For what I need to tell you concerns him as well as you."

"How so, grandfather?" said Madeleine. There was a hard edge to her voice that had not been there an instant before.

"Do you recall the night I summoned you here, shortly before your battle with Don Caravelli?" asked Pietro.

"I remember perfectly," said Madeleine. He knew she had not forgotten. Madeleine never overlooked a slight. "You suggested my loyalty to Clan

Giovanni was suspect. The implication was that I had fallen in love with Elisha and was about to abandon my family honor."

"Not true, my childe," said Pietro. He disliked discussing the matter, but he had no choice but to continue. "I was worried that Rambam might have tempted you with an offer to restore your lost humanity. It was foolish of me to doubt you."

"You are never foolish, grandfather," said Madeleine, her tone neutral. "No offer was made, nor would I have accepted such a bargain. Elisha and I were friends and I thought he would make a powerful ally for our clan. I still feel the same. You were misinformed about my motives."

Pietro bared his teeth. He removed his hand from the grandfather's clock. In his anger, he might damage its fragile workings. "I was told a deliberate falsehood," he snapped, his temper rising for a second time that night. "One of Rambam's associates came to me and accused you of deceit. This man, a powerful sorcerer totally lacking in scruples or honor, had sold me secrets in the past. He swore that what he told me about you was absolutely true."

"He lied," said Madeleine. There was a dangerous glint in her eyes. "I do not know his motive. But I will learn it. What was his name?"

"I made an oath that night," said Pietro, "that if I discovered the wizard had played me for a fool, he would die a horrible death. Months have passed. The time has come for revenge."

Pietro paused for only an instant. "His name was Ezra."

Madeleine smiled, her bloodless lips curling with pleasure. "I suspected as much. He and his sister, Judith, were very close to Rambam. It follows that one or the other had tried to turn you against me. I just was not sure which."

"Yet you acted against neither," said Pietro. He walked up to his childe. She rose to her feet. They stood, eye to eye, separated by a few feet. "You are very patient, Madeleine."

"It took me many long years to destroy Don Caravelli, grandfather," said Madeleine, her gaze never wavering. "I am not concerned with time. Vengeance comes due at the proper moment. It seemed best to wait until you decided to honor me with your trust again."

Pietro chuckled. "You are too devious even for me, my childe. I want this Ezra to pay for his insult to you and our clan. This assignment is much more dangerous than the one I gave to Montifloro. As a wizard, Ezra controls great forces and can twist reality with his mind. He will not be easy to kill."

"I am very persistent," said Madeleine, with the slightest of smiles. "As Don Caravelli discovered. Ezra will be a challenge. But he shall not escape the Dagger of the Giovanni."

With a harsh laugh, Pietro walked over once

again to the huge tinted windows that looked out across the city. He peered into the darkness as if searching for answers. "Locating him may prove more difficult than you realize," he stated, gazing at the sleeping metropolis.

"He no longer serves Rambam?" asked Madeleine. The young woman in black had moved soundlessly to Pietro's side.

The master of the Mausoleum shook his head. "Not since the night he visited me. He evidently realized that in making his accusations he was cutting off all ties with the past. Instead, Ezra has forged a new alliance, with influential figures in the business world." The words rolled off his tongue. "Friends in the oil industry."

"Endron International," said Madeleine in disgust. "How do you know so much about these affairs, grandfather? Since when does a Giovanni elder interest himself in the doings of scum like Ezra?"

"By now, I thought you would have guessed," said Pietro, with a dry chuckle. "Why do you think I summoned you and Montifloro here tonight? Your two assignments intersect. Years ago, it was Enzo who introduced me to his friend and confidant, the rogue sorcerer, Ezra.

"Last week, my spies in Rochester reported that Enzo received an important visitor in his offices at the Everwell Chemicals in Rochester. They sent along a photograph to be identified. Needless to say, it was his boon companion, Ezra. The two were obviously engaged in some new intrigue."

"*The devil never sleeps*," declared Madeleine, quoting an old Italian proverb.

"So it appears," said Pietro. All trace of humanity was gone from his voice as he spoke. "*Find the mage and kill him*, my childe. If you discover that Enzo was plotting with him against our clan, destroy the traitor as well. I sent Montifloro on his mission merely to serve as a distraction. You are the true hunter. Stamp out the enemies of our family without mercy. *You are my dagger. Strike deep.*"

<u>Chapter Five</u>

The steady rumbling of the huge transport lulled Seventeen to a state of near sleep. Safely hidden in his narrow space between boxes, he half-dozed as the big trucks made their way to their destination, a place he believed was named Rochester. The hum of the tires on the highway was peaceful and steady. Now that the excitement of his escape had worn off, a sense of strangeness gripped him. Somehow, he knew that sauroids were rarely defeated in unarmed combat— especially by a human opponent. Yet, the beast had done no damage. His body was unharmed, unmarked. Seventeen felt fine, except for a gnawing hunger that burned in his belly.

He was starving. The sharp pain in his stomach made it clear that he needed to eat as soon as possible. His metabolism had shifted into high gear during the attack and he was burning calories at an incredible rate. As soon as the transports reached their destination, Seventeen planned to slip away and find some food. He wasn't exactly sure how he was going to pay for it. But, minor details like that were the least of his concerns.

The truck holding him had been speeding along for well over an hour when gears suddenly whined and brakes screeched. Seventeen grunted in pain as several of the boxes surrounding him shifted with the abrupt change in momentum. The big trailer truck vibrated violently as it rumbled to an unexpected stop. Seventeen wasn't sure of the reason. However, he thought it highly unlikely that the trucks had reached their final destination. An unplanned delay meant only one thing: trouble.

Careful not to disturb any of the crates, Seventeen unwound himself from his hiding place. It was pitch black inside the truck. Cautiously, he crawled over the boxes to the rear of the vehicle. He wanted to be at the rear door of the transport when it opened. There was no question in his mind that he would have only seconds to act. He was correct.

Steel thumped against steel and the rear cargo door of the truck slid upward. A thin beam of moonlight splashed across the cartons. "No way someone could be in my vehicle," a man was saying, his voice indignant. "We're very careful at the..."

In an instant's grace, Seventeen's eyes registered a short, heavyset man talking to a much taller, powerfully built figure wearing a long black trench coat. A surge of adrenaline rushed through his body as he leapt forward with the ferocity of a hunting tiger. There was no question of his intended target. He needed to take advantage of the second's worth of surprise to do some damage. The newcomer was a HIT Mark cyborg, the most deadly killing machine in the world. Possessing a man's brain, the HIT Mark was impervious to his control over computers. It had to be destroyed physically.

The driver's sentence ended in a scream of absolute panic as he spotted Seventeen's form flying out of the truck. He stumbled backward, off the concrete highway. The HIT Mark stood his ground, his mechanical form whirling in a desperate effort to meet Seventeen's attack. Covered by a combination of real skin and imitation flesh and disguised by the billowing coat, the cyborg appeared almost human. But there was no hiding the flicker of red laser light blinking every few seconds in the cybernaut's eyes.

Seventeen slammed into the cyborg's head with his right shoulder. Though it weighed well over three hundred pounds, the angle and momentum of Seventeen's attack knocked it sprawling to the pavement. With a skill that bordered on magickal, the prisoner flung himself on top of his victim. Acting entirely by instinct, Seventeen grabbed the

HIT Mark's left arm at the elbow with both of his hands and wrenched with all of his strength. Metal snapped and the limb collapsed, useless.

"You cannot escape," declared the cyborg, swinging its other arm at Seventeen's back. The cybernaut moved with lightning speed. An ordinary man would have been smashed to pulp, but Seventeen was not ordinary. Effortlessly, he dropped beneath the clublike hand. Rolling off the machine, Seventeen wrapped his fingers around its upper arm and jerked. The elbow crunched like a piece of rotted wood. Joints were the robotic killer's one weak spot. Red laser eyes blinked in astonishment. The HIT Mark had obviously never been forced to engage in hand-to-hand combat before. It was not trained in the deadly art of street fighting.

The cyborg, however, was not one to give up. Driven by a human brain merged with an artificial body, it was conditioned to continue the fight at all costs. Arms hanging uselessly at its sides, the machine man kicked up and out with its powerful legs. Seventeen leapt to his feet, barely avoiding the blows. The cyborg was damaged but definitely not disabled.

From the direct center of its chest, a whiplash tentacle of steel slashed out at Seventeen's face. He jumped back as a serrated claw snapped shut an inch from his nose. "You cannot escape. No matter how hard you struggle, you are a dead man."

"Everyone dies," replied Seventeen, without thinking. He answered as if by rote. "But the spirit is immortal. That's what matters."

"Damned sonofabitch stowaway causin' me trouble," screamed a man from behind Seventeen. Again, acting reflexively, Seventeen dropped flat to the ground. A laser beam flared where he had been a second before. Pain seared across his back, but the feeling disappeared almost immediately. Ten feet away, the heavyset driver of the truck waved a high-intensity laser gun. "I'll kill you."

Gripping the pistol with both hands, the trucker fired a second blast. But Seventeen was already on the move, scrambling toward the enraged driver. Instead of hitting the stowaway, the beam sliced into the face of the HIT Mark cyborg as it struggled to regain its footing, its flesh bubbling and splattering as its face collapsed. The cyborg halted as it attempted to clear its vision. The laser fire had temporarily blinded it, but it was still functional. The blast had merely given Seventeen a few seconds of breathing time.

Taking immediate advantage of the moment, Seventeen wrenched the gun out of the trucker's hand. A twist of Seventeen's fingers and the man was dead. Hurriedly, he ripped the wallet out of the driver's back pocket and stuffed it inside the neck of his uniform. It might prove useful later—assuming there was a later. Seventeen felt no moral qualms about killing; there was no time now for mercy or pity. Death was part of life. And he seemed to possess a talent for murder.

Thoughts whirling, he assessed his situation. He realized he was in extreme danger. The HIT Mark was already clearing its eyes with its metal claw, and would be after him again in an instant. Behind him, heavy steps pounded the pavement. There had been a total of four trucks in the convoy, which meant there must be at least four cyborgs close by. Luckily, his transport had been last in line, which bought him precious seconds. The noise of the scuffle had caught the attention of the other HIT Marks, and they were heading his way. But he knew that this time there was no chance for surprise.

"Termination mode," snarled the partially disabled HIT Mark behind him. It was on its stomach, crawling toward him, arms dragging uselessly at its sides. Like the tentacled claw from its chest, a chain gun had popped up from its back. The automatic rifle chattered death.

Seventeen leapt to the left, out of harm's way. The cyborg was unable to shift position quickly enough to follow. Hitting the ground in a forward roll, Seventeen came to his feet running.

The escaped prisoner knew he could never outrun the HIT Marks. They weren't extremely fast, but they were tireless, and he was already nearing the limits of his endurance. A straight dash down the highway was out of question: Their chain guns would nail him before he had gone a hundred yards. His only hope for escape was to go somewhere they could not follow. Which meant taking advantage of the dangerous terrain.

The highway cut through the slope of a mountain. To Seventeen's right, the ground rose at a near forty-five degree angle. To his left, the earth dropped away at a much steeper incline. Rocks and small bushes randomly dotted the landscape but offered little hope of shelter. It was either up or down and he had to make his decision immediately. Seventeen chose to go left. The cyborgs might be able to climb up—but climbing down could pose a problem.

Leaping over the low, metal guardrail, Seventeen scrambled in a zigzag pattern across the cliff face. It was nearly impossible to maintain his footing on the shifting earth. Pebbles and stray clods of dirt flew from beneath his feet. He moved as fast as he could without losing his balance—one misstep and he would tumble into darkness. From here, he could not see the bottom of the gorge; the mountain descended into blackness.

In less than a minute, he was shrouded in shadows, a hundred feet from the road. The angle of descent made every movement precarious. Finding a small outcropping of rock, Seventeen paused for breath. It was then that his enemies stepped into view.

Three cyborgs, all near-exact duplicates of the one he had attacked, were positioned at the guard rail, hesitant to attempt the steep mountain grade. Though they looked human, the cyborgs did not have the balance or agility to chase Seventeen across the face of a cliff.

Three pairs of red eyes gleamed brightly in the moonlight. "You cannot escape," called one of the trio, raising an arm. The dark barrel of a chain gun emerged from beneath the black overcoat. "Death is the only possible end."

"Like hell," cursed Seventeen and flung himself to the left. Light seared his eyes as the cyborg fired. A sharp pain raked his back as the earth around him exploded. Face first, he slammed into the rocky face of the cliff. Desperately, he clawed for handholds in the earth. If he started rolling, he knew it would be impossible to stop.

His fingers had just wrapped around the edge of a half-buried boulder when a second hail of bullets raked into his side. Seventeen's body arched in torment. Hands and feet twitched uncontrollably and for an instant, his mind went blank. He began to fall. Another jolt of pain stabbed him in the back, and then, yet another. As he fought to stay conscious, he heard one of the robotic killers declare confidently, "That finished him."

Round and round Seventeen fell, his body bouncing and rebounding off the hard earth. A blood red haze clouded his every thought. Yet, through it all, a small center of reason remained. The robots thought he was dead. His only chance to survive was to convince them that they were right.

Seventeen tumbled down the bleak face of the mountain with horrifying speed. He made no attempt to stop or even slow his descent—doing so would alert the cyborgs that he was still functional. It was the longest minute of his life.

The fall came to an abrupt stop when he slammed with stunning impact into a huge boulder. He remained there, unmoving, plastered like a flattened bug to the side of the stone. His body was ripped and cut in a thousand places. The prisoner's uniform from Gray Compound was in shreds. Four laser blasts had struck him. Blood was everywhere. A small pool was forming on the rock, while a crimson streak on the side of the mountain marked his path down the slope.

Dead proclaimed his thoughts. Extending his will, he broadcast the idea upward at the cyborgs. A human mind controlled each biomechanical body. As such, the HIT Marks were susceptible to intense mental suggestion. *Dead, dead, dead,* Seventeen proclaimed with the full force of his intellect. *The target has been eliminated.*

"The human is dead," declared the lead cyborg. The sounds drifted to Seventeen through the night air. He remained unmoving, displaying no signs of life. "Our mission is complete."

"We were instructed to destroy the prisoner entirely," said a second machine man. "His form remains intact."

Robert Weinberg

"I can sense no indications of life," declared the third cyborg. "My readings of his life signals are nil. The man is dead. The angle makes any further laser blast futile. Any attempt to better our position or reach the body could cause our destruction. There is no logical reason to take further risks."

"Automobile traffic approaches from the west," declared the lead cyborg. "If we remain, we will be spotted. The convoy drivers are anxious to continue on to their destination. Our intervention has already delayed them. We must leave, before anyone stops to see what is happening. Discovery by ordinary mortals would be a major disaster, requiring further killings. We have no authorization to take such action."

"His breathing has stopped," said the second machine man. "I accept your conclusions. He is dead. Let us depart."

Seventeen waited for five minutes after he heard the roar of the departing trucks before he let his bodily processes return to normal. Even then, still concerned that the HIT Marks might make an unexpected reappearance at the railing, he waited another fifteen minutes before he actually moved.

Finally satisfied that he was alone, Seventeen rose shakily to his feet. He drew in several deep breathes, clearing the dark mists from his mind. His body ached from the enormous punishment it had endured, but the damage was nowhere near as bad as he had originally believed. Obviously, his magickal combat skills had saved him from major injury. And his amazing ability to control his body had enabled him to fool the cyborgs' senses.

Carefully, Seventeen checked his wounds. Though his clothes were badly charred, his skin was hardly singed. What he thought to have been major hits must have been mere grazes. He was bruised all over but nothing felt broken. The blood on the rocks came from cuts caused by collisions with the debris on the slope. Despite all of the action, or perhaps because of it, he still felt enormously hungry.

Miraculously, the wallet he had stolen from the trucker remained stuffed inside the shirt of his prison outfit. It had survived the chain gun attack and the long fall without damage. Seventeen opened the billfold and counted seventy dollars. Enough cash to buy him food to satisfy the ever-present pangs in his stomach. Though first he had to escape from this gorge and get a ride to someplace civilized. He planned to eat, then try to locate Prisoner Fourteen's brother. How he was going to do that he had no idea. He had a name to trace—Alvin Reynolds—and nothing else. He suspected it was going to be a difficult assignment.

Chapter Six

It was a hot, humid night on the shores of Lake Ontario. Though it was hours after midnight, the beach was still crowded. Most of the action was clustered around the boat dock that stretched like a long wooden finger out into the stagnant water. The lake was covered with a foamy green rot, born of more than a century's worth of pollution. No one cared. Dead, bloated fish were scattered all across the beach, their moldering bodies filling the air with a noxious smell. No one noticed. Life on the beach reflected the same corruption and decay that gripped the city itself. Rochester had died years before, but the rotting corpse refused to remain still.

Thugs and hoodlums ruled the sand. Men wore tight black sleeveless muscle Ts and baseball caps turned backward, though the temperature was still in the nineties. They carried knives openly at their sides and concealed guns in their waistbands or in shoulder-holsters. Many wore gang colors, though the beach was considered neutral, safe territory.

The women dressed in bikinis with thong bottoms and push-up tops. Some wore wrap-around skirts, not for modesty, but to protect their legs from sparks from the blazing fires. Their faces were heavy with makeup and eyeliner. None of them ever went in the water. Though most of them were still in their teens, their expressions were as hard as the grim faces of their male companions. And most of them carried knives as well.

Two huge bonfires kept the shadows at bay. The Latino gangs controlled this section of the beach. Most of the regulars had come to the northwest from Puerto Rico in search of work. Poorly educated, speaking only Spanish, they found the only jobs were working at the Everwell Chemical plant on the lakefront or selling drugs. Dealing paid better but the mortality rate was a lot higher than working at Pentex.

Loud music, driven by an intense Latin beat, blared from an old sound system on the pier. Young couples danced wildly to the demanding beat, their sweating bodies pressed close together. Others, many of them high on wine or drugs, writhed passionately in the shadows beneath the dock. Few worried about whether they would be seen. Their lust pushed all other concerns away.

Robert Weinberg

A short distance up the beach, in the shadow of a broken-down lifeguard station, a large, heavyset man watched the proceedings with the slightest smile on his thick lips. He stood a few inches over six feet tall and weighed close to three hundred pounds. Dressed in a black suit, white shirt, and black tie, the observer had ruddy red cheeks, bushy hair and a dark goatee and mustache. The glare of the fire reflected off his unblinking eyes. Enzo Giovanni often came down to the beach to watch the revelers' late night celebrations. Their antics provided him with much amusement. He enjoyed watching the puppets dance.

His gaze was fixed on a young, dark-haired woman, perhaps twenty years old. For the past three nights he had spent the entire evening gazing at her. She intrigued him. Tonight he had decided to speak to her. He had been looking for someone like her for a long time.

The girl wore a white bikini top with a thong bottom covered by a transparent white lace beach robe. The skin-tight bathing suit clung to her wide hips and large breasts like a coat of paint, barely containing her short, trim figure. As in nights past, she stood at the edge of the crowd, her lush body swaying to the music. During the past hour, three men had approached her. Two she had sent scurrying away with a withering glance and a few sharp words. A third had tried to grab her by the arm. The girl easily evaded his clutching fingers and then kneed him in the groin. As the thug bent over, screaming in pain, she sliced off part of an ear with her switchblade knife. After that, no one else bothered her.

Enzo glanced down at his Rolex watch. It was late and the caravan from the Gray Collective was due in shortly. Much as he enjoyed watching the foolish play of the living, it was time for him to make a decision. His eyes focused on the girl in white. He admired her brazen attitude and wild courage. She was a cruel, merciless fighter, just like him. Enzo nodded. She would have her say. If the girl proved to be disappointing, human life was cheap.

His eyes narrowed in concentration. The girl pursed her lips, then frowned as if remembering something forgotten. Gathering her purse and skirt off the sand, she stepped away from the crowd and walked into the darkness. She moved slowly, deliberately, almost as if she were guided by another's thoughts. No one seemed to notice her departure. Which was exactly what Enzo wished. And, in most cases, his wishes usually came true.

The girl came to a stop a dozen feet away from him. Moving with uncharacteristic grace for a man his size, Enzo walked across the short distance of sand separating him from the dark beauty. "Good evening, my dear," he said, softly. "It is a beautiful night."

The girl in the white bikini blinked, as if

suddenly coming awake. "Who the fuck are you?" she asked. Though her words were coarse, her voice was sultry and deep. Enzo liked its sound, the cadence of her speech. "Keep your fuckin' distance, scum bum. I'm no cheap-shit beach whore looking to fuck around with grease-balls out for an evenin's entertainment."

"Be quiet," said Enzo, the slightest snap of authority in his voice. He disliked profanity and found modern street talk offensive. "Speak only when I command. Otherwise, remain silent. I wish to ask you some questions. I want you to answer me. Tell me the truth." He grinned, revealing a row of gleaming white teeth. "Answer as if your life depended on it."

The girl said nothing. Without Enzo's permission, she couldn't speak. The young woman stood motionless, as if frozen in place. Her eyes were the size of saucers, wide with shock and sudden fear.

"Do you understand my orders?" asked Enzo.

"Yes, I fuckin' understand, you motherfuckin' bag of piss," replied the girl.

Casually, Enzo slapped the young woman with the back of his hand. Knowing his own strength, he did it with just enough force to make an impression but not enough to break her jaw. The mark of his fingers left red welts across her cheek.

"Respect," he said smoothly. "I demand respect from my inferiors. I realize you cannot speak without cursing. But, taunt me again and I will split your body wide open and scatter your insides across the beach while you are still breathing. Do I make myself clear?"

"Yeah," said the girl. She might be brash and aggressive, but she wasn't stupid. "What's happenin' to me? Why can't I move? Who the fuck are you?"

"I will ask the questions," said Enzo. "What is your name?"

"Esperenza," said the girl, a trace of panic in her voice. Unable to move, unable to speak other than at her captor's command, she was finally starting to realize how helpless she was. "Esperenza Morales."

"Esperenza," repeated Enzo. "A beautiful name. My ravishing young Hope. You live here in the city, Esperenza?"

"In the barrio," said the girl. "With two other..."

"Yes," said Enzo, cutting her off before she could continue. "With two young women, like yourself, working on the assembly line at the Everwell Chemical plant. They are beauties as well, though not as brazen. The three of you became friends when you attended Catholic school. Faith, Hope and Charity you like to call yourselves. How charming."

Enzo chuckled. In the moonlight, he looked almost benevolent, a concerned uncle speaking to a wayward niece. Except that there was a certain bestial slant to his jaw, a strange glimmer in his eyes.

"They have boyfriends, these two, and you don't," he continued. "You're jealous, insanely jealous of their luck. That's why you come to the beach and taunt the young men. Envy eats at your insides like a worm."

"That's a fuckin' lie," spat out Esperenza, angrily. "I ain't fuckin' jealous of nobody. Who the fuck cares about anybody else. I'm the only one who matters. I do what I want, when I want, how I want. I can have all the men I want, anytime I want. And that's the fuckin' truth.

Enzo nodded. "I believe you. One of my talents is sensing when one of your kind is lying. I think I have a job for you, my dear. With a little training, you will do quite nicely. Come with me."

Enzo turned and headed away from the lake. The girl, Esperenza, her face twisted into a combination of frustration and fear, followed.

A solitary couple, sprawled out on a blanket on the sand, raised their heads as they walked by. Drugs and lust clouded their eyes. Neither said a word nor made any move to stop Enzo and his unwilling companion. The man, some small measure of intelligence in his face, hurriedly formed the sign of the cross on his chest. Enzo chuckled.

"Superstitious peasants," he declared. "If I had the time, I'd show them how much that silly gesture bothers me. But, not tonight. Work comes before pleasure."

"Wh-where are you taking me?" asked Esperenza, her voice thin and whispery. She seemed surprised that she could speak without having been given permission.

"Tell me, my dear," said Enzo, ignoring the girl's question, "what matters the most in the world. Love, honor, sex, happiness? Speak honestly, my little Hope, for I will know immediately if you are lying."

"Power," said the young woman immediately. "Nothing is as important as power. If you've got power, the rest falls into your lap. The fuckin' world is your toy."

"Very good," said Enzo. "I judged you correctly. I think you will serve me quite well."

"Serve you?" said Esperenza, her voice growing shrill. "What the fuck are you saying? I don't remember takin' no fuckin' job interview?"

Enzo turned and stared at the girl. "You still don't seem to understand, dear Hope. There is no choice involved. My wishes matter. Yours don't."

A jagged line of low cement blocks separated the beach from the parking lot. A layer of broken glass, the debris of a thousand beer bottles, littered the cracked black pavement. Esperenza was not wearing shoes or sandals.

"My limousine is over there," said Enzo. "Come, my men are waiting. Remain absolutely silent. You are not allowed to scream, no matter how much pain you feel. I need to concentrate on important business matters."

Robert Weinberg

Together, they walked across the lot. Esperanza moved as if in a trance, unable to avoid the shards of glass, rusted nails, and smashed concrete that covered the ground. Jolts of pain slashed across her face, but she could not make a sound. Nor could she stop walking. By the time she reached the limo, the skin of her feet was cut to ribbons. A trail of red footmarks crossed the lot.

"Pain is an effective teacher," said Enzo. "Consider this brief stroll your first lesson."

Two short, stocky men leaned against the side of the shiny black stretch limousine. Brutish hairy faces, wide shoulders, and arms that nearly touched the ground gave them the appearance of gorillas. They wore crisp black chauffeur's uniforms, complete with caps, but no jacket could conceal their bulging biceps. Gray eyes peered at Esperanza without curiosity or desire. Their expressions remained indifferent and cold. The men had no interest in her lush body or her bloody feet.

"Any word about the shipment?" Enzo asked the taller of the two.

"Not a word," the man replied. His voice was so low, it was barely audible. "It's late."

"Obviously," said Enzo, not sounding pleased. "An unusual occurrence. Did Ms. Hargroves call?"

The bigger man shook his head. A man of few words, he had evidently used up his vocabulary for the evening.

"These are the brothers Grim," said Enzo to

Esperenza. "They're my most loyal servants. Don't bother wasting your charms on them. As you can see, they lost what little sex drive they possessed many years ago."

He pulled open the rear door of the limo. "Get in," he commanded the girl. "Be careful with your bloody feet. I value my carpets. Bloodstains are difficult to remove."

Enzo stared at Mark, the taller Grim brother, as the girl slid into the limo. "She's not for you. I have other plans for her. I know I promised you and Jacob a reward for recent services: After we return to the factory, you have my permission to hunt down and pull a few vagrants off the streets. Do what you want with them. Just be careful not to be seen. My police bill is high enough without adding blackmail to the list."

"We'll be careful," said Mark. Behind him, Jacob, shorter and heavier, nodded agreement. "You know us, Mr. Giovanni. We don't cause no trouble."

"Get me back to my office," said Enzo. "I want to know why the shipment is late."

He slipped into the car beside a trembling Esperenza. The girl's feet were crossed, yoga style, so that the soles didn't touch the floor. The skin had been sliced and cut to ribbons, and red blood oozed across her knees and thighs. She shuddered as Enzo entered the auto, but did not speak. Until he gave her permission, she was mute.

"Very good," said Enzo. "You know the value of obedience."

Robert Weinberg

The limo started moving, its engine a dull, sullen hum.

Carefully, Enzo pulled back the edge of his right shirt sleeve, revealing his wrist. Like a surgeon, he drew the sharp nail of his left index finger across a large vein. The white skin parted like paper. A few drops of black blood glistened beneath the dimmed lights of the car's interior.

"Drink," said Enzo, raising his hand to the girl's lips. "Drink my blood."

Unable to resist Enzo's will, the girl obeyed. She opened her mouth and started to suck blood from the wound. Slowly at first, her eyes filled with revulsion. Then, as horror turned to incredible pleasure, the girl drank greedily.

"Enough," said Enzo after a few seconds. He wrenched his wrist away. Instantly, the jagged cut closed. In seconds, there was no trace of any wound. "Look at your feet."

Esperenza gasped. Her soles were no longer ripped into bloody fragments. The skin was smooth and whole. All trace of blood had vanished.

"Your second lesson," said Enzo. "Serve me and you will be rewarded with power beyond your wildest dreams. Control even over the forces of life and death."

He settled back on the black leather seat. "Did my driver look familiar? Perhaps you remember his face from the television news?"

"Um," said Esperenza, gifted again with the

ability to speak, "I kinda thought I saw him before."
She sat quietly for a moment, concentrating, then
shook her head in disbelief.

"It ain't possible," the girl muttered. "It ain't
fuckin' possible. He's dead. Him and his lunatic
brother were blown away by the fuckin' cops a year
ago."

Enzo laughed. "Never believe what you read in
the newspaper or see on television, sweet Hope.
Manipulating the media is child's play for anyone
with talent.

"The Grim brothers are incurable psychopaths.
They derive their only pleasure from making others
suffer pain. Torture involving knives and fire are
special favorites. I believe the police linked them
with twenty-seven slayings before finally tracking
the pair down to their hideaway in an abandoned
warehouse in the old section of town."

Satisfaction filled Enzo's voice. "Afterward, the
law officials discovered more remains that told
them that they had vastly underestimated the
number of kills made by the Grims." He laughed.
"Seventy-three heads in freezers convinced them of
the error in their calculations."

Esperenza stared at Enzo. "If you fuckin' think
you're scarin' me with stories of those shitfaces,
you're damned fuckin' crazy. One of those mothers
lay a finger on me, I'll fuckin' chop his hand off and
shove it up his ass."

"An intriguing concept," murmured Enzo. "Your

attitude is perfect, my lovely Hope. All that is necessary is to change your presentation. It will be a challenge, but one that I believe can be accomplished with some effort."

"Who the fuckin' hell are you?" asked the girl. For the first time, she seemed to notice the lush interior of the limo. "Sure got plenty of fuckin' cash. You the devil like the Sisters talked about?"

Enzo laughed. "Would it matter?" he asked. "Would it really matter?"

"No," said the girl. "Not a fuckin' bit."

"Then don't trouble yourself with such questions," said Enzo. Reaching forward, he uncorked a glass bottle from the portable bar. The thick red liquid he poured into his glass was definitely not wine. Esperenza licked her lips nervously as she watched Enzo sip his drink.

"I would offer you some refreshment," said the big man, "but I think you would find the taste unpleasant."

His eyes, red as the blood in his glass, stared deep into hers. "I can force you to obey my wishes," he declared. "You've seen how easily I can bend your will to mine. But I require a willing servant, not a mindless slave. Cooperate with me and everything you have ever desired will be yours."

"For a price," said Esperenza.

"Of course," said Enzo Giovanni, recognizing the acceptance in her voice. He smiled, pleased with the outcome of the evening's endeavor. "*Everything has a price.*"

Chapter Seven

" I will pass along the information to Comptroller Klair," X344 said into the telephone receiver. He could not disguise his anger. "I am sure that he will want to discuss the matter with you personally."

Snorting in disgust, the cyborg slammed the receiver onto the base. Chips of plastic shot across the room as the unit exploded into fragments. Too often, X344 forgot his own strength. Anyone capable of bending steel bars needed to control his temper better. He had already destroyed three telephones this month and there was still more than a week left. His record was five.

With the barest whir of machinery, the cyborg headed for the hall outside his office. Comptroller Klair was meeting in the conference room on the next level with the Progenitor Research Director,

Sharon Reed. Neither of them were going to like the news he brought.

The entrance to the conference center was closed. X344 extended his left claw and rapped hard on the duralloy door. The synthetic material was supposedly stronger than steel, though it weighed less than plastic. The cyborg felt confident that he could smash the stuff to smithereens with his artificial hands, however. Someday he hoped to have the opportunity to try. He liked smashing things.

The door slid to the side as Klair sensed his presence from inside the chamber. Four Technomancers clustered around a conference table. It was circular to signify that they were all equal: No one could be said to sit at the head of the table. X344 thought the concept was stupid. Everyone knew that Iteration X was the most important branch of the Technocracy. Comptroller Klair was the true leader of Gray Collective. Maybe Sharon Reed felt differently, but her opinion, and that of her damned assistant, Velma Wade, meant nothing.

Klair nodded as X344 rolled into the room. Reed, who made no secret of her hatred of machine-enhanced humans, sneered at him but kept her mouth shut. X344 smiled at her. She knew he wouldn't take insults from anyone, even a Director.

Velma Wade, the freak who changed her appearance as often as some people changed their outfits, ignored him. X344 was positive she was Reed's lesbian lover. Not that sex mattered much at the Gray Collective. The only thing that counted was getting your work done on schedule. Wade never failed to be the first to finish her assignments. Comptroller Klair despised and feared Sharon Reed, but X344 thought Velma Wade was the more dangerous of the two.

The fourth Technocrat at the gathering was Terrence Shade. A short, fat man, with a beet-red face, full black beard, and puffy cheeks, he belonged to the Technocracy Convention known as the New World Order. Along with Reed and Klair, he was the third member of the Triumvirate that ruled the Gray Collective. Shade served as the chief administrator of the compound. He was the only mage in the entire complex who was not a member of either Iteration X or the Progenitors.

The New World Order were masters of propaganda and deception. Their job was to neutralize any random factors that disrupted an orderly and controlled existence. Among their fellow Technocrats, the NWO specialized in coordinating efforts between various branches of the Technocracy. They acted as the glue binding the five Conventions of the Technocratic Union into a whole.

Shade was a Mission Specialist. He worked hard to keep things running smoothly between the Progenitors and Iteration X mages assigned to the

AW Project. Some thought he worked a little too hard. A suspicious Armature had once suggested to X344 that Shade was actually the one behind the entire top-secret enterprise. Knowing that such brilliance could only have been the result of Dr. Klair's efforts, X344 had rejected the lunatic idea without a second thought. The fat man was a glorified pencil pusher, nothing more.

"I assume you are here with news, X344?" said Klair. The tone of the Comptroller's voice indicated to the cyborg that a violent argument had been going on for the past few minutes. "We are all waiting with bated breath for your report. Mission Specialist Shade feels I overstepped my authority by sending the HIT Marks after Prisoner Seventeen. He thinks I overreacted. Do you bring information that will make him eat those words?"

"Umm, I don't know sir," said X344, distinctly uncomfortable with the news he brought to the gathering. "I just finished speaking with Richard Gill, the supervisor of the Syracuse Collective. Following our request, he sent out four of the HIT Marks to terminate Prisoner Seventeen. The mechs stopped the truck convoy a few miles outside the city of Rochester and located the escapee. Somehow, he partially disabled one of the four. The remaining three shot and killed him using their high-powered chain guns. They left his lifeless body lying on a cliff and returned to base."

"That sounds satisfactory," said Shade, nodding.

"Despite my misgivings about excessive force, it seems like all went well."

"No, it did not," said Klair, his hands tightening into fists. His forehead reddened with anger. With the isolated tufts of brown hair sticking out from his head at wild angles, his bald dome, and his big, bulging eyes, the Comptroller reminded X344 of a circus clown. A maniacal, demented circus clown. His voice was shrill. "The garbage I have just heard is *not* satisfactory."

"I'll say," declared Sharon Reed. Her features were snow white. Nelson had spent enough time with the Research Director to recognize that she was just as disturbed as his boss. "I warned you that those metal heads couldn't be trusted."

"This fool, Gill, is entirely to blame," said Klair, trembling with rage. "I was very specific in relaying my instructions to him. *Very specific*. I told him that not only were the HIT Marks to kill the prisoner, but they had to utterly destroy the body as well. I even insisted that he repeat his instructions to me so that there was no question as to what I meant."

The Comptroller stared at X344. "Remember Mr. Gill's name. His status needs to be reviewed."

The cyborg nodded. He understood Klair's hidden meaning. Sooner or later, Iteration X cyborg X344 and Richard Gill would meet. It would be the last time Mr. Gill disobeyed specific orders.

"Well, now that your man has fucked up royally," said Sharon Reed, "what do you intend to do, Klair?"

Robert Weinberg

"I'm not sure I'm following the thread of the conversation," said Terrence Shade. Despite his blustery appearance and piglike features, the Mission Specialist spoke with a calm, measure voice. He never got angry or upset no matter how bad the news. His gaze traveled from Klair to Reed, then back again. "Would either of you care to explain to me what is wrong?"

"Prisoner Seventeen was perhaps our most successful attempt at full body modification and enhancement," said Sharon Reed, tapping a finger on the table-top as if to emphasize each word. "Many of the changes made to his form were incorporated in the final AW prototype. Seventeen served as our test case for some of the more involved procedures. Though the bioconstructs were not as complex as those used in the pattern-clone, the prisoner was still transformed into one of the most advanced life forms in all existence."

"Among his many enhancements," continued Velma Wade, "the prisoner possesses near absolute command of his physical and mental attributes. He has conscious control of most of his physical processes. Feigning death is child's play for him."

"But chain guns are deadly," said Shade.

"Seventeen's recuperative powers are beyond your limited imagination," said Reed impatiently. "Remember, we put everything *possible* into his reconstruction. He is a physical and mental superbeing. This man, without weapons, killed a sauroid."

The Road to Hell

"Gill said Seventeen broke both the arms of the HIT Mark that was partly disabled," added X344. "Those robots have bones made from Primium. They are nearly indestructible."

"Then what you're saying," declared Shade, "is that this escaped prisoner is probably still alive? That the HIT Mark's only thought he was dead?"

"Exactly," said Klair, whose color had returned to normal. He seemed to be in control of himself again, though X344 could still detect a note of panic in his voice. "Don't forget that along with the modifications to his system, Seventeen also possessed powerful paranormal skills. If necessary, any of us in this chamber could fool a HIT Mark into thinking we're dead. They are intelligent but not immune to mental manipulation. Seventeen's will is obviously as strong as ours."

Shade sighed heavily. "Explaining this disaster to the Symposium is not going to be easy. Obviously, one thing that we must do immediately is locate and destroy this Prisoner Seventeen. The longer he remains at large, the greater the chance of him revealing details of this operation. The whole project could be in jeopardy."

"That," said Velma Wade with confidence, "is not a major problem. Maximum security measures are always in effect when dealing with the prisoners in the cell block. None of them have any notion of what we are doing at the Gray Collective. Some may have an intuitive idea of our plans, but I feel quite certain that our secret is safe. Seventeen cannot discuss what he doesn't know."

"Sure," said X344, unable to resist jabbing at Wade. The shapechanger gave him the creeps. "Why would anyone in the Nine Traditions be curious about a near superhuman bioengineered mage who turns up one night telling stories about a secret research center in an offworld Construct?"

He laughed, the sarcasm dripping from his tongue like bile. "Yes sir, nobody would be interested, even when he mentions the prison block filled with kidnapped wizards that are used for our experiments."

"A depressing but acute observation, Mr. Nelson," said Shade. "We must assume the absolute worst case scenario and proceed from there. Prisoner Seventeen has been on the loose for hours. There are Tradition mages in the Rochester area. Our working hypothesis is that he has made contact with them and they have obtained some knowledge of our existence. It is conceivable that our enemies will mount an attack on the Gray Collective. How do we react?"

"The project must proceed as scheduled," said Dr. Klair, his face a mask of determination. "We can't let this incident force a delay. Too much effort has gone into this project to shut it down because of one man. The AW experiment is crucial to the future of the Technocracy. It could be the key to our eventual destruction of the Nine Traditions."

"I'm in complete agreement with Comptroller Klair," said Sharon Reed. "We're close to an astonishing breakthrough in pattern-clone development. I refuse to let a mere possibility of danger destroy a year's work."

"How soon before the actual completion of the AW pattern-clone?" asked Shade.

"Ten to twelve days, assuming Dr. Klair has no further modifications to the nervous system," said Reed. "We are about to initiate the final growth sequences."

Klair grimaced. "Unfortunately, we must still make one minor revision." From the inside pocket of his uniform, the Comptroller pulled out several pages of hastily scribbled notes. "If we connect the mainframe directly with the nanotech drivers, I believe this alteration can be completed in less than a day."

Sharon Reed glared at Klair. She snatched the papers from his hands. Staring at the instructions, she shook her head in bewilderment. "When do these ideas come to you, Klair? In your sleep?"

The Comptroller's features turned ash gray. X344 couldn't help but notice that Klair's voice was shaking when he replied. "These plans are the result of long hours spent trying to maximize the pattern-clone's efficiency. At least that has always been my goal."

"Mine too," said Reed, sneering at the Comptroller. "Don't pull any of that smug superiority crap on me, Klair. I've worked as hard on this project as anyone."

"Enough bickering," said Shade, loudly. "The leaders of the Symposium have expressed their satisfaction with both of your contributions to this important project. It is not a topic for discussion tonight."

It was a subtle but effective means to remind everyone that Shade was their link to the Technocratic Symposium, the board that governed all Convention undertakings. The wrong word from him would bring the AW project to an immediate halt. Or cause anyone involved in the operation to be replaced.

The red-faced man stared at Sharon Reed. "You will make Dr. Klair's changes and then start the growth sequences. Ten days. No more. Agreed?"

"Agreed," said the Research Director.

Shade turned to Dr. Klair. "You will assist Dr. Reed's efforts. I expect your total cooperation."

"Of course," said the Comptroller. "Whatever you say, Shade."

"Very good," said the Mission Specialist. He looked at Velma Wade, and then finally at X344. The cyborg found Shade's gaze vaguely disconcerting. It was like staring into the eyes of a reptile. There was an absolute coldness hidden by those ruddy cheeks and black beard that the machine-enhanced man found frightening. It was an aspect of Terrence Shade's personality that X344 had never seen before.

The Road to Hell

"I assume the two of you will cooperate to your fullest to make sure that there are no further foul-ups or disasters?"

"My loyalty is with the Technocracy," said Velma Wade. "There will be no complaints about my work."

"Nor mine," said X344. The thought of cooperating with Wade turned his stomach, but the completion of the AW project was all-important. As Klair had said, the pattern-clone might be the weapon that could destroy the Nine Traditions. He could ignore his feelings for a few weeks. Sooner or later, his chance to strike back would come. "You can count on me."

"Excellent," said Shade. He was pleasant and smiling again, the coldness gone from his voice as if it had never been. "I think we are on the right track here. We can discuss tightening security measures later in this meeting. At present, our first concern is what to do about Prisoner Seventeen. Obviously, based on the remarks made here, the longer he remains at large, the greater the chance of attack from the Traditions. The man must be eliminated."

"I can lead a squad of sauroids after him," suggested Wade. "The beasts are spectacular trackers. They'll pick up his trail with no problem and track him down." She smiled viciously. "The creatures are bred with a strong pack loyalty. They would tear Seventeen into tiny pieces."

"A half-dozen HIT Marks under my direction would handle the task equally well," said X344. "The cyborgs are relentless and do not tire. They merely need close supervision. Using their chain guns at close range, they can burn Seventeen to ashes."

"I appreciate your suggestions," said Shade, "but neither venture is feasible. Prisoner Seventeen is no longer offworld but on Earth. The task forces you mentioned would be difficult to hide from the general population. We cannot disturb the Sleepers' worldview. If they spotted your hunting teams, their disbelief and astonishment would cause a tremendous Paradox backlash. We cannot risk such a disaster."

Reluctantly, X344 nodded. Like most Technomancers, his knowledge of Paradox was limited. No one really understood exactly what caused it or when it happened. In most cases, though, it was the result of normal humans, the Sleepers, observing reality reshaped and twisted by magick. Their disbelief caused a tremendous psychic backlash that badly damaged the mage involved and his work. It was the main reason why mages avoided using strong spells and magick among ordinary people except for in extreme circumstances. Static reality had a nasty trick of paying back with a vengeance those who toyed with it with impunity.

"What do you suggest?" asked Klair. "Send

acolytes after him? Mere mortals would be helpless against him. Remember, while most of Seventeen's powers are magickally fueled, since they are internal, he appears perfectly normal to the Sleepers. Except in the most extreme cases, he will not generate Paradox."

"I have the perfect solution," said Shade. "The New World Order has its own branch of enforcement agents. They are notorious among the Sleepers, especially the most paranoid of them, but no one suspects their true magickal nature. They appear to be nothing more than secret government operatives. Their powers are formidable; they are ruthless, efficient and quite deadly."

The Mission Specialist smiled. To Nelson, the red-faced, black-bearded man looked positively satanic. "I will contact our branch office in the northeast. It is time that the New World Order takes charge of this operation. I assure you our operatives will not fail. The Men in Black are trained for such search and destroy missions. They will handle the operation swiftly and efficiently. By tomorrow night, Prisoner Seventeen will be nothing more than an unpleasant memory. And the AW project will be able to continue undisturbed.

<u>Chapter Eight</u>

It took Seventeen nearly an hour to climb the distance it had taken him seconds to fall. Though he was in perfect physical condition, the ex-prisoner was beginning to feel dizzy when he finally reached the flat plateau of the highway. After the incredible amount of activity he had experienced tonight, his body needed fuel. Otherwise he would collapse.

Dragging himself over the edge of the slope, Seventeen collapsed on his hands and knees on the grass fronting the metal guard rail. It required several minutes of deep breathing before he could rise to his feet—and found himself staring into the eyes of a white-haired stranger less than a yard away.

"Took you long enough to get here, son," growled

the man. Seventeen figured him to be around six feet tall and weigh about two hundred pounds. His face was gnarled with age, his forehead heavily wrinkled. A shocking mass of pure white hair crowned his head, while a long waxed mustache covered his upper lip beneath a huge tomato-red nose. His blue eyes twinkled with good humor. His voice sounded like seeds rattling in an empty gourd. "We've been waiting for twenty, thirty minutes at least. Me and Albert would have played a coupla hands of gin rummy if we knew you were gonna crawl all the way up."

Several feet behind the white-haired man, another figure moved forward in the moonlight. A scrawny black man with a shaved skull, he towered nearly seven and a half feet in the air. He was dressed in a flowing blue and purple robe that stretched from his neck to his ankles. Seventeen's gaze was drawn immediately to the mysterious sigils painted in blue on the giant's cheeks. He knew that the symbols meant something, but he couldn't remember what.

"We didn't want to startle you," said the black man, his deep voice rumbling like a kettle drum. "My presence has a disconcerting effect on most people. They immediately assume that I am a cannibal headhunter. Or a freak escaped from a circus sideshow. It gets tiresome explaining that I am actually a not a freak."

"Damn bigots in this country judge a man by his

color or his appearance," said the oldster with a snort. "You ain't stupid, are you, son?"

Seventeen shook his head. "Your friend looks fine to me," he declared. "Other than that he's pretty damn thin. But that's no crime."

The white-haired man chuckled. "When Albert turns sideways, he casts no shadow. I've been trying to put some meat on his bones for years. Darned fool only eats vegetables though. Can't get fat munching on leafy green things." The old man peered intently at Seventeen. "Looks like you've had a rough night, boy. You need some help?"

Seventeen licked his lips. He sensed that he could trust this oddball old man and his giant companion. He couldn't explain his feelings but at the moment his instincts were his only guide. In this situation, he felt he had no choice. "Since you're speaking of food, you wouldn't happen to have anything to eat?" he asked. "I'm very hungry."

"There's a loaf of Italian bread in our van," said Albert. The black man spoke his words precisely, with an accent that Seventeen could not place. "The cooler has cheese and roast beef for sandwiches for Sam, and there's a salad for me. You are welcome to that."

"Better bring the jug of lemonade, too," said the man who had to be Sam. "I think our battered friend might appreciate a drink. He looks like he's been torn up pretty damned good."

"I'll be fine after a meal," said Seventeen. He

meant what he said. All he needed to recover fully from the night's adventures was food. Despite his recent injuries, he felt perfectly fit.

"Better let me take a look at you while Albert fetches the grub," said Sam, stepping up to Seventeen. "I've got the touch. You know what I mean? I can sense a man's injuries and wounds, even if they ain't visible or hurting. Albert's the medicine man of the two of us. Once I do the findin', he performs the healin' rituals."

"If doing this will make you feel better," said Seventeen with a smile, "then go ahead." He raised his hands over his head. "I assure you, though, that I'm in perfect health. Except for terrible hunger pains, I feel fine. I'm not even tired."

Sam pushed aside the remnants of the scorched uniform and placed both his hands on the skin of Seventeen's chest. "Heard the exact same words from a friend seconds before I discovered he was bleeding like a pig inside and would have died within the hour, son. Let me do the judging, okay?"

Seventeen sighed. "I don't think you understand. I'm not like an ordinary man."

"I realize that," said Sam. "You're one of the Awakened, just like Albert and me. That's how we came a-searching for you on this god-forsaken stretch of road. We sensed your presence and started hunting. I got a talent for finding orphans in need. Sorta sixth sense or seventh. Lose track after a while. Whatever, no one ever said that Sam

Haine, the Changing Man, doesn't speed to the aid of his fellow magick makers."

"Sam Haine, the Changing Man," repeated Seventeen. The name sounded familiar, as if he had heard it spoken before. But, like many other things, he was not sure when or by whom. It was quite frustrating. "You don't know a man named Alvin Reynolds, by any chance?"

The white-haired man frowned. Muttering incomprehensible phrases under his breath, he shifted his hands to touch Seventeen gently on each side of his neck. "Reynolds?" he replied. "Alvin Reynolds? The name doesn't strike a chord with me. Don't mean a hell of a lot, 'cause I meet lots of people and can't remember all their names. Memory is shot to hell, son. Growing old does that to you. Albert's the one for names. Better if you ask him."

"Ask me what?" said Albert, returning from a large blue van parked fifty feet down the road. In his arms he carried the promised food and drink. Hungrily, Seventeen held out his hands.

"Go ahead and eat, boy," said Sam, removing his fingers from Seventeen's body. "Damn it all if you weren't tellin' the truth. Never before encountered a specimen so damned healthy in my entire life. Ain't nothin' wrong with you."

Albert handed Seventeen the food. The next few minutes were silent as he devoured every single scrap of bread, cheese and meat. It was as if a fire burned inside him that could only be quenched by the provisions. The others watched him with a mixture of amusement and astonishment.

"How long you been without supplies, boy?" asked Sam as Seventeen gulped down the last of the lemonade. "Never saw a man go through a round of food so fast in my entire days. And I ain't no youngster."

"My body required the energy," answered Seventeen honestly. "I can't explain it any more clearly. It's just the way my system functions."

Sam and Albert exchanged odd glances. Seventeen could sense their discomfort but he could offer no other explanation.

"Albert," he said, turning to the giant, "do you know a man named Alvin Reynolds? It's desperately important that I contact him as soon as possible."

The black man shook his head. "I do not recall anyone with that name," he declared. "Besides, Alvin Reynolds is not an unusual appellation. There may be hundreds, perhaps thousands, of individuals who are called by that name living in this country. Do you know anything more about him?"

"According to his sister, he's a computer hacker," said Seventeen, not exactly sure what the term meant. "She also said that he was one of the Awakened. He's definitely not a member of the Technocracy. But that's all I know."

"If he's a major computer geek, this Reynolds probably belongs to the Virtual Adepts," said Sam. "Not that all the Traditions don't have their share of software soldiers, but your best bet is to try the Adepts first. Though, they're a pretty anarchistic bunch. Getting information from any of them is like trying to pull out your own teeth."

The white-haired man beckoned to Seventeen. "We better get back to the van and start driving. Yakking by the side of the road here might attract some attention. Latest scandal in the papers concerns gangs of teenagers roaming the highways looking for broken-down cars. The young thugs rob the stranded motorists, raping the women, most times killin' the men. Freeway bandits, they're called. Around a scum hole like Rochester, they're a real problem. Better we be moving than find ourselves their next target."

Sam stared at Seventeen. "I'm making the assumption you're coming with us, son? Seems like you need a lift. Correct me if I'm bein' too forward or anything like that."

Seventeen shrugged. "What other choice do I have?" He pulled the truck driver's wallet from his pocket. "I only have seventy dollars. It's not much, but any help you can lend me in finding Alvin Reynolds would be appreciated. I'm sure he will give you more once I contact him."

Sam shook his head. "Keep the change, boy. Albert and I don't take money for helpin' nobody.

We're perpetual do-gooders." The old man laughed. "Besides, seventy bucks don't buy spit these days. Me and Albert are goin' to a big shebang tomorrow night. That's why we're in this stretch of territory. Lots of mages goin' to be present. Maybe someone there will know about this Reynolds character."

"If he belongs to the Virtual Adepts," said Albert, as they climbed into the van, "contacting him may prove to be quite difficult. The Technocracy hates their order and members of the Tradition usually work in isolation. They love deception, intrigue and trails that lead nowhere. I've heard talk of a universal database that lists the location of every Adept, but I doubt there's much truth to the story."

Albert gestured for Seventeen to take the passenger seat in front. Sam was the driver. The rear seat was pushed as far back as possible for the giant. Vans were not made for men his size.

"There's a small Verbena Chantry House about twenty miles up the road," said Sam as he turned the key in the ignition. "We were planning to spend the rest of the night and tomorrow there. They're holding a big celebration for Summer Solstice. Hope our little detour didn't set the Casey cabal worryin' too much. We were due to arrive hours ago."

"I doubt it," said Albert as Sam steered the van onto the highway. "They know what you are like."

Sam chuckled. "They do at that. Good thing,

too. Nobody'll be surprised to see me turn up with a stray puppy in tow. Folks will just shake their heads and say it's another typical day in the life of the Changing Man."

Albert laughed, a booming sound that filled the van. "Since half the members of the Casey cabal were found by you in similar fashion, I do not think they will be very upset."

"Yeah," said Sam. "Never occurred to me, but that's the truth." He looked at Seventeen, his bright blue eyes twinkling. "I'm a trouble magnet, son. Everybody agrees. Seems like I'm always rescuing wayward mages in dire straits and helping them solve their problems. Me and Albert's been keeping our curiosity in check so far, but I think it's time you do some talkin'. Care to explain what you were doing in Watkins Glen gorge during the middle of the night, with nothin' round to show how you got there? It's a long walk to the middle of nowhere, son."

"You may find my story rather hard to believe," cautioned Seventeen. He needed allies in his search for Alvin Reynolds and Sam Haine and Albert seemed the most likely prospects. He couldn't expect them to help without knowing the dangers they faced.

"Try us," said the white-haired man. "We've heard some pretty wild tales in our day. Fightin' this damned Ascension War, life can get awfully strange. Nobody knows more about crisis management than the Changing Man. Part of my blessing. Or my curse. Depends entirely on the point of view."

"Don't cry any tears for poor Sam Haine," added Albert, chuckling. "He thrives on disaster. Life without a crisis would bore him to tears."

"Whatever you say," declared Seventeen. Without further hesitation, he related his adventures, beginning from the moment he awoke in his cell to when the HIT Mark Vs agreed that he was no longer a threat and walked away from the cliff edge. By the time he was finished, they were traveling on a backwoods dirt road that wound a circular path to a huge old farmhouse glowing with lights. Nearly two dozen people—men, women and children—were waiting outside. Many were waving, some were singing a song without words.

"Son," said Sam, shaking his head, as he steered the van slowly along the rutted path, "do me a favor and keep this tale of yours quiet while we visit with the Casey Cabal. Let me do all the talkin'."

"Then you don't believe me?" asked Seventeen, wondering what he would do next.

"Just the opposite," said Sam Haine, his cheery voice deadly serious. "I believe every word. No fool would dare make up a story like that and tell it to the Changing Man. You're not lying. That's what scares the hell out of me. Albert?"

"An amazing story," said the giant. "But, like you, my old friend, I believe our unusual comrade.

Robert Weinberg

Which, of course, leads to numerous questions that need answers."

"Questions?" said Seventeen. "About what?"

"You, for example," said Albert. "I do not think I have ever before met a mage, no matter how powerful, who could kill a sauroid with his bare hands and a few hours later badly damage a HIT Mark cyborg. What Tradition do you follow?" The black man chuckled. "Is there perhaps a new Order from the planet Krypton?"

"Forget the witchy trappings and ritual stuff," interrupted Sam Haine. "Ain't important right now. You're missin' the obvious, Albert. We need an answer to the real big question." The white-haired man stared at Seventeen. "What's your name, son? What do you call yourself?"

"I-I-I'm prisoner Seventeen," said Seventeen, feeling slightly bewildered by the query.

"Sure, that's what you were in that Gray Collective's cell block," said Sam. "But who were you before? What's your real name?"

"Name?" repeated Seventeen, warily. Slowly, he shook his head. "I'm Seventeen. That's all I remember. I don't have a name."

An uneasy feeling crept over him. Concentrating, he realized his memory only extended back a few weeks. He had no recollections of his life before the laboratory. Never before had he questioned his apparent lack of a history. It didn't seemed important. It was as if he had been programmed not to worry about the past.

"Who am I?" he asked, the edges of panic stirring in his soul. "And why did they wipe out my memory?"

"That, son," said Sam Haine, "is the real big question. That's the one we got to answer."

Chapter Nine

"There is a van stopped in the middle of the road up ahead," said Shadow of the Dawn, nudging her half-dozing companion in the ribs to get his attention. She eased a foot onto the brake, slowing down the speeding rental car. "Emergency flares burn around it. I see a young woman, just a teenager, waving at us. She appears anxious for aid. From what we were told at the agency, this stretch of highway is quite dangerous. Do we pull over and lend assistance?"

The bearded mage, who preferred to be called Kallikos, yawned and glanced at the clock on the car dashboard. "The celebration is not until tomorrow night. Our rooms at the hotel in Rochester are guaranteed for the evening. We can afford the delay if it means helping someone in distress. Pull over."

Shadow slowed the car to a roll, steering it onto the shoulder of the highway. The big van was less than twenty feet away. The girl behind the emergency lights stood waiting, the expression on her face a mixture of hope and despair. As best as Shadow could determine in the glare of the flares, the young woman was shapely and blond. A very dangerous combination to be standing alone on the road signaling for help. Wolves roamed these byways. Human wolves.

"I think," said Shadow of the Dawn, as they unbuckled their seat belts, "I will take Whisper and Scream with me. By chance, do your farseeing powers hint at anything unusual occurring in the next few minutes?"

Kallikos shook his head. "Sorry, but as I have explained more than once on our trip, my visions normally come to me during otherworldly dreams. When they do occur, they are powerful portents of possible futures." The hawk-faced mage sounded amused. "They rarely cover changing a tire."

"I assumed as much," said Shadow, "but I thought I would ask anyway. If any fighting takes place, stay well out of reach. I would not want to accidentally hurt you."

"Don't worry," said Kallikos, with a slight smile. "I can hold my own. But I am quite content to leave the real fighting to an expert."

They approached the stalled van slowly. The blonde made no effort to come and meet them. She was either very cautious, very afraid, or very dangerous. Shadow could not decide which.

"Hello," called Kallikos. "What's the problem? We mean you no harm."

"Two—two of my tires are flat," replied the girl from behind the flares. "There were spikes in the road a few miles back. It had to be a gang trap. I was afraid to pull over so I drove on the rims as long as I could. My CB's busted and no one else has come by since. You're the only people I've seen in the past hour."

"Do you have any spares?" asked Kallikos, starting to walk a little faster. Shadow laid a restraining hand on his arm as he came up to her side. She felt uneasy about this situation. "We can give you a hand changing them."

"Would you?" said the blonde. She spoke slowly, almost as if reciting dialogue learned by rote. Shadow of the Dawn suspected that was exactly the case. "I've been going crazy watchin' and waitin' for someone to come along. I was starting to worry that nobody would ever stop. But now everything'll be just fine."

"Down!" hissed Shadow and shoved Kallikos to the ground. She dropped to the earth as fire and lead roared across the spot they had occupied an instant before.

A mechanism clicked loudly in the blackness a

dozen feet away. A man's gruff voice cursed. "Shit, fuckin' gun's jammed."

"Motherfucker," swore a second man. Metal struck metal but nothing happened. No one ever succeeded in firing twice at a wizard.

"Enough fuckin' around," said someone. "We'll do it the old-fashioned way. With our fuckin' hands."

Wordlessly, five hulking figures materialized out of the darkness. Big, powerfully built men, one carried a metal rod, two carried shotguns, another held a knife, and the last was armed with a long piece of thin steel chain ending in a sharp metal hook. All were dressed in blue jeans and muscle Ts. Several sported large tattoos on their arms. Two had shaved heads, while the third had a full beard and thick black hair. The fourth wore a black eye patch and was missing an ear. The fifth, the man with the chain, wore thick brown gloves and a battered old leather hockey mask over his face like a character from a horror movie.

"Odds look just fine," growled the masked man. "Five against two. Fair fight."

Shadow, back on her feet, shuddered in revulsion. "Nice bunch of fellows," declared Kallikos from behind her. "Think you can take them?"

"Just stay out of my way," said Shadow softly. "See to the young lady. She may be an unsuspecting innocent. Or she could have been acting as bait for these monsters. Be careful."

Kallikos disappeared beyond the flares. Shadow stood alone, her feet slightly spread, facing the five men.

"Barbecue," said the thug with the knife. All five men were moving forward slowly but steadily. None of them had much to say. Shadow didn't care. Insults and curses couldn't kill. Cold steel was the only thing that mattered.

"Don't rush," said the masked man, speaking to his companions. He held the chain like a lariat, a coil of it dangling from one gloved hand, the section ending in the hook swaying from the other. "We got plenty of time."

"Gentlemen," said Shadow, her voice steady. "I offer you your lives. Depart now or die without mercy. The choice is given only once."

The man with the black beard giggled shrilly, revealing a mouthful of yellowed teeth sharpened to points. "Oh, oh," he declared in a high-pitched voice. "I'm so worried."

None of the others said a word. Instead, they crowded forward, eager to be the first to the attack. Shadow accepted this as an unspoken refusal of her offer. With the faintest whisper of steel, she drew her two swords from their sheaths. Whisper and Scream blazed with red fire in the glow of the emergency flares.

The gang's sudden rush came to an abrupt halt as they caught sight of the twin blades. Shadow stood ready to attack, her left arm raised, her right arm parallel to the ground, the two swords crossed to form a steel X. She could feel the *Do* energy channeling from within her mind, filling her body with mystic power. The black-bearded man giggled again, but this time terror tinged the sound.

"What the fuck?" snorted the skinhead holding a tire-iron. "I'm not scared of a babe with big knives. There's five of us and only one of her."

With a roar, the man leapt forward, swinging his metal rod in a downward arc that, if it had connected, would have smashed Shadow's head to a bloody pulp. However, the bar cut through empty space. True to her namesake, only a shadow remained. The *Do* warrior-maiden moved with a pantherlike grace, the swords in her hands dancing with a music only she could hear. And each time they came to rest, fountains of blood erupted.

Shadow twirled in death's ballet. Her long and short swords flickered to near invisibility as she swung the blades with astonishing speed. Acting with a precision and expertise born of years of training, the young woman attacked her enemies in order of greatest menace.

First to die was the thug with the steel bar. Whisper, Shadow's katana, sliced effortlessly through the wrist of the offending arm. The metal rod and the hand that clutched it, dropped to the ground with a thump. Blood gushed out of the man's stump in a torrent. He screamed once, half turning to his companions. A red spray splattered across several of them before Shadow's wakizashi caught him in the neck and put him out of his misery. The swordswoman was neither cruel nor merciful. Her victim deserved his end; a slow death was proper punishment for his crimes. But she didn't want him stumbling about in his final agony while she was engaged in deadly combat.

She intended to finish the man in the hockey mask second. Killing your enemies' leader early on was basic strategy. But, before Shadow could engage the chain-wielding gangster, the black-bearded psycho stepped into her path, laughing wildly. Gripped in his hands was a sawed-off shotgun that he continued to pump ineffectively.

"Oh, oh, oh," he mewed as Shadow swung her katana at his neck. Reacting faster than she expected, the bearded man jerked his gun up to meet the blade. Metal sparked against metal as Whisper glanced off the tempered steel of the rifle barrel. The man giggled madly as Shadow spun away, whipping her long sword in a swirling arc over her head.

His laughter turned into a gurgle of shock as Shadow dropped to her knees at the end of her turn and let her momentum guide her swing. Whisper sliced a diagonal cut from the bearded man's belly to his abdomen. He gasped in unexpected pain and stumbled forward. He never saw Scream extended straight out in his path until he rammed himself onto the razor sharp blade. Without another sound, he collapsed to the earth, a massive hunk of dead meat. Shadow whipped her short sword out of his body before he touched the ground.

"Sonofabitch," muttered the thug with the eye patch. He stared at the bowie knife in his right hand and then at the twin blades Shadow held. For a second, he seemed to be weighing his chances. Shadow gave him little opportunity to make a decision. The man was armed and dangerous, a killer lacking in morals or honor. She had no mercy in her heart for cannibals. Her katana arced so fast that the air whistled with its passage. The criminal's head tumbled to the earth, a puzzled expression still on his face.

At the same instant, Shadow twisted her wakizashi in a narrow loop, catching the descending shotgun barrel of the remaining skinhead. It was an impossible feat for an ordinary sword fighter, but the supernatural energy of *Do* fueled Shadow's attack. The rifle went flying out of the stunned criminal's hands. Two of his fingers also paid the price of folly.

"Mother of mercy," whimpered the man, clutching his mutilated hand close to his chest. He didn't hesitate. Whirling around, he scrambled off into the darkness. Shadow let him go. She still had the man with the chain to dispatch.

The gang leader had shifted position. Now, he stood at the edge of the highway, framed between the headlights of the rental car. The bright beams made it difficult for Shadow to see the masked thug clearly. His chain, held as before in his gloved hands, swung back and forth in a shallow arc just above the pavement. The sharp, rounded hook at the end of the loop gleamed in the lights.

"Not my night for pickin' suckers," the man said with a hoarse chuckle. "I shoulda fuckin' stayed home and played cards."

Cautiously, Shadow stepped forward. The gang leader could have fled while she was engaged with his companions. He had chosen not to. She felt certain that he was not suicidal. The thug had to have something nasty planned.

"Watching you was like seeing one of those chop-socky movies from Hong Kong," said the leather-faced man. The end of the chain swung in slightly wider arcs. His voice, gravelly and low, betrayed not a trace of fear. "You know, the ones where nobody's mouth moves when they talk."

Shadow said nothing. Deftly, she slid her wakizashi back into its scabbard. She gripped Whisper with both hands. In single combat, she preferred using one blade. Two hands gave her much sharper control of the sword. Cautiously, she took another step forward. The leather-faced thug was no more than five yards away. The steel chain in his hands swung back and forth, almost hypnotically, in the glare of the car lights.

A sixth sense, born of years of *Do* training, warned Shadow of peril an instant before she was attacked from behind. She flung herself to the right, her body dropping into a backward somersault, as a big man hurtled forward, rifle butt held head high to club in her skull. It was the skinhead who had supposedly fled into the night. Evidently, his departure was part of a ruse the gang had used before. This time, however, the trick didn't work.

Without a wasted motion, Shadow was back on her feet, her katana pointed straight out from her body like an arrow aimed at the eight-fingered hoodlum. Her attacker, off-balance from the missed contact, was just regaining solid footing as Shadow stepped forward, raising her katana for a killing stroke. That was when the leather-masked man struck.

He whirled the chain once around in the air to gain some speed and then whipped it at Shadow. The attack wasn't unexpected. Shadow had guessed immediately that the masked man intended to use the chain in such fashion. However, caught in motion, she was unable to perform the proper defensive moves. With a snap of steel against bone, the chain wrapped itself around Shadow's extended arms, the hook on the end locking into an open loop. Sharp pain cut into the young woman's limbs: A thick strand of barbed wire ran through the chain, and the hooks clung to her flesh like a horde of vermin, tearing her exposed skin. That was why the masked man wore padded gloves.

Laughing cruelly, the lead gangster wrenched

hard on the chain, pulling Shadow off balance. She stumbled. Blood spurted from a dozen wounds on her arms. The katana sagged in her suddenly numb fingers.

"Kill her quick," the leather-masked man ordered his stooge. He kept the chain taut, the end of it wrapped around his gloves. His voice was no longer calm and cool but filled with excitement. The thought of murder obviously gave him a thrill. "Don't give her a fuckin' second to recover."

His head bobbing up and down like a toy, the skinhead reached with his good hand into his pocket and pulled out a six-inch switchblade. The hand missing two fingers was wrapped in a blood-soaked bandanna. With a click, the blade emerged. "I'm gonna cut off your face for slicin' my fingers," the thug swore as he stepped close to Shadow. "First your nose, then your ears, then I'll carve my initials in your cheeks."

"I think not," murmured Shadow of the Dawn. Dropping her sword, she yanked her arms back across her shoulder. Blood gushed from her wounds, but the motion caught the leather-masked man by surprise. He flopped forward onto the pavement, his grip on the chain loosening slightly.

Calling upon her *Do* abilities, Shadow leapt high into the air. At the top of her jump, her feet level with the skinhead's face, she lashed out with a spinning windmill dragon kick. The blow slammed into the side of the thug's face like a thunderbolt.

Bones shattered like rotten wood as blood and brains spurted across the man's shoulders. The skinhead remained standing, a horrified look in his eyes, an entire portion of his skull smashed to pulp, dead on his feet.

Desperately scrambling erect, the leather-faced man tugged impotently on the barbed-wire chain. It no longer mattered. Shadow was already on the ground and running forward, keeping the chain slack. She moved faster than he could pull. Her arms raised, she had as much control of the steel links as the gangster. He screamed in horror as he suddenly realized what she intended to do. Though he tried to disentangle his gloved hands from the barbed wire, it was already too late. With a surge of speed, Shadow swung the chain over the man's shoulder. In an instant, a barbed-wire necklace circled the gang-leader's head, anchored by the thread wrapped around his fingers.

Blocking the pain from her mind, Shadow jerked her arms downward. The leather-masked man shrieked as the hooks ripped into his skin, and flopped face-first onto the pavement of the highway. "You fuckin' bitch!" he screamed. "I'll rip your heart out for this. I swear it!"

"Maybe in the next circle of Drahma," said Shadow calmly. "But not in this turn of the wheel."

Placing one foot on his back, she jerked the chain tight. The gangster gurgled in horrible pain as the barbed wire bit into his throat. His arms flailed wildly as he tried to wrench loose, but there was no escape. With a savage twist of her wrists, Shadow wrenched the steel chain high into the air. The man's neck snapped like rotten wood, the hooks in the wire digging deep grooves into his skin.

Seething with annoyance, she untangled her arms from the deadly links. Shadow was angry with herself for letting the man catch her with the chain. She should have dealt with him earlier in the fight. A well-directed slash from Whisper would have rendered the steel useless. The battle had lasted much longer than she had planned. The young woman shook her head. Though she had trained for years as a Dragon Scale, she still had much to learn. Actual combat was a harsh but effective teacher.

It wasn't until Shadow reached over to retrieve Whisper that she remembered Kallikos. The time-master had left to deal with the blonde who had lured them into this trap. Shadow felt certain that the girl was no innocent. She worked as bait. Which meant that she was as dangerous as her companions, and perhaps even more so. Quickly, the young willworker hurried over to the van.

The golden-skinned mage waited for her, a slight smile on his lips. In his hand, he held a bowie knife. A thin trickle of blood stained his purple silk shirt. A few feet away, her back pressed against the metal of the big van, stood a tall, slender blonde dressed in a halter top and black bike shorts. With wide baby blue eyes, red lips, and dimpled cheeks, she appeared the soul of innocence. Shadow estimated the girl to be no more than eighteen years old. A bloody X across the bare flesh directly beneath her breasts indicated that Kallikos had gotten the better of their exchange.

"Trouble?" asked Shadow, keeping a wary eye on the blonde. There had been enough surprises for one night. If the woman moved, she was dead.

"A little," admitted Kallikos. "My long years out of touch with society have rendered me helplessly naive. I could not believe this young woman was associated with our attackers. She claimed she was their victim, forced to do their bidding or be killed. I assumed she was telling the truth until, when I turned my back on her to see how you were managing, she tried to slip this blade between my ribs."

The dark-haired mage held up the bowie knife. "Fortunately, even after my long exile, I am not entirely helpless. I wrenched the weapon from her hand, and in the ensuing struggle, paid her back double for my wound."

Left unsaid was that Kallikos most likely aided his cause with a small dash of magick. It was impossible to stab the bearded man in the back.

"What happened with our other friends?" asked Kallikos. "Since you are here and they are not, I assume the outcome of your struggle was satisfactory?"

Shadow shrugged. "I learned a lesson in humility tonight," she declared. "Still, I survived and will benefit from the experience. They did not. Their bodies litter the road."

"Dead?" said the blonde, her jaw dropping. "They're all dead?"

Shadow of the Dawn nodded. "They attacked me. I offered them the chance to retreat. They did not take it and thus paid the price for their arrogance. The wheel turns."

Tears trickled down the young woman's cheeks. "They-they were the only family I ever had. Now, I'm alone. All alone!"

Momentarily forgetting the knife Kallikos held, the blonde took a step away from the van. Instantly, Whisper was poised beneath her throat, just touching the soft white skin of her neck.

"Take one more step," said Shadow, "and you can offer your regrets to them personally in hell. While I dislike the thought of killing anyone without a fight, in your case I would make the rare exception. Your hands are covered with the blood of too many innocents for me to feel any sorrow in terminating your worthless existence."

"Wh-what are you going to do with me?" she asked, shuffling backward so that her shoulder blades once more touched the metal of the van.

"We are going to release you," said Kallikos, the eyebrows knitting over his face as his expression grew stern. "In that fashion, you can inform your fellow cannibals that there are those of us who are tired of their attacks on the helpless. Enough is enough. Rabid animals cannot be allowed to live. Death rides the highways."

Kallikos' tone turned sharp. Hypnotic in intensity, his voice demanded attention. "Justice is slow, but it is relentless. Go and warn your comrades wherever they gather in this god-forsaken region. Tonight was only the beginning. These deaths were but the first of many. They are next. No mercy for them, no forgiveness. Only death."

Trembling with fear, the blonde staggered to the front of the van. In seconds, the vehicle was barreling along the highway, where it was soon lost in the darkness of the night.

"You made a strong impression," said Shadow, sheathing Whisper, "projecting in such a manner. However, I did not realize that we planned to bring relentless justice to this section of the country."

"We don't," said Kallikos. "And, even if we did, I fear that it would take a small army of mages to accomplish the feat. The world is filled with predators like the ones you killed tonight. Destroy a handful and dozens more will take their place. Ours was a hollow victory. Still, I thought a stern warning, while the memory of her departed companions was still fresh, might have an impact upon the child. For the near future at least, she'll preach the gospel of repentance. If even one life is saved, it will have been worth the effort."

Robert Weinberg

"Maybe," said Shadow. "More likely, she'll return in an hour with a new pack of headhunters. I think it best for us to depart. The further we are away from this place, the better I will feel. Once we are safe, I need to concentrate on healing my wounds."

"We will see that girl again," said Kallikos, an odd note in his voice. "I feel certain of it."

By now, Shadow knew better than to mock the mage's words. He rarely made outright predictions. But, when he did, they invariably came true.

<u>Chapter Ten</u>

The intercom on Pietro Giovanni's desk buzzed. Standing in front of the huge glass window overlooking St. Mark's cathedral, the vampire lord of the Mausoleum stared at the communications unit in annoyance. He had left strict instructions not to be interrupted tonight. Pietro scowled. The master of the Mausoleum intensely disliked when his commands were disobeyed. There had better be a good reason for the call.

Madeleine had left an hour ago. Most of the time since he had spent staring out across the city. Though he managed an enormous financial empire, Pietro Giovanni dreamed of even greater glories. He wanted more power for his family—and for himself. Incredibly ambitious, he was relentless and

148

patient. He understood that it might take many years before his goals were realized. It mattered not at all. The Undead didn't worry about time.

"Yes?" he growled into the intercom. "What is it?"

"My apologies, chairman," answered the receptionist forty floors below. Pietro had used many titles over the centuries. Chairman fit him best for the present. "Your gardener, Antonio Quastro, needs to speak with you immediately. I informed him of your wishes to remain undisturbed, but he insisted. He claims that it is an emergency and that any delay will mean disaster. Knowing your concerns, I decided it best to disobey your orders."

"You acted correctly," said Pietro. Antonio was the one person whose calls he never ignored. "Patch me through to him. Immediately."

Pietro waited impatiently for the transfer to be completed. The gardener was one of his oldest and most trusted retainers; he had tended Pietro's flowers for decades and was a superb horticulturist. An emergency call from Antonio could mean but one thing: Plants were dying. He was not someone who panicked easily.

"Antonio," said Pietro as soon as the connection was made to his country estate, "what is happening? Why did you phone?"

"The blood roses, Signoro Giovanni," said Antonio, his voice cracking with emotion. "The

The Road to Hell

bushes, they are dying. I cannot explain why. Nothing has changed here. The roses, they were fine until a few hours ago. Then, for no reason, the plants began to shrivel and perish. I've checked everything two times. The conditions all remain the same. The water, the light, the blood, all are perfect. Yet, the roses are dying."

Pietro gritted his teeth together in suppressed rage. Two hours ago was approximately when he was giving instructions to Montifloro and Madeleine. He knew beyond any doubt that the events had to be related.

"Do what you can," said Pietro, his voice reflecting a calmness he did not feel. "The dawn approaches. It is impossible for me to be there before sunrise. Save any bush if possible. The fault is not yours. Tomorrow night, I will come out to the gardens as soon as I am able. Do not despair, Antonio. What can be grown once can be grown again."

"I will try my best, Signoro," said Antonio. The gardener's voice held little hope. "It is a terrible mystery. I can find nothing wrong. Nothing. It is as if the plants are cursed."

Eyes glowing in anger, Pietro clicked off the intercom. He had devoted thousands of hours to developing the Blood Rose. Despite what he had said to Antonio, he knew that duplicating his success would not be easy. Too many factors contributed to growing the perfect flower. Softly, he cursed in frustration.

A low chuckle, coarse and grating, echoed through Pietro's office. Startled, the chairman raised his head. He saw no one. Yet, he was sure that he had heard something. Frowning, he pushed himself out of his chair.

Slowly, carefully, he circumnavigated the floor of his chambers. The vast room was empty. The thoughtful expression on Pietro's face deepened. Just as he settled back into his leather chair, the voice laughed a second time. Not loud, yet sharp and clear enough that there was no mistaking it for a recording or transmission. Someone was in the office with him—a person who could remain hidden unless he willed himself to be found. A being whose powers could defy Pietro's own heightened senses. The master of the Mausoleum had no doubts as to the identity of his enemy.

"Well?" he asked the empty air, "are you planning to make yourself visible? How long do you wish to continue this foolish charade?"

"The emergency call button you are pressing with your foot no longer functions," said the short, husky man who suddenly appeared in front of Pietro's desk. His hair and beard were steel gray, his eyes pitch black. In visits past, he had always been impeccably neat. Tonight, his thick hair appeared tangled and uncombed, while his white shirt was wrinkled and creased. "All of the protective devices on this floor ceased to work the moment I arrived. Nor will the elevators rise to this level. Downstairs, the indicators signal all is well. They'll continue to do so until I depart." The short man smiled, the grin of a maniac. "I thought it best if we spoke in privacy, Pietro. Just two old friends conversing without any interruptions."

"What do you want, Ezra?" asked Pietro. Centuries old, incredibly powerful, the chairman was not easily intimidated. Ezra, however, scared him.

Wizards were notoriously unstable. Their obsessive quest for Ascension, for mental perfection, drove many of them mad. Such lunatics, armed with vast powers to warp reality, were extremely deadly. And they were entirely unpredictable.

"What do I want, Pietro?" said Ezra, leaning forward so that his hands rested on the desk, his wild eyes staring directly into those of the vampire elder. "*I want to be left alone.* That's all. I merely wish to not be disturbed by meddling outsiders while I pursue my interests."

"We've had no dealings in months," said Pietro. "I have no idea what you're doing at present. Nor have I or any of my clan interfered with you in any manner."

"So you say," declared Ezra, his lips curling into a sneer. "*So you say.* What about your two underlings who came here earlier this evening? Did they stop by your office merely to pay their respects—or was there a more sinister purpose to their visit? You think to keep secrets from me, Pietro, but I'm not easily deceived. Not even by a master of lies like yourself."

The willworker laughed. An uneasy feeling swept over Pietro. In the years that he had been dealing with Ezra, the wizard had always been accommodating, anxious to make deals. He had spoken carefully, using words designed to avoid friction between himself and Pietro. That was no longer the case. The mage's personality had undergone a major transformation. He was arrogant, self-assured, and unafraid. While Pietro assumed much of this change in attitude came from encroaching madness, there had to be another reason.

"Once I feared you," said Ezra, as if reading Pietro's mind. "But no more. In the past few months, I've forged an alliance with a mentor whose power far exceeds your might."

Ezra's face twisted into a mask of hate. "The rules of conduct have changed drastically. I am no longer bound by that fool Rambam's code of honor. The only law I now obey is my own. Step in my path, Pietro, and I will crush you. The female assassin, the woman-childe named Madeleine you sent out hunting for me, shall be utterly destroyed. So will be the one she holds most dear. Eliminating them both will be my great pleasure. One by one, I will destroy all that you hold dear."

"The Blood Roses," said Pietro, comprehension dawning. "You poisoned the bushes."

The Road to Hell

"It was a simple matter to suck the life out of the plants," declared Ezra, chuckling. "Knowing how dearly you treasured those weeds, I derived immense pleasure out of destroying them. But, their elimination was not enough. A final lesson is needed."

The madman walked over to the ornate grandfather's clock standing against the inner wall of the office. "A beautiful antique," said Ezra. He placed a hand on the wood, as if caressing the fine veneer. "August LeClair was a true genius. I find it amazing that a mere mortal could build such a magnificent piece of work. This clock is truly a piece of art. I know it is one of your greatest treasures. It is irreplaceable. Too bad."

Pietro was on his feet. "No!" he shouted angrily. But he was talking to empty air. Ezra had disappeared. It was as if he had never been in the room.

A moment later, the LeClair clock began to chime, its full, deep notes filling the room. Pietro sagged against his desk in despair. The hour was still twenty minutes away. Again and again, the mighty grandfather's clock tolled, each note seemingly louder than the last. Sound piled upon sound, the echoes of the previous note mixing with those of the next. The walls shook with the vibrations. Pietro's desk shifted inches across the carpet. The chairs in the room tumbled over, as if knocked askew by a giant hand. Tiny spider web cracks appeared like frost across the thousands of square feet of tinted glass in the office.

Reaching out with the full force of his tremendous will, Pietro tried to discover what Ezra had done to the clock. There was no sign of the madman's tampering. Whatever spell he had used, it was beyond Pietro's abilities to stop it.

With a thunderous roar, the LeClair Clock struck twelve. The sound was so overpowering that all of the windows in the chamber exploded. Most of the glass fell outward, sending thousands of pieces hurtling to the earth. A small number of fragments dropped into the room. Prepared for the worst, Pietro had hardened his body to the consistency of steel and was unharmed. Surprisingly, the clock remained intact, completely unaffected by the note. The sound of the twelfth note was just dying when it struck thirteen.

Thirteen o'clock. The hour of madness. The sound it made was shrill, piercing, the tone of absolute insanity. The universe seemed to pause for an instant, as the unbearable agony of the discordant note rode through the air in a wave of ultimate madness.

With that sound, the LeClair Clock collapsed in on itself, a steaming mass of gears and bolts and springs. Like a year-old corpse unexpectedly exposed to the air, it dissolved into a pool of bubbling putrescence.

Tears of black blood stained Pietro Giovanni's

cheeks. There could be no compromise, no retreat. Honor governed his actions. It was to be war between Ezra, the insane wizard, and the Clan Giovanni.

<u>Chapter Eleven</u>

The meeting between the three members of the Gray Collective Triumvirate stretched on for another hour, as they thrashed out new precautions to prevent any repeat of the breakout. Velma suppressed a yawn. She found the eternal bickering between Sharon Reed and Comptroller Klair tiresome. Their constant fighting transformed every conference into a battle of wills which neither could win. If it wasn't for the patient efforts of Terrence Shade, no important decisions would ever be reached. As it was, it took hours to resolve matters that should have been settled in minutes.

Her boss, the leader of the Progenitors at the Gray Collective, and Comptroller Klair, chief among the mages of Iteration X, exemplified to

Velma the worst faults of Technocracy leadership. Both were convinced beyond doubt of the superiority of their own beliefs over anyone else's. Compromise or negotiation was impossible for them because they knew they were right and everyone else was wrong. Velma found Reed and Klair unintentionally funny. They hated each other, but personal beliefs aside, their personalities were almost identical.

Fortunately, the highest leaders in their Conventions wanted the AW Project to succeed. Outside pressure, along with the incessant badgering of Terrence Shade, forced the two to cooperate. Inwardly, Velma nodded in satisfaction. Though it had taken years of effort and sacrifice, the great plan was proceeding as predicted.

Casually, she glanced across the room at the cyborg they had dubbed Ernest Nelson. The freakish mech man appeared to be as bored as she was. Nelson, with his tank treads and claw hands, looked more machine than human to Velma. The rest of his body was as hard and firm as the steel of his artificial limbs. Klair's assistant's expression was cold and devoid of human emotion. When he spoke, his voice sounded artificial, almost robotic.

Velma knew that he hated her. Those people he could not categorize and put into specific groups worried Nelson. As a shapechanger whose personality shifted with each transformation, she presented the ultimate puzzle to the cyborg, and he made no secret of the fact that he did not trust her. Velma found Nelson amusing. More than anyone else in the complex, Nelson sensed a small measure of the truth about her schemes. But no one believed him.

"I believe that wraps up the last detail of the revisions," declared Terrence Shade, breaking through the haze of her daydreams. The Mission Specialist's tone was weary. "These added precautions should eliminate any possibility of further escapes."

"If they don't," declared Sharon Reed, "then we follow my earlier suggestion and kill all of our captives, saving tissue samples from them to grow clones as needed."

"Absolute nonsense," retorted Klair. This argument, in one form or another, had been the chief roadblock between the two leaders all night. "Such action could seriously delay the project for months. We cannot risk any further setbacks while you tinker with genetic codes. Scientific expertise is the answer, not more mumbo jumbo gene splicing."

"Quiet," said Shade, rising from the table. His face was so red it appeared ready to explode. "I've listened to enough of your pointless debates tonight to last me a month. The Men in Black must be set on Prisoner Seventeen's trail this morning. Any possible damage he may have caused the project needs to be counteracted. I have plenty of work to occupy my time. I suggest that the rest of you get moving. There are specific deadlines for this project. See that they are met. No one here cannot be replaced by another. Fail me and someone else will end up claiming credit for the work you have put in for the past year of your life."

From the tone of Shade's voice, it was quite clear to everyone in the room that the Specialist meant exactly what he said. As the representative from the Technocracy Symposium, he wielded supreme power over the personnel in the Gray Collective. Anxious to get things done and knowing he had the best team possible, he had used velvet gloves in dealing with problems in the past. But, there was no question that steel fists were beneath the softness.

The rest of them stood up. The meeting was over. Still muttering beneath his breath, Shade exited. The Mission Specialist was not a happy man.

"Let's go," said Sharon Reed, gathering up her notes from the table. There was a determined look in her eyes that Velma sensed had nothing to do with the decisions made at the meeting. "We can discuss the new work schedule on the way to my quarters. I need some more rest. It's been a long night."

They exited without a word of goodbye to their companions. Sharon was never polite or diplomatic. As Reed's second-in-command, Velma knew better than to say anything. Her boss made the decisions. She just carried out her orders like a proper assistant. At least until the appropriate moment arrived.

"Before we head back," said Sharon as they walked through the corridors of the huge complex, "let's make a quick side trip and check on our experiment in the growth tanks in the lower level. With all of the attention to the AW Project, we've neglected our little pet."

Velma smiled. The Research Director had something to tell her that could not be communicated with playing cards. The growth tank area was one of the few places in the Gray Collective where they felt reasonably safe from Iteration X spies and microphones. A horde of genetically enhanced rats patrolled the region and killed anything that moved. The creatures served to ensure that no miniature bugging devices made it into the secret laboratories.

"Semok looks fine to me," declared Velma fifteen minutes later. She stood with Sharon Reed on a long narrow catwalk located on the lip of a huge container of development fluid, twenty feet high by thirty feet wide by sixty feet long. The liquid was dense and murky with numerous growth compounds and chemicals. A large control panel, monitored by two mages twenty-four hours a day, was located at the base of the tank. Careful attention was paid to the mix, maintaining a proper balance of nutrients and hyper-growth hormones.

Six months of hard work had gone into developing the monster the Director referred to fondly as her "little pet." Velma, who disliked sentiment and nicknames, preferred the acronym, Semok.

The AW Project was the main focus of all work at the Gray Collective. However, as Research Director for the Progenitor faction in the complex, Sharon otherwise had free reign to conduct whatever experiments she wished, as long as they did not interfere with the primary objective. Charles Klair spent his free time designing new computerized limbs, several of which he had grafted onto his own body. Terrence Shade conducted psychological testing on the mages, charting their reactions to various subliminal messages. Sharon Reed had Semok.

The Research Director had dreamed of the project for over a decade, but never before had she possessed the necessary resources or time to make her vision reality. Now, the bizarre creature was nearly complete. The final evolutionary step, requiring a magickal linkage of all the Progenitor mages in the compound, was scheduled to take place approximately a week from now. Velma, who trusted no one, suspected that Sharon had planned Semok's emergence to coincide with the completion of the AW Project. Though she had been Reed's assistant for years, the Director did not trust her with all of her secrets.

"He appears quite healthy," said Sharon.

"However, that is to be expected. While not common, cephalopoids have been employed by our underwater units for years. I was never concerned about whether we could grow one here; I only wondered about the question of mobility. And whether he will be able to exist outside of the tank for more than a few minutes without dying."

"The monster's awake," said Velma. "Shall I drop in a few dummies and see how it reacts?"

"Why not?" said Reed. She grinned. "I can at least pretend that one of them is Comptroller Klair."

The dummies were life-size mannequins dressed in heavy-duty diving gear. The clothing was used for the most dangerous undersea missions and was built to withstand tremendous underwater pressure. The feet of the suit were filled with cement so that the phony aquanauts quickly sank to the bottom of the tank. The outfits were painted black, so as to be almost invisible in the murky water.

Nearly a dozen mannequins were lined up on the catwalk near where Velma and Sharon stood. Choosing figures entirely at random, Velma pushed the third, fifth, ninth, and tenth dummies into the tank. They dropped, hardly making a ripple, into the solution. The question was not whether Semok would react—it always did—but when, and how much damage the celaphopoid would inflict on the pretend divers.

In seconds, the water erupted. One mannequin

came flying out of the tank, its suit and body nearly ripped in two. A second followed, instants later, legs and arms missing. The third and fourth remained in the pool, but the thrashing of huge tentacles made it quite clear that the two dummies were being smashed to shreds.

Semok was a giant squid, approximately thirty feet long, with the brain and features of a man. The face rested at the center of the cluster of gigantic tentacles, with the human mouth replaced by the squid's beak. The man's eyes were adapted for underwater use, but Semok retained the squid's eyes on each side of its head. A hard shell surrounded its body, making it extremely difficult to kill. What it had done to the mannequins was only a small demonstration of the astonishing strength of the monster's ten tentacles. Semok was one of the strongest creatures in the world. And, because it also had a human mind, it was among the most destructive.

"It's getting faster," said Sharon with satisfaction. "Putting the brain of a mass murderer in its body was a stroke of genius. Semok doesn't attack the diving suits because its territory has been invaded. The monster enjoys killing."

"Controlling the thing during a fight may be difficult," said Velma, always focusing on the practical matters. "I suspect once it goes berserk, the beast won't be able to distinguish friend from foe."

"That's why we won't use the cephalopoid in situations where such things matter," said the Director. She smiled. "Mindless destruction can be quite useful in certain circumstances."

The Progentiors had used monsters like Semok for years to scour the sea bottoms for useful life forms and treasure. Sharon Reed saw them as something more. Using the latest developments in Progenitor procedure, she intended to give the squid/human monstrosity the ability to move on land. Couple that power with an ability to exist for short periods of time without water, the cephalopoid became a nightmarish engine of destruction. Semok was short for *semi-mobile octopoid killer*. It was an insane, improbable idea. But some of the Progenitors' greatest triumphs came from equally unlikely concepts.

"I assume you wanted to discuss something other than our octopoid friend?" asked Velma. Because of genetic body modification, she required less sleep than most. Still, even her body needed some rest. "More news about the final situation?"

"That's why I summoned you to my quarters," said Sharon, "before this entire fiasco started. I had some good news to share. Final word came this evening from the executive branch."

Velma smiled. "Nothing unexpected, I assume."

The Research Director's face glowed with satisfaction. "We are to finish the AW Project as swiftly as possible. Once we know the results are positive, the pattern-clone is to be destroyed except for tissue samples for EcoR growth tanks. The sauroids, as you guessed correctly months ago, are to be given orders to execute every nonessential person in the Gray Collective. Knowledge of this collaboration between us and Iteration X will die with Klair and his cronies."

Velma stared deep into the tank. Semok's human eyes, bright blue and filled with intelligence, looked up at her. It was almost as if the giant squid were trying to speak to her. Shaking her head, Velma looked away. She needed to concentrate on the matters at hand.

Though she had been expecting such orders for weeks, tonight Velma felt a trace of unease. A great deal hinged on the upcoming conversation. "The sauroids love to kill," she said, picking her words carefully. "It's bred into their genes. Yet, after the events this evening, I'm not sure that they will be enough to finish the job."

"What are you implying?" asked the Research Director.

"We can't make the mistake of underestimating our opponents," said Velma. "Remember, Prisoner Seventeen dispatched one of the snake men with his bare hands. Ernest Nelson may be a freakish nuisance, but those steel claws of his are deadly. He won't be easy to kill. Several other Iteration X technicians working on the project are equally tough. The sauroids are flesh and blood. I'm not convinced they'll be able to obliterate all of our enemies in the Collective. In the battle, one of the machine men might escape to static reality. If that happens, we would be faced with an all-out war between our Convention and Iteration X."

"I hate to admit it, but your worries about the snake men makes sense," said Reed, a thoughtful expression on her face. "The sauroids were never meant to be shock troops for our Convention in the manner that the HIT Marks serve Iteration X. Overconfidence can be a dangerous trap. I'm well aware of Comptroller Klair's feelings about me. That metalhead would like nothing better than to smash me to a pulp."

The Research Director laughed, a harsh, cruel sound. "Of course, that's the least I would like to do to him."

"Nelson's the one who frightens me," said Velma. "Klair believes in the basic goals of Iteration X. Though obnoxious, he is a true scientist in the proper Technocracy tradition. Logic governs his actions. He's an idealist at heart; he truly believes in Unity and works tirelessly toward that goal. That's not the case with his assistant. Nelson worships the machine without thought or reason. Faith alone guides him. Klair understands the need for justice and order in the world. Nelson does not. Nothing matters to him other than metal. He's a fanatic."

"My orders were quite clear," said Reed.

"Anything less than total destruction of the pattern-clone and Klair's forces would be considered failure." The Director's features hardened. "I'm not prepared for failure. You have an idea?"

"I have several," said Velma, licking her lips. She enjoyed talking about her hobby. "All of them involve lethal chemicals. With your authority, I could begin manufacturing the compounds tomorrow. For example, a timed hallucinogenic in the water supply would produce spectacular effects. Making sure it only affected metalheads might take a little work, but I'm sure I could find a way."

"Do whatever you think necessary," said Reed. "I'll issue the requisitions for supplies tomorrow. Just make sure the drugs are ready in time. And make sure Klair doesn't have a clue as to what we're planning."

"He'll never guess," said Velma. "Not until it's much too late."

"Very good," said the Director. "Any other worries?"

"One more," said Velma, cautiously. After months, she finally had the subtle opening to raise a question that needed to be answered. Velma forced herself to relax. Director Reed was extremely suspicious. If the query was phrased the wrong way, it could mean serious trouble. "I'm concerned about managing the destruction of the AW pattern-clone."

Sharon Reed frowned. "The artificial being? Why are you concerned about it?"

"Perhaps I'm jumping at shadows," said Velma, gaining confidence as she spoke, "but according to these new instructions, we're supposed to eliminate the AW pattern-clone once we know it is fully functional. Which means that the being must first be brought fully to life. What happens if our newly energized creation does not agree to his termination?"

She stared directly into Sharon Reed's eyes. "You've spent the past year directing the growth of the most powerful humanoid pattern-clone in existence. Our creation possesses regenerative powers that make it nearly unkillable. Its every mental and physical power has been enhanced a hundred times over that of a normal human. Comptroller Klair has programmed the being to have astonishing control over computer systems. Actually, no one is sure exactly how powerful this creation might be. Prisoner Seventeen possesses only a small measure of the pattern-clone's strengths and look at what he's accomplished already. His exploits make clear the problems we could face. I repeat. *What happens if when the AW pattern-clone is brought to life, he doesn't want to be destroyed?*"

The Research Director shook her head in mock dismay. She smiled. "Don't be naive, Velma. The pattern-clone has no intelligence or personality.

Upon awakening, it will be a functioning body without a mind to guide it. Besides, don't you think I know my business? If somehow the clone developed a functioning mind, killing it would still be child's play. When I supervised the initial growth of the pattern-clone form, I programmed into the basic DNA patterns a sequential self-destruct code. Once begun, there is no way for the AW bioconstruct to stop a total system collapse within minutes. I voice-coded the string. One sentence from me and our otherwise indestructible toy is finished."

"And that sentence is?" asked Velma.

"For me to know and you to wonder," said Sharon, with a laugh. "I'll tell you when necessary, Velma. But there's no reason to discuss it now."

"Of course," said Velma. "Just curious."

She knew, though, that before the project was complete, she would have to learn the self-destruct sequence. Velma was going to have the initialization string. Or make sure that Sharon Reed would not be able to use it.

Chapter Twelve

As she did every morning at exactly eight a.m., Ms. Millicent Hargroves signed the entry log at the front security desk of her apartment building. She was dressed in a conservative blue suit, entirely without makeup, her hair pulled back tightly in a no-nonsense bun. Joe Steeger, the officer on duty, studied her handwriting, matching it against the official template. A big, fat man, stuffed into an official blue security patrol uniform, Steeger enjoyed making people wait. When any of the residents complained, he merely told them that he took his job seriously. He liked to brag that no deadbeat had ever gotten into the apartments during his tour of duty at the front desk. Ms. Hargroves suspected the record was due more to luck than any efforts by the overweight and underintelligent officer.

"Checked out last night and now you're back kinda early in the morning?" he declared for perhaps the fiftieth time in the past few months. The security guard leered at her. "Got insomnia or something?"

Ms. Hargroves sighed. Steeger was a tiring nuisance. She had told him time after time that she worked the night shift for Everwell Chemicals. It never made any difference. The guard had little memory beyond what he ate for lunch.

"I work the midnight circuit for Everwell Chemical Corporation, the company that owns half this stinking city," she said, her tone flat and honest. "I'm tired and I want to go to bed. Is my signature okay?"

"It looks fine, ma'am," Steeger declared pompously, peering up at Ms. Hargroves. Her icy tones were lost on the guard. "You can go up. Use elevator three."

"Thank you, officer," said Ms. Hargroves mockingly, knowing she was wasting her effort. Steeger was too dumb to recognize sarcasm if it hit him over the head.

"I'll buzz the entrance door when you get to the end of the hall," he said, shifting his weight on the huge chair behind the security desk. He liked to move around when residents were present to display the .45 automatic he wore strapped around his huge waist. Not that he had ever drawn the gun. Or knew which end to use in case of a real emergency.

Lips pressed tightly together, Ms. Hargroves walked briskly to the inner portal. The buzzer sounded when she was five feet away. Hurrying her steps accordingly, she grabbed hold of the doorknob and twisted it open an instant before the noise stopped. Steeger was not only dumb but incompetent.

As she stepped into elevator three, Ms. Hargroves wondered if she should go to the trouble of having Steeger replaced. It wouldn't be difficult. As private secretary to Enzo Giovanni, she wielded tremendous influence. A word from her to the owners of the apartment complex and Mr. Steeger would be back on the street, working as a part-time guard in some dilapidated public school. Or a more direct comment to the Grim brothers and the fat security officer would be at the bottom of the lake, held in place by a pair of cement handcuffs around his wrists.

Ms. Hargroves smiled, thinking exactly how bloated Steeger's face would look after a few weeks under water. Knowing the Grim brothers, the guard's death wouldn't be pleasant. They delighted in torturing their victims before finishing the job.

It was a tempting notion. Her only concern was that the guard's replacement might be even worse. As a single black woman, she had dealt with intolerance and prejudice all her life. For all of his faults, Steeger did not treat her any worse than he did anyone else in the building. He wasn't a bigot, just a fool. It was a small but significant mark in his favor. Stepping out of the elevator on her floor, she decided she would let the guard live a little longer. Until, at least, he did something that really annoyed her.

Opening the door to her apartment, Ms. Hargroves immediately kicked off her shoes. She was bone-weary and after hours of pollution and rot, her feet needed freedom. Physically exhausted, she walked into the suite's small kitchenette and grabbed a beer from the refrigerator. She emptied half the can in a single gulp. Enzo Giovanni might need human blood to survive, but Millicent Hargroves needed beer.

"You're a minute late," came a soft, sultry voice from the parlor. "That imbecile doorman give you problems again?"

Ms. Hargroves padded into the living room, her toes sinking into the thick white shag carpeting. The entire room was decorated in black and white. Those were her favorite colors. The furniture was entirely white, while the walls were jet black. Ms. Hargroves found the stark contrast pleasing to the eye. To her, the world existed entirely in black and white, so it made sense to decorate her surroundings accordingly. A woman of strong tastes and opinions, Ms. Hargroves got whatever she wanted.

Robert Weinberg

Seated in a large, plush sofa was a slender young woman. She wore a man's pin-striped suit, complete with a red necktie and matching handkerchief. Cut short, her hair was the same deep red as her tie and curled around her face like a snake. Her sexless, inhuman face glowed with unnatural vitality. Dark eyes burned like hot coals. Though she had many names among many peoples, she preferred to be called Aliara. A being from the Deep Universe, she was one of those mysterious creatures known to the Technocrats as Those Beyond. Others, of more occult leanings, called them the Dark Lords. Whatever her title, she was Ms. Hargroves' mentor.

Though Aliara appeared solid, she was nothing more than a ghostly illusion. Physically materializing on the Earth required hundreds of spells and thousands upon thousands of human sacrifices. As an inhabitant of the Deep Universe, she could touch the real world only with her mind.

"Steeger raises the definition of stupidity to a new level," said Ms. Hargroves, settling in a thick armchair directly across from Aliara. As usual, with her mentor present, the gaunt woman felt extremely uneasy. Ms. Hargroves liked to be in control of every situation. That was never the case when she dealt with Aliara. "He's annoying but harmless."

"It wouldn't be hard to bend his will to mine," said the red-haired figure. When she spoke, the air about her twisted as if unseen figures writhed in pain. Ms. Hargroves wanted to close her eyes but dared not. Aliara demanded absolute attention. "A short, whispered conversation with me and he'd be ready to do anything I ask. It's a gift of mine."

Aliara laughed shrilly. The sound hurt Ms. Hargroves' ears. It was inhuman, unnatural. "My words would stir dormant passions lurking just beneath the surface of the fool's mind. Most men are filled with such primal, savage urges. I'd just weaken the psychic bonds in his brain a little. It might take days or weeks before he'd finally snap. Suddenly, for no reason, he'd attack. Mr. Steeger would go berserk and murder someone he thinks looks suspicious."

Aliara's face was a mask of uncontrolled lust. Ms. Hargroves bit her tongue to keep from screaming. "Or he might just run out on the street and start shooting at cars driving past," continued the Dark Lord. "When such men snap, there's no predicting their actions. The fool would be caught soon enough. He doesn't possess the cunning to escape. His bout with insanity would probably get him shot if he was lucky. Or executed if he wasn't."

"Leave him alone," said Ms. Hargroves, trembling. She hated Aliara's vicious games. Her mentor delighted in tormenting her, upsetting her view of an ordered universe. Aliara offered endless temptations, but there was always a price for her favors. Ms. Hargroves had to be very very careful.

She knew that if she yielded to lust, it would engulf her life. The possibility of losing control of her senses frightened her more than Aliara's most vicious schemes. "I can deal with Mr. Steeger if necessary. I assume you materialized here because you want my report?"

"Of course," said the red-haired woman. "Manifesting myself as a shadow on Earth is difficult. It takes a great deal of energy and concentration to maintain even this illusory body. A dozen men and women died last night in an orgy of blood to allow me these few hours. I surely didn't come here to watch soap operas." Aliara laughed again, gesturing at the television. "Though, I must admit their plots and characters have a certain appeal."

"I'm sure they would to one such as you," said Ms. Hargroves, heading to the kitchen for another beer. She needed a few seconds away from Aliara. Reality twisted around the unearthly figure, surrounding her with an invisible curtain of insanity. "Though I doubt if any of the scriptwriters are aware of your existence, they practically worship your attributes in their compositions. Uncontrolled passion is a mainstay of daytime television."

"I've inspired more writers than most of my kind," said Aliara. She sneered. "Authors hunger for money, power, and fame just like the rest of mankind. They like to brag about how they are different, inspired by the muses. But, deep within, they are the same greedy, lusting animals as their subjects."

Sipping at her second beer, Ms. Hargroves made herself comfortable in her chair. "Enzo Giovanni continues to scheme. He is obsessed with power. His ambition grows as he becomes enmeshed in the coils of the Everwell Corporation."

"He doesn't suspect your influence?" asked Aliara. "Remember, our Cainite puppet is no fool. As a member of Clan Giovanni he belongs to one of the most cunning and ruthless groups of schemers to walk the face of the Earth. He is suspicious to the point of paranoia."

Ms. Hargroves shook her head. "Nothing. He trusts me. I'm extremely careful in everything I do. He knows I know some hints of the truth, but he considers me the perfect secretary. I arrange things for him so he doesn't need to deal with the busywork. A typical boss, he hates paperwork. The fool never suspects that my efficient operations are aimed at ensuring he follows our wishes."

"*Our* wishes?" said Aliara, laughing softly. There was a subtle edge of menace in her voice.

"Your wishes, of course," said Ms. Hargroves immediately. She nearly choked on her beer. A creature of the Deep Universe, Aliara was nothing more than a ghostly manifestation in static reality. Yet, even in this incorporeal form, the Empress of Lust could twist mortal minds with ease. One wrong word from her mentor would doom Ms. Hargroves to an eternity of torment and unceasing pain. "I am but your humble servant."

"Servant, yes," said Aliara, "though humble hardly describes your demeanor. No matter. I need human tools to further my ambitions on this world. You are the best I have ever discovered." The boyish woman's voice hardened until it was nothing even remotely human. "Your rewards will be great, Ms. Hargroves. But cross me and your punishments will be beyond imagination."

"Enzo took another step forward in his plan to control and corrupt the mayor's office tonight," said Ms. Hargroves, anxious to change the subject. "He recruited a beautiful young woman to aid his subversive campaign. With her good looks and total lack of morality, she will serve him well. Enzo plans to give her a touch of polish and then set her loose on those few city officials who have remained off the Everwell payroll. The girl is named Hope, which Enzo finds quite amusing."

"Excellent," said Aliara. "Each action he takes entirely for his own purposes leads him one step further away from his family elders in Venice. The ties that bind him to the rest of the Giovanni are nearly broken. A little more pressure and he will pull free from his clan."

"If that's the case," said Ms. Hargroves, "then won't you and Enzo serve the same master? Why are we engaged in this subterfuge?"

"Do not worry about matters that don't concern you," advised Aliara, her tone sharp.

"There was news of the AW project tonight," said Ms. Hargroves instantly. Dealing with Aliara was like dancing on quicksand. One wrong step and you were pulled under. "A man escaped from the research lab."

"A prisoner broke free from the Gray Collective?" said Aliara, arching one eyebrow. "I don't remember you mentioning this fact earlier."

"I didn't have a chance," said Ms. Hargroves, quick to cover for her mistake. Conversing with Aliara always proved a test of her wits. "Evidently, a man managed to smuggle himself onto one of the transports carrying chemicals from the Gray Collective to our factory. A team of heavily armed Technocracy agents stopped the convoy en route. According to the truck drivers, the squad blasted the man to pieces when he tried to escape."

"So?" asked Aliara. "Why does this encounter concern me?"

"Enzo somehow sensed that something was wrong," said Ms. Hargroves. "He sent a group of our best men to the location. They searched the scene thoroughly, but found no body."

"Interesting," said Aliara. "The hunters were positive they had the right location?"

"No doubt," said Ms. Hargroves. "They found minute traces of primium steel on the highway where the trucks had pulled over. The gorge nearby was torn up from chain-gun fire."

Robert Weinberg

"This escapee begins to interest me," said Aliara. "Especially considering that he comes from the Gray Collective."

"Enzo didn't seem very concerned," continued Ms. Hargroves, "until he learned of the marked rock."

"Rock?" repeated Aliara. "You know I do not appreciate drama, my dear. To what rock are you referring?"

"When the Technocracy agents shot the stowaway, his body crashed into a large boulder far down the mountainside," said Ms. Hargroves. "Evidently, he was bleeding badly from several wounds."

"And?" said Aliara, licking her lips as if in anticipation.

"The First Team found no traces of blood on the rock face," said Ms. Hargroves. "However, there were a number of markings in the stone, as if drops of acid had spilled onto it. The holes extend deep into the rock. Very deep into the rock."

Aliara burst into wild laughter. The sound rocked the apartment like thunder. Glass shattered in the kitchen. Ms. Hargroves flew back in her seat, stunned into near unconsciousness. The red-haired figure wavered, almost dissolved. Then, evidently realizing her peril, Aliara quieted. Her face contorted into an impossibly wide grin, she giggled softly. "How did Enzo react to the news?"

"He appeared to be in shock," said Ms.

Hargroves. "I heard him mutter some words about blood that burned like molten fire. For a minute or two, I thought he might recite a prayer."

"The Giovanni were once pillars of the Church," said Aliara. "Perhaps this situation will push Enzo into the priesthood. Though I strongly doubt it. I assume he has men hunting for this mysterious stowaway?"

"The First team found fresh footprints in the ravine," said Ms. Hargroves. "What little evidence exists points to the prisoner departing with newcomers who arrived on the scene after his escape. Before retiring for the day, Enzo ordered a massive search for the stranger. Hundreds of agents for Everwell Chemical and its sister companies are scouring the region for him. I cannot imagine that he will be hard to find."

Aliara licked her upper lip, her tongue much longer than any ordinary human tongue should be. "What wonderful news. Agents of the Technocracy and Enzo Giovanni working together to hunt down an escaped prisoner. They make an interesting mix. Needless to say, both organizations want him dead, though for entirely different reasons."

Aliara clapped her hands together like a small child excited by an unexpected gift. She giggled. "A tangled web indeed! I don't want this man destroyed. His continued existence will gnaw at both parties, diverting their attention from my efforts. Besides, knowing he is free, they will work all the faster!"

The red-haired woman's eyes glimmered with crimson flames. "The prisoner is a perfect foil for my own pursuits. We must do everything we can to ensure his survival. At least until the AW Project is nearly finished. After that, he will no longer matter."

"It won't be easy," said Ms. Hargroves, shaking her head, "especially since I have no idea what Enzo plans to do, and I won't know anything until the prisoner is actually found."

"Do whatever is necessary to prevent the prisoner's elimination," said Aliara, rising from the sofa. The plush cushions showed no outline of her body. Nor did her feet make any indentation in the thick carpeting. The red-haired woman was a realistic illusion, nothing more. "The events at the Gray Collective are my concern. Everything there is progressing much according to my plan. You no longer need concern yourself with the matter. The escapee is your only responsibility: He must not die tonight. I am counting on you. Do not fail me."

"Have I ever?" replied Ms. Hargroves.

"Of course not," said Aliara, her androgynous features cracking a demonic smile. She laughed. "If you had, you would no longer be alive. Give me your hand."

Trembling, Ms. Hargroves stretched out her right hand, and Aliara grasped her fingers with her own. The gaunt woman gasped in unexpected pain as a jolt of pure energy coursed through her body. Her blood felt as if it were on fire. Her muscles twitched in agony. The feeling lasted less than an instant, then disappeared.

"I've transferred a small amount of my being to you," said Aliara. "Using my power, you should have no trouble protecting the escapee. But be warned, dear Ms. Hargroves: My strength also carries with it my lusts. If you are not firmly in control of your senses, it might cause you to lose control. And I know how desperately you don't want that."

Laughing cruelly, the red-haired woman vanished from the parlor. Ms. Hargroves remained standing. Terrible, forbidden desires raged inside her. She needed a few moments to regain her self-control.

Finally, she was able to sit down. Reaching for a scratch pad on a nearby end table, Ms. Hargroves sighed as she started scribbling some quick notes. Sleep seemed a remote possibility today. She needed to make preparations for the evening. It was going to be a long, difficult night.

Ms. Hargroves felt as if she were balanced on a tightrope stretched between two supernatural entities of near godlike powers. One false step meant disaster. She was engaged in a dangerous venture—but the stakes were worth any risk.

With a shrug, Ms. Hargroves chugged the rest of her beer. Staring at the can for a moment, she decided another drink was in order.

<u>Chapter Thirteen</u>

As always, Seventeen awoke with a clear mind, his senses alert. His eyes snapped open and he glanced about the small room where he had been sleeping. As he stared out the window near his cot into the green meadow just beyond the glass, a feeling of unreality swept over him. He had no memory of waking to anything other than the cold, steel walls of his prison cell in the Gray Collective. The riot of color outside, seen for the first time in daylight, was a shock to his vision. He blinked several times, mentally trying to adjust to the greens, browns, reds and yellows that seemed almost unnaturally bright.

There was a knock on the wood door of the bedchamber. Instantly, Seventeen was on his feet, braced for trouble. He was clad only in a pair of faded boxer shorts, which he had found on top of the blankets last night when he stumbled exhausted into the room. His clothing from the Collective had disappeared off the floor sometime while he had been sleeping. "Yes," he said. "Who is it?"

The doorknob twisted and a young woman who looked to be about seventeen or eighteen years old stepped into the room. She was slender, with flowing blond hair, blue eyes, and a healthy glow to her skin. The girl wore a long billowy blue dress, decorated with large pink flowers. A shard of crystal hung from a rawhide thong around her neck.

In her hands the young woman carried several thick towels and a small stack of clothing. She stared at Seventeen, her expression curious, her eyes lingering over his powerfully built torso.

"I sensed that you were awake, so I brought this stuff so you could take a shower and put on some real clothes," she declared. "The shirt and slacks are pretty worn but they should fit okay. They're a lot better than that uniform you were wearing. We burned that already. Too many bad vibes to keep it around."

Seventeen nodded, not sure exactly what to say. He understood what she meant about his garments. The psychic residue from his outfit could be disturbing for a community of mages.

"I appreciate your concern," said Seventeen. "A

shower sounds good. Afterward, could I get something to eat? I'm starving.

The girl grinned. "Of course. There's always food around, a necessity considering the strange hours some of us keep. My name, by the way, is Jenni Smith. Sam Haine suggested that I show you around our enclave before the celebration tonight. Think of me as your own private tour guide."

"I'm called Seventeen," said Seventeen. Sam Haine had assured him that among willworkers, using a number for a name, especially a prime number, would not attract any notice.

"Seventeen," repeated Jenni. She laughed. "That'll be easy enough to remember. I'm seventeen too, age wise. Why don't you clean up and change? It's three in the afternoon and the ceremony won't begin until night falls, so we have plenty of time to talk."

The young woman stepped closer to Seventeen, handing him the towels and the clothing. "Sam mentioned your amnesia to me," she whispered. "When we're alone outside, I'll refresh your memory on the Traditions so you don't seem out of place tonight."

Louder, she declared, "The shower is down the hall. While you're washing, I'll rustle you up some food."

"That sounds wonderful," said Seventeen. "Afterward, maybe we can go for a walk outside. This area looks so peaceful, I'd enjoy seeing more of it."

The Road to Hell

An hour later, feeling well fed and more relaxed than he had been since he could remember, Seventeen slowly followed Jenni along a wooded path to a circular glade surrounded by immense oaks. Thousands of brightly colored flowers covered the ground with patches of red and purple and yellow. Their sweet smell filled the air like perfume. There was no order to the blossoms, giving the place a sense of untouched and unplanned beauty.

In the center of the grove, surrounded by a ring of bright green grass, sparkled a pool of crystal-clear water. In the bright sunshine, the liquid glistened like soft spun gold. The even placement of the massive trees made it quite clear that the existence of the open area was not mere coincidence.

"This grove once served as a gathering place for Iroquois Indian shamans," said Jenni, as if reading Seventeen's thoughts. "Hundreds of years of tradition and worship have centered on that pool. As one of the Awakened, you sense the energy focused in this place of power. It is a holy place, filled with the essence of life energy. That primal force takes material form as the water in our sacred spring. We call it *Tass*. Drinking it strengthens a mage's power, heals our wounds, cleanses our spirits. Our cabal settled here to be near this holy place."

Seventeen nodded. "I can feel the dynamic energy in the glade," he said. "The trees resonate with life."

The big man paused, lost in thought. Dressed in faded jeans and a checkered red shirt, he looked like a woodsman. Standing here, he felt as if at long lost, he had finally returned home. For the first time in his memory, he understood what it meant to be Awakened. The world about him was alive and he was an integral part of it. A sense of well-being filled his mind and he knew that the world was not as dark as it sometimes seemed.

He drew in a deep breath, exhaling it slowly. His body throbbed with the natural force of the grove. "What happens here this evening?" he asked.

"It's Midsummer Night," said Jenni, "the longest day of the year. For those of the Verbena Tradition, this eve marks the half-way point of the year. We celebrate the event with a festival around the pond. Willworkers from all Nine Traditions will be in attendance. Later, toward dawn, when things quiet down, some of our members will pass into the Horizon to meet with Verbena elders from other cabals."

"The Nine Traditions," said Seventeen. The words sounded so familiar. But when he tried to remember exactly why, his thoughts were blank. It was as if certain portions of his memory had deliberately been wiped clear. He suspected that was exactly what had been done. "Tell me about them."

Jenni laughed. A free spirit, she laughed a lot. Seventeen found her enchanting. Reaching down to the ground, she swept up a handful of flowers in her arms. Peering out at him across a sea of colors, she grinned. "What do you want to know?" she asked.

"Everything," said Seventeen. He shook his head, dismayed by his lack of knowledge. "Start from the beginning and tell it all. Tell me about mages and Sleepers and the Traditions." He hesitated, but just for an instant. "I also want to know about the Technocracy. Everything that as a member of the Awakened I should know."

"Well," said Jenni, "Sam said you would have a lot of questions. I guess you summed them all up in one. Let's sit beneath this tree; it's very peaceful here. Be prepared for a long lecture. It's quite a bit, even giving you the condensed version."

"The more you tell me," said Seventeen, "the more I think I'll remember. I've noticed it before. Certain encounters seem to awaken skills I never knew I possessed. It's like someone whispering knowledge directly into my brain. Here, in this grove, I feel like there's someone watching over my shoulder, guiding my actions."

"Your avatar," said Jenni, with a knowing smile. She nodded, as if agreeing with herself. "It's communicating directly with your subconscious."

Seventeen's eyes narrowed. "My avatar?"

"Let me start at the beginning," said the girl, with a long sigh. "That's the only way to make things clear."

Jenni leaned back against a massive oak tree, her legs tucked underneath her body, her long dress spread across the ground. With the bright sun shining on her face, she looked like an enchanted princess. Seventeen, though he was not sure exactly what it meant, hoped he was not a frog.

"Pardon me if I use all sorts of formal terms and archaic phrases," said Jenni. "It's hard to explain a lot of the more complicated stuff in common language. Nobody uses this language in normal conversations."

"I understand," said Seventeen. "I'd rather suffer through a lot of terminology than remain uninformed."

"You and I are Awakened Ones," Jenni began, her features serene. "We are mortals who have learned the truth about reality. In this world of Sleepers, mages are the few who understand the truth about the shifting nature of reality. Within each of us dwells a shard of undying divinity known as the Avatar. Religious people call this spark the soul. Others believe that Avatars are inner devils, while hard-headed materialists think of them as their id and superego. No one knows for sure what's the truth, but one thing is certain: An Avatar serves as the magickal consciousness that gives willworkers their power."

"Where do these Avatars come from?" asked Seventeen. "Do all mortals have them? And if they are undying, what happens to them when their host dies?"

"They pass from one Awakened One to another," said Jenni, answering the last query first. "As to your first two questions, there are as many theories as there are willworkers. No one knows the truth, though mystic speculations abound. Today, let's stick to the basic stuff and avoid the philosophy."

"A wise decision," said Seventeen. There was only so much he could learn in an afternoon. Yet, he had the feeling that he was making a mistake in not pressing further with his inquiry. He leaned forward, staring into the girl's beautiful eyes. She blushed under his unwavering gaze. "Please continue."

"Willworkers have the power to change reality by the force of their will," said Jenni. "This great gift makes them active participants in shaping the direction of mankind's continued evolution. As you can imagine, Awakened Ones take this responsibility quite seriously. Over the centuries, four factions of magick makers have emerged in an ongoing battle to control humanity's destiny. They are the Council of Nine Mystick Traditions, the Technocratic Union, the Nephandi, and the Marauders. The struggle which engages them all is called the Ascension War."

"The Nine Traditions," said Seventeen, the words spilling out of his mind. "I know them all. There are the Verbena, your Tradition, who believe that Life is the most powerful force in the universe. Thus some of you worship the ancient Goddess, others weave mythic strands of past beliefs into reality, and still others change their shape to become one with all living things.

"The Akashic Brotherhood believe in the perfect union of mind and body. They blend martial arts and meditation into a path to Ascension they call *Do*, 'the Way.'

"Then there are the Virtual Adepts," continued Seventeen, as one thought led immediately to another. "They believe that the alternate reality of the Digital Web is mankind's next step in evolution. Once they belonged to the Technocracy. Now they work with the Traditions. They are loners, surfing on the borderlands of our known universe."

"For someone who doesn't know anything," interrupted Jenni, smiling broadly, "you sure seem to know a lot."

Seventeen laced his fingers together, placed his hands behind his head, and laid back on the soft ground. Surrounded by flowers, he felt at peace with nature. The grove affected his mind, released inner tensions that he had not even realized were there.

"The Cult of Ecstasy follow the path that heightened awareness can only be brought about by stimuli and passions," continued Seventeen, information cascading like a raging torrent from his subconscious. He closed his eyes, so he could better concentrate on what he was saying. "Numbered among them are the greatest Time-Masters of the Nine, men and women who can see the future and work to change from one reality to another.

"The Dreamspeakers," he went on, as if reciting a lesson memorized years ago, "are among the most ancient of all the Traditions. They speak with spirits and change into animal shapes.

"The Order of Hermes traces its roots to ancient Egypt. Members of the society practice ritual magick in all its forms. They are the greatest enemies of the Technocracy, whom they see as the destroyers of uncertainty in the universe.

"The Sons of Ether are strange characters who believe that True Science is Art, an inner vision producing creation. They use their powers to create bizarre devices and crazy machines to further their goals." Seventeen shuddered, remembering the prisoner who had been brought back to the cell block in a bloody sack. He had obviously been a follower of that Tradition. "They lack practicality, but their dreams can yield amazing results."

Seventeen paused, his eyes open again, his brow crinkling in concentration. "Last is the Celestial Chorus. They see magick as a religious experience. The particular religious beliefs are not important to them, just the actual believing. More than any other Tradition, they are concerned with the well-being and safety of humanity."

"You left one out," said Jenni. Smiling, her face hovered over his. "You named only eight of the mystic Nine."

Robert Weinberg

"Which one?" asked Seventeen. He sat up. The girl, slightly startled by his sudden motion, scurried a few feet back. "That's odd. I thought I listed them all."

"You missed Euthanatos," said Jenni, scowling. "The Death Mages."

Though his eyes were wide open, Seventeen had a sudden vision of himself standing tall, clad entirely in black, with a swirling dark cape and a brace of pistols buckled to his belt. His features were drawn and melancholy. A lifeless body lay at his feet.

"Euthanatos believe that death is a natural part of existence," said Seventeen slowly. "They understand that entropy must be served to keep the universe functioning properly. Thus they are killers of those who must be slain. Each good death puts the victim one step further on the path to redemption. They do not fear death, knowing that it leads again to life."

Jenni shivered. "They give me the creeps. Verbena hold life sacred. Euthanatos treat death as a reward. Our Orders are at two ends of a vast spectrum of belief."

"Nine Traditions," said Seventeen. "The number remains unchanged since the origin of the Council many hundreds of years ago. Yet, there were no Virtual Adepts or Sons of Ether in centuries past."

Jenni nodded. "When the Council met in the Grand Convocation of 1466, there were nine existing Traditions. The Ahl-i-Batin occupied the seat now held by the Virtual Adepts. The Sons of Ether took the place of the so-called cursed Tradition, the Solificati."

"I'm not familiar with either group," said Seventeen. "Obviously, whoever I once was, I didn't know everything about the Nine Traditions. Neither name means a thing to me."

"No surprise," said Jenni, sounding somewhat distraught. "Today's mages prefer not to discuss the mistakes of the past. The leaders of the Nine Traditions have their faults. They seek to rewrite history by ignoring it. A few of us feel that's extremely unwise."

Seventeen rose to his feet. Jenni shook her head, then smiled. "Don't mind me," she declared, her voice softening. "It's just a pet peeve. Nothing of any significance."

"No problem," said Seventeen. He stretched, letting the bright sunshine warm his skin. "I need to walk about for a few minutes to clear my head. The sudden rush of memories has me a bit shaken. Let's take a break."

"Whatever you say," declared the girl, standing beside him. She pointed to the sparkling brook. "Let's go down to the pool. Staring into it, feeling the blaze of primal energy, serves as an intense stimulant. You'll feel better once you gaze into the water's depths."

Jenni wasn't lying. Gazing at the water was like

walking into a room filled with mirrors. A hundred reflections stared back at him. Each one was a part of the whole of his being, revitalized and renewed by the mystick life-energy of dynamic reality. The mirror images called out in a language without words and his inner self heeded their cries.

Like a bird in flight, his mind soared out of his body, joining with the life that filled the glade. Seventeen's identity fragmented as he became one with the trees, the flowers, the grass, even the tiny insects that were beneath his feet. For an instant, he understood perfectly the true meaning of being Awakened. Reality took on new dimension as his consciousness expanded toward infinity. For a bare instant, he grasped the true meaning of life, of existence itself. Then, in a blur, the concept slipped out of his thoughts and he was once again merely Prisoner Seventeen, sitting on the grass, captivated by a hundred reflected images in the pond.

With a sigh, he rose to his feet. While talking to Jenni, Seventeen had thought he understood magick. Now, he realized how little he really knew. Still, he felt more alive than he could ever remember. The dark vision of himself in black faded, though it remained on the fringes of his consciousness.

"If this *Tass* is so important to mages," he asked, looking at Jenni, smiling mysteriously at him, "isn't it unwise to leave this magic pool unprotected here in this clearing?"

The young woman laughed, a wild untamed sound that sent shivers of pleasure up Seventeen's back. It had been a long time since he had heard such a joyful noise. "You are so-o-o naive," the girl declared, shaking her head in amusement. "Look closely at the spring with your inner eye, your psychic sense. I'm sure you have the power to do it. Afterward, talk to me about the lack of safeguards."

Tentatively at first, then with more confidence, Seventeen stared at the pool, striving to see what existed beyond the material world. Gradually, a mesh of a thousand glowing strands of light took shape around the sacred spot. Many of the ribbons stretched to the huge trees that formed a circle around the grove. Others sank deep into the soil, while a few stretched out toward the large farmhouse in the distance. "This pool is sacred to the earth," said Jenni, softly. "It is well protected. Would you care to test its defenses? I assure you that touching the waters is not as easy as it appears."

"I see that now," said Seventeen, wondering how many other mystick powers he possessed without his knowledge. "Can we discuss the Technocracy?"

"What better spot than before the pool of life," said Jenni. She sat down, crossing her legs in lotus position, her back to the pool. Seventeen sprawled out on the ground next to her. By now, the sun was starting to sink in the sky. Evening was approaching.

Robert Weinberg

"The Nine Traditions," declared Jenni, "believe in the freedom of the individual and that reality should be fluid. Not so the Technocracy. Still, like the Traditions, the Technocracy feels that it is working for the good of all people. Its leaders feel that that mankind needs to be guided by the strong, that humanity must be protected from the supernatural and the supernormal. To this end, they have worked hard over hundreds of years to establish a static reality. They studied the basic laws of creation, then focused all of their efforts on making those rules the only ones allowed. The Technocrats built a wall around the world and then started locking the doors with bars they named *science*."

"The Road to Hell," said Seventeen, an old saying rising from his subconscious, "is paved with good intentions."

"Exactly," said Jenni. "The mages who belong to the Technocracy believe just as strongly as the mages of the Nine Traditions that they are striving for the betterment of mankind. The Technocrats believe that the path to Enlightenment, what they call Ascension, lies in statis and an absolute belief in the laws of science. They seek to define *everything*, with no hints of the unknown permitted. To them, rational and logical behavior will bring order to the universe. Only when total tranquility is achieved will mankind reach perfection. It sounds nice until you realize that lack of change leads eventually to stagnation and death.

"The mages of the Technocratic Union dislike the fact that they rely on the same forces used by willworkers of the Nine Traditions, so they disguise their efforts with the trappings of technology and science. They talk about gene research, or tinker with machinery. Or, they may act like they are a counter-espionage agency. But, if you probe deep enough, in the end, it always becomes clear that they use magick and twist reality in a very similar manner to Tradition mages. The problem is that with the Technocracy's tight grip on the Sleepers, they are steering society in a direction that will give them absolute power over the future. If we're not careful, they'll wipe out the Nine Traditions and rule over a sterile and bleak future."

"You seem to know quite a bit about the Technocracy," said Seventeen.

"The only way to defeat your enemy is to know them, inside and out," said the young woman, a serious expression on her face. But she couldn't stay grim long. A grin lit up her features. "Besides, I had a great teacher. He knows more about the history and beliefs of every sort of spellcaster than anyone I've ever met."

"Sam Haine," said Seventeen.

"The Changing Man," said Jenni. "He's Verbena, though he hates to be reminded of it. Sam's not typical of our Tradition. He's a unique individual. Don't let him fool you with his folksy manners and attitudes: He's really terribly sharp. Together with Albert he travels throughout the country battling the distortions and lies of the Technocracy. As a sideline, he helps Tradition wizards in trouble or on the run. Like many of us here at the Casey Cabal, I consider Sam my best friend and mentor. There's no one like him in the whole wide world."

"He does appear to be unique," said Seventeen. "So, tell me about the Five Conventions of the Technocracy."

"It seems to me," said Jenni, "that your memory is kicking into gear faster and faster. I never mentioned that the Technocratic Union has five branches. Or that they call them Conventions."

Seventeen shrugged. "I'm not sure if it's past memories or recent ones. I may have heard..."

He stopped, realizing he was about to mention his captivity. Sam Haine had warned him emphatically not to mention his imprisonment to anyone. Though Seventeen suspected the white-haired man wouldn't be concerned if Jenni knew the truth, he felt it would be better to err on the side of caution. "...the word from Albert."

"Do you remember anything about the different branches of the Union?" asked Jenni.

"Not much," said Seventeen. "There's the Progenitors and Iteration X. Those two groups I know. The first specializes in genetics and mind-altering drugs. The second believes that ultimate Ascension can be achieved through mankind's merging with machinery. They are convinced that humanity's future lies in a technology gone berserk."

"Remember your remark about the Road to Hell?" said Jenni. "I've met quite a few Progenitors in my time. You'd be surprised who you run into at clubs when you're a wild teenager. I had a close girlfriend who I discovered belonged to the Convention. She was a sweet, wonderful kid. Her brother was born with terrible birth defects; that's what propelled her toward the Technocracy.

"Someday, the Progenitors will wipe out birth defects. It's one of their stated goals. Everyone will be healthy and never suffer from disease. We'll all live to see a hundred years or more. At least, that's what my friend believes."

"You don't?" asked Seventeen.

"No," said Jenni. "The ordinary mages who make up most of the Technocracy are decent, dedicated people, striving toward Enlightenment, the perfection of the human spirit. Like I've said, they want a better world. It's their leaders I don't trust. Unlike the Traditions, which are mostly democratic, the Technocracy has a rigid chain of command. Decisions are made on high and followed without question. Maybe I'm just not the trusting type, but no matter what miracles the Progenitors, or any other branch of the Technocracy, promise, I suspect there'll be rules attached. Lots and lots of conditions to be satisfied.

There will be gifts for sure, but those gifts come with high price tags."

"The Progenitors want to remake the world in their own image of perfection," said Seventeen. Saying the words felt odd, as if he was stating a message that had a special meaning. Looking down at his strong hands and powerfully muscled arms and legs, he wondered yet again about his own incredible physical gifts. "The same holds true for Iteration X. Their way of coping with an ever-more-complicated world is to restructure humanity to deal with faster and faster data transmission. No one dares raise the thought of just trying to slow everything down slightly instead. They're certain that mankind will one day achieve a melding of man and machine and are doing everything in their power to hurry that day's approach."

"And you said *I* knew a lot about the Technocracy," said Jenni, smiling. The girl's expression was thoughtful. Seventeen reminded himself that Sam Haine was no fool. In subtle fashion, Jenni was learning all she could about Seventeen. He didn't mind. Whatever secrets he held were buried in the deepest realms of his subconscious. He doubted anyone, including himself, could draw them out so easily. "You're more of an expert than I."

"I just know something about the philosophies of the two groups," said Seventeen. "Tell me about the others. I'm not familiar with any of them."

"That's not surprising," said the young woman. "They maintain much lower profiles than Iteration X or the Progenitors. But, they are equally dangerous.

"The New World Order coordinates the activities of the Technocracy. They also manipulate the vast majority of sleepers through the mass media and subliminal suggestions. They're the worst dreams of George Orwell come to life."

Seventeen shook his head. "I view them as dangerous, but not as frightening as the Progenitors or Iteration X. Who's left?"

"The Syndicate is a mystery to everyone," said Jenni, "even members of the Technocracy. They handle money for the Conventions. Using their vast financial network, this group controls mainstream popular culture—everything from movies to paperback novels to television. Sam Haine says the Syndicate wields a lot more power than anyone, including their fellow mages in the Technocracy, realize.

"Last and perhaps the least threatening to the Traditions are the Void Engineers. They're dedicated to exploring the final frontiers that exist in the Tellurian—the entire sphere of existence. Void Engineers explore the Umbra, surf the virtual reality nets, and map the final unexplored areas of the world. They're interested in order and stability, but they still possess a strong desire to discover what lies beyond the farthest reaches. Most

Robert Weinberg

Tradition mages don't consider the Void Engineers much of a threat. The Technocracy probably distrusts them as much as we do, if not more."

The young woman looked skyward. "It's getting late. The festivities will start when the sun sets. Lots of spellworkers will be arriving shortly. We should return to the farm so we can change our clothes for the celebration."

"Whatever you think best," said Seventeen. "I can use the exercise. Talking with you has been a pleasure, but I need to move around more. Most days I work out for several hours."

He saw no reason to add that in the Gray Collective prison, exercise was one of the few activities permitted in the cells. Many days he had spent six or seven hours engaged in pushing his body to the limits. Prisoner Fourteen had jokingly referred to his workouts as "test to destruction," though Seventeen more than once thought he detected a note of fright in her tone.

They were half way back to the sprawling farmhouse when he remembered two more questions. "The Nephandi," he said. "You mentioned their name but never said anything about them. And another group known as the Marauders?"

Jenni shivered. There was no hiding the fear in her eyes. "The Nephandi are absolute evil in human form. They're willworkers who believe in Darkness instead of Light. Their masters are monstrous demonic forces who dwell in the Deep Umbra. They are called the Dark Lords in whispered tales. No one knows much about them other than that they are enemies of all life."

"The Dark Lords seek to enter our world and gain control of humanity," said Seventeen, the thought rising from his subconscious. He spoke as if in a dream. "Known as the Maeljin Incarna, these powerful beings exist in the Deep Umbral Realm of Malfeas. They seek to bring final Entropy to the universe—absolute and total destruction to all life."

Jenni licked her lips. "Uh, whatever you say, Seventeen."

He shook his head, trying to clear his thoughts. "Sorry. I can't explain what happens. You say a word, or a phrase, and suddenly I'm overwhelmed by a bit of knowledge I didn't know I possessed. Maybe you're right. It may very well be my Avatar trying to communicate with me in a basic but effective manner." He shrugged his shoulders in bewilderment. "I just don't know."

"If anyone can help you," said Jenni, "it's Sam Haine."

"I hope so," said Seventeen. "Who are the Marauders? My Avatar seems pretty quiet concerning them."

"I'm not surprised," said Jenni. "No one, not even Sam, knows much about the Marauders. They're the greatest mystery of the Tellurian. I've been told that they're insane mages of tremendous power who can warp reality with their mere presence. Supposedly, they live in the Deep Umbra. I've never met one and hope I never will. Marauders are totally self-absorbed and care little for mankind. They're amoral, existing utterly without regard for anyone else. Unlike the Nine Traditions or the Technocracy or even the Nephandi, the Marauders don't organize into groups to accomplish their goals. They're crazed lunatics, to be avoided at all costs."

They were close to the farmhouse now. More than a dozen mages, dressed in outlandish and garish clothing, stood outside, carrying on a heated discussion. None of them had been there the night before. They had to be guests who had arrived early for the celebration.

Seventeen, with his sharp ears, heard the word *Everwell Chemicals* repeated more than once as they approached the crowd. Evidently, the newcomers were concerned with the company's growing influence in the region. Remembering the final destination of the boxes from the Gray Collective, Seventeen felt certain that the menace of Everwell was much greater than anyone realized.

"Thanks for being so patient with me," he said to Jenni as they reached the rear door of the farmhouse. "I appreciate your help."

"No problem," said the girl. Unexpectedly, she stretched up on her tiptoes, put her hands around

Seventeen's neck and kissed him gently on the lips.

"I've been wanting to do that all day," she said, giggling. "Consider the debt paid in full. Now, go change. I'm sure Emma's found some exotic outfit for you to wear tonight. Catch you later."

Still smiling, the young woman disappeared into the crowd. Seventeen, his mouth tingling, shook his head in astonishment. His life was getting more complicated by the minute.

Chapter Fourteen

Terrence Shade arrived at the main office of Dynamic Security at exactly five p.m. After he presented his identity card and submitted to a retinal check and brain wave scan, two armed guards escorted him to the office of Winston Graves, chief of operations for the company.

Like all NWO front corporations, Dynamic Security actually operated as a full-time business, providing bodyguards for politicians, gangsters, lawyers, doctors and anyone else wealthy enough to afford their services. Less publicized but equally profitable were their industrial espionage and surveillance branches, which worked for many of the same clients, but in different capacities.

None of their usual clients, however, were aware that the twelve story corporate headquarters located in Albany, New York, was connected to an equally large site beneath the foundation. It was in that underground labyrinthine maze of offices and corridors that the New World Order supervised the affairs of the Convention throughout the entire northeastern corridor and Canada. It took twenty minutes of weaving through hallways and registering at several secondary security checkpoints before Shade finally reached coordinator Graves' office.

A tall, thin man in his late fifties, with graying hair and a constant nervous twitch, Graves ground out a cigarette in a butt-filled ashtray as Shade was shown into his headquarters. Though he was responsible for hundreds of operatives in the region, Graves was well aware that Shade, one of the higher-ups in NWO, had the authority to replace him in an instant if he was dissatisfied in any way with his work.

"Mission Specialist Shade," said the operations chief, hurriedly standing and holding out a hand, "a pleasure to meet you, sir. A visit from a top field agent is always an honor."

Shade shook hands with Graves and settled into an easy chair across the desk from him. "I've heard plenty of good things about your operation here, Graves," he said, smiling. "The Convention considers you to be one of our best field commanders. That's why I selected your office to serve as my base of operations for tonight's assault."

"An honor, sir," said Graves, his face beaming.

"We at Dynamic Security are prepared to do anything necessary to make sure your mission is a total success. I've put the entire base on alert. We await your orders."

"Excellent," said Shade. "I assume from your call this morning that the dragnet I ordered was successful?"

"Yes, sir," said Graves. "Since we were speaking on an unsecured line, I thought it best not to mention any details. I employed effective procedures as instructed, working with an amalgam of Men in Black. Our search combed through databases and witnesses until we located the specific Reality Deviant. The printout you sent describing his physical characteristics proved to be quite useful. Our location in the state capital also helped.

"The politicians are extremely paranoid here and we can tap into their lines and let the government do half our work. A detailed scan of satellite surveillance photos, police records, CB radio reports, and counter-intelligence feeds provided the necessary information to pinpoint the fugitive's exact location."

"Which is?" asked Shade, suppressing a smile. Graves talked too much but he was anxious to please. After months of dealing with Comptroller Klair and Sharon Reed, it was a pleasure having someone suck up for a change. "Where are we going?"

"Your fugitive has taken refuge with a Verbena cabal located several miles outside of the city of Rochester. He's still with them as far as we can ascertain. According to our latest intelligence reports, the eco-terrorists will be celebrating one of their pagan holidays tonight. Since your primary concern is that the Deviant will reveal classified information to the enemy, I suggest we strike as hard as we can with everything we've got. Make sure that anything the target reveals never leaves their so-called 'magic grove.' My agents are ready, Mission Specialist. They're just waiting for your authorization to attack."

Shade nodded, his expression thoughtful. "Knowing Verbena customs, I expect they are planning a major celebration for most of the Tradition willworkers in the area. Their Chantry will be filled with reality deviants of all persuasions. Do you have enough Men in Black available to handle the situation? There can be no mistakes. This fugitive must be utterly and totally destroyed, so that not even his ashes remain. What the other mages learn from him is of secondary importance. Once the information leak is plugged, the Traditions will only have vague half-told tales with which to reconstruct the truth. Your main objective—the only objective that really matters— is to eliminate the man referred to as Prisoner Seventeen. If you manage to kill some Tradition mages in the process as well, all the better. But, if

Prisoner Seventeen is not destroyed, the mission will be considered a failure. I will be extremely unhappy with such a scenario."

Beads of sweat popped out on Graves' forehead and his cheeks lost all their color. "I assure you, Mission Specialist, there will be no mistakes."

"Good," said Shade, smiling. He rubbed his hands together, briskly. "Like I said, the Convention has absolute faith in your ability, Graves. We know you won't underestimate the opposition. Now, you were going to tell me how many Men in Black have been assigned to the mission?"

The Coordinator licked his lips. "Um, let me check on that number for you personally, Mission Specialist. I don't have the exact information in the amalgam; my assistant has those figures. I assume you'll want to know how many of the group are bioclones and how many are independent operators?"

"Of course," said Shade, folding his hands across his ample stomach. "Please do check. I think we should be leaving shortly. You've already assigned a Gray Man to supervise the Men in Black amalgam?"

"Yes, sir," said Graves, heading purposefully for the door. "Field agent Murray Helman, the top Gray Man in the Collective. He's an ex-CIA operative our agents recruited several years ago. Helman is a master technician without a trace of foolish sentimentality. He uses the Men in Black like chess pieces, sacrificing them as necessary to achieve the stated objective. His operations are models of efficiency."

"Wonderful," said Shade. Purposefully, he glanced at his watch. "Time is passing, coordinator. I really think we should be leaving soon."

"Yes sir," said Graves, his voice a gasp. "Yes sir. I'll return in a moment, sir. Just one minute."

Shade sighed heavily and closed his eyes. Behind him, the door slammed shut as Graves went scrambling to double the size of his strike force. The Mission Specialist shook his head in despair. Intimidation worked best when done with a gentle hand. Graves was terribly easy to manipulate. The man was an excellent administrator—his record indicated that—but he was not top echelon material for the NWO. The Albany office was a good place for him. Enough responsibility for him to handle but not so much that he could cause any system foul-ups. Shade, however, was starting to wonder if putting Graves in charge of the attack tonight had been a bad idea.

The Mission Specialist sighed for a second time. If only Sharon Reed and Comptroller Klair were as easy to manipulate. Despite their irritating lack of rationality, both members of the Triumvirate possessed strong minds and refused to bend to the various subtle mind control measures that were Shade's specialty. Seizing control of the AW Project upon its completion was going to require a healthy dose of brute force. The Mission Specialist shrugged. What had to be done had to be done.

Coordinator Graves returned to the office in two minutes, thirteen seconds. Outwardly calm, he could not disguise his short breath and red-tinged cheeks. Settling behind his desk, he took a few moments to readjust his tie and straighten his shirt before he spoke.

"Everything checks out fine, Mission Specialist," said Graves, trying to project an image of a cool, calm executive. Shade found the attempted deception annoying but said nothing. He was starting to lose patience with coordinator Graves' ineptitude. "Helman's team consists of forty Men in Black. Two dozen of them are bioclones. Another ten are Sleepers—tough, hard-working thugs on Dynamic Systems payroll. These men are professional killers who know nothing of the goals or beliefs of the NWO, but are motivated by money, and we pay them very well. The other six are independent operators, minor Technomancers belonging to the Convention, hoping to perform well enough in the field to be promoted to a higher level."

"A diverse collection," commented Shade. "Does Helman use a Hive Mind with the bioclones?"

"It depends on the situation," said Graves. "I'm not sure what the Gray Man plans for tonight. I suspect it will depend on who we face when we arrive. The group mind functions well in battle scenarios when coordinated firepower is the only consideration. However, when fighting a cabal of reality deviants, independent action is probably the wiser path."

Graves seemed to have regained his composure. His voice was calm and unhurried. "We have a fleet of eleven limos waiting. Four Men in Black per auto, with you, Helman and myself in the command car. Are you ready to depart, sir? Our working schedule estimates time of arrival at five minutes before midnight."

Helman, a short, thin man, with bland features and watery blue eyes that seemed permanently out of focus, awaited them on the garage level of the corporation headquarters. He stood in front of a massive black Cadillac El Dorado, the preferred vehicle of the Men in Black. Behind the car, their motors growling in the underground garage, were ten other identical limos.

Each vehicle was equipped with armor-plated doors, darkened bullet-proof glass windows, and puncture-proof tires. Persistent rumors—many of them spread by NWO operatives—linked the mysterious black cars with a secret government security agency. Their appearance in a neighborhood spread waves of fear for blocks. No one knew exactly who employed the Men in Black or what their objectives were, but their connection with numerous disappearances made it quite clear that they were a force to be avoided at all cost. Like Bigfoot, alligators in the sewers, and welfare queens dining every night on fancy steak dinners, they had grown to become part of modern urban mythology. With their black limos in the east and midwest, and their black helicopters in the west, they had become the focus of urban paranoia. It was a reputation well deserved.

"Agent Helman," said Shade, stepping forward and offering a pudgy hand. "Glad to meet you. I'm Mission Specialist Terrence Shade."

"Honored," said Helman, his voice clipped and precise. His fingers were cold, his grip like a vice. "My team is ready, Mission Specialist. Our advance crew, a small emergency contingent located in Rochester, is already on the scene, monitoring activity. They'll keep your quarry pinpointed until we arrive in force. Plan's a simple one. We go in, blasting away, concentrating our primary fire on the main target. Anyone gets in our path, we blow them to hell and beyond. Scorched earth policy, if you catch my drift. My men are armed with handguns, assault rifles, and flame-throwers. By the time we're finished, your fugitive will be charred to a crisp. The same goes for any of the tree lovers who make trouble. Nice and simple is the way I run my operations. I get results."

Graves pulled open the rear door of the limo and Shade slid inside. The seat was covered with black leather. Directly in front of him was a portable bar.

In stark contrast to the luxury of the interior, a weapons rack holding a half-dozen laser rifles and submachine guns hung from the roof.

Helman took the wheel, with Graves beside him holding a double-barreled shotgun on his lap. The coordinator took his title seriously. Like many Technomancers of the NWO, the weapon served as a focal point of his procedures as well as a necessary part of his persona. Shade carried a .357 Magnum in his coat holster.

The Gray Man turned the key to start the auto. A half-dozen computerized gadgets on the dashboard lit up as the mighty V-8 engine roared to life. His hands flickering over the instrument panel with unnatural speed, Helman programmed in the coordinates of their trip.

"The on-board guidance system projects an ETA of 11:57, Mission Specialist," said Helman, as he steered the black limo out of the garage and onto the street. Behind him, a line of duplicate autos followed. "We'll break formation driving through the city. Too many people think it's some bigwig's funeral when they see a convoy. We don't want that to happen. Curiosity and idle talk will raise questions we prefer not to answer."

"Good thinking," said Shade, resting back on the cushions. In one hand he held a scotch and soda. As expected, the bar was stocked with only the finest brands. "You are aware, Mr. Helman, that our quarry this evening, on his own, disabled a HIT Mark cyborg?"

Robert Weinberg

"No sir," said Helman, his tone unchanged. He glanced for an instant at the coordinator sitting next to him. "Mr. Graves did not mention that to me."

"I assume then that he also forgot to tell you that the escapee killed a powerful biological Progenitor lab creation as well," said Shade, sipping his drink.

"A sauroid, sir?" asked Helman, the slightest hint of annoyance in his voice. He looked again at his boss. Graves stared straight out the front window, his eyes never wavering.

"Yes, Mr. Helman," said Shade. "I wasn't sure if you were aware of such beings. Their existence is a closely guarded secret."

"As a Gray Man," said Helman, "it's my job to be informed about all aspects of Technocracy security, sir. I am cogent of such creatures, though I have never encountered one. From what I read, I gather that ordinarily they are quite difficult to kill."

"Your assumption is valid, Mr. Helman," said Shade, closing his eyes and savoring the texture of the fine whiskey. "I felt that you needed to understand exactly why we required such a large troop of Men in Black for this mission. Our quarry can be extremely deadly. He also heals with unnatural speed. I am not sure that ordinary bullets will stop him. But I highly doubt it."

"Yes sir," said Helman. "I appreciate your concern. What you've told me calls for a revamping of my strategy. Instead of controlling all of the bioclones with my thoughts through the use of a Hive Mind, I'll just set them loose with a general command to create as much carnage among the Reality Deviants as possible. They'll serve as a diversion, while I lead our independent agents and hired guns on a quick strike aimed at finding and destroying our target. It'll be brutal work, but it should do the job. If not, I'm pretty good at improvising. If necessary, I'll sacrifice the rest of my entire team. No matter what the cost, I won't fail."

"Good," said Shade, draining the last of his scotch. Helman's competence made his next decision much easier. Shade pulled his handgun from his shoulder holster. Casually, he turned it over, examining the barrel as if searching for an imperfection. Finding none, he raised the gun, pointed it at the back of coordinator Graves' head and pulled the trigger.

The blast shook the car. Blood splattered the inside windows, as Graves slumped forward onto the dashboard, the entire back of his skull blown away.

"A terrible mess," said Shade. "Let's get it cleaned up as quickly as possible. I don't want any delays. Mr. Graves is no longer in charge of Dynamic Security, Mr. Helman. You are. Make sure you do a better job. I want no screw-ups tonight. Understand?"

"I understand, sir," said Helman. "Perfectly."

Robert Weinberg

Chapter Fifteen

The executive offices of Everwell Chemicals in Rochester were located in a dilapidated brick building that covered an entire block of the crumbling industrial section of the city. Once the vast structure had been a coffin factory, and now the smell of death and decay hung over it like a fetid, unhealthy fog. It suited Enzo Giovanni's personality perfectly.

Unlike his relative, Pietro, Enzo preferred to locate his headquarters in the basement of his hideaway. In a massive room that had once served as a storage area for caskets, he directed the fortunes of Everwell Chemicals and dozens of other smaller companies that formed parts of the secret Pentex empire. As a member of the Board of Directors of the huge multinational corporation that schemed to rule the world, Enzo wielded incredible power. But, it wasn't enough. He wanted more. He wanted it all.

Having risen from a deathlike sleep only an hour before, he sat alone in his office reviewing reports of the day's activity. His massive chair was made from the finest mahogany and covered with purple velvet sewn up with gold thread. To Enzo, it was a throne.

Frowning, he skimmed the reports from the search teams sent out to look for the prisoner who had escaped from the Gray Collective. The results were inconclusive, with only vague clues as to the fugitive's possible location. Enzo was not pleased. The AW Project posed a serious threat to his plans for the future. It had to be eliminated. For months, he had been working on a complex scheme to destroy the Compound and all of its inhabitants. For his strategy to be a total success, the fugitive would have to be found and killed. Immediately.

"Busy as usual," came a man's voice out of nowhere. "You work too hard, my friend. You should learn how to delegate authority."

Enzo looked up from the stack of documents. The only door to the room remained closed. Behind the concrete walls of the chamber were hundreds of tons of dirt and stone. It should have been impossible for anyone to gain entrance to the office. Unless that person possessed mystick powers.

"Not using the regular entrance tonight?" Enzo asked, with the slightest of smiles. "I thought you wanted publicity."

"No need for photo opportunities anymore," said the short gray-haired man who now stood on the other side of Enzo's desk. His thick hair was tangled and uncombed, while strange sparks glistened in his dark eyes. His voice, though, was calm and relaxed. "Pietro knows that we are working together. He swallowed the bait exactly as expected."

"You're sure," said Enzo, placing the papers on his desk. They could wait. This conversation was much more important. "He is no fool. The clan elders have absolute faith in Pietro. My cousin is not easily deceived."

"Perhaps," said Ezra, smirking, "but he has his blind spots. Pietro has assigned Madeleine the task of eliminating me. And, he has sent Montifloro to America to check on you."

"Montifloro?" repeated Enzo. He shook his head in amazement. "How utterly droll. My cousin is a perfect choice for what we plan. Twisting his thoughts to our purposes will be child's play. What about the girl?"

"The Dagger of the Giovanni has earned her reputation," said Ezra, "but her powers are no match for mine. More importantly, she is engaged in her own plot against Pietro. Madeleine is loyal only to herself. She will unwittingly be her sire's doom."

"It can't be this easy," said Enzo. "Pietro is a master of double-dealing and treachery. He must realize that we are plotting against him."

"Of course he does," said Ezra, "but he has no idea what our real goals are. He thinks me mad and you power-hungry. The fool has no grasp of the extent of our ambitions. By the time he finally understands, the trap will have snapped shut and he will be ours."

"You destroyed the clock?" asked Enzo.

"I did," said Ezra. He shrugged his shoulders, as if in dismay. "It was a beautiful piece of art, but it had to be done. I killed his blood roses as well. The greater Pietro's anger, the greater the chance of his overlooking our machinations."

Enzo's hands knotted into fists. He grinned savagely. "The power of clan Giovanni combined with the resources of Pentex. The world will be ours, Ezra."

"Don't grow overconfident," cautioned the gray-bearded man. "Madeleine must be turned against her sire. And Montifloro's will must be broken and then reshaped."

"Last night, I found a young woman who'll be perfect for the task," said Enzo. "I know my cousin's tastes. He has a weakness for dark-haired women. The girl's name is Hope."

"How appropriate," said Ezra. "Now, we…"

A knock on the door of the office silenced the gray-haired man. Without a sound, he vanished into nothingness.

Robert Weinberg

"I hate that damned trick," Enzo muttered, lifting the stack of papers back into his lap. "Enter."

Ms. Hargroves walked into the room. As always, she wore a blue suit, no makeup, and her hair pulled back in a tight bun. The tall, gaunt woman seemed nervous, ill-at-ease, filled with unnatural energy. Normally, his secretary was in complete and absolute control of her senses. Enzo wondered what was bothering her. In her hand, she carried another stack of documents.

"I thought I heard you talking to someone," said Ms. Hargroves, looking around but seeing no one. Her voice was as steady as ever. Hearing her speak, Enzo dismissed his concerns about the gaunt woman's composure. He should know better than to think anything could rattle her. "These reports just came in. The First Team thinks they've located the fugitive. I assumed you would want the news immediately."

"You assumed correctly," said Enzo, taking the papers from Hs. Hargroves' hands. He scanned the documents quickly.

"Madron!" he declared after a moment. "Of all places, he ended up with that gang of ecological lunatics who've been fighting our expansion into the suburbs. What a mess."

He glared at Ms. Hargroves, who returned his stare without flinching. The gaunt woman had a heart as cold as ice. "I assume you've taken the proper measures?"

"I contacted the Knights of Pain," declared Ms. Hargroves, "through our usual sources. A reward's been posted: one million dollars for our quarry's head. For that kind of money, they'd ride straight into hell."

Enzo's features twisted in annoyance. "I don't know. Mattias and his followers are unreliable at best. Can't we use some of our own men?"

"Not on such short notice," said Ms. Hargroves. "There's some sort of festival taking place out on that farm tonight. If we don't strike immediately, a lot of people are going to hear your fugitive's story."

"Issue the order, then," said Enzo, gritting his teeth.

"I already have," said Ms. Hargroves. There was a brittle edge to her voice. "I assumed you would realize it was the only choice."

Enzo laughed, a harsh, inhuman sound. "Some day, my dear secretary, you will assume too much. And then, you will be very very sorry."

Ms. Hargroves shrugged. "Try running Everwell Chemicals without me," she declared calmly. "Balance the books. Juggle the accounts. Pay the bribes. Then make your threats."

"Enough," said Enzo hastily. "You've made your point. Hopefully, Mattias and his gang won't botch the job."

"They know the price of failure," said Ms. Hargroves. "I made it quite clear that we will accept no excuses."

"Good enough," said Enzo. "How goes the education of the girl, Hope, I brought in last night?" he asked, changing the subject.

"Considering that she is a cheap, vulgar slut, with little education and a sadistic streak that frightens even the brothers Grim," answered Ms. Hargroves, "surprisingly well. Esperanza is not stupid and learns quickly. Properly trained, she will cause quite a stir in influential circles."

Enzo smiled. "Excellent. One of my relatives from Italy is due in the city shortly. I think he will find her fascinating. They will have to be introduced under the proper circumstances. Now, leave me. I wish to be alone with my thoughts."

Seconds after Ms. Hargroves exited, Ezra reappeared. "There's something odd about that woman," said the gray-haired man. "Can she be trusted?"

"Without question," replied Enzo. "Ms. Hargroves is quite reliable. Entirely without emotion, she worships only money. And I pay her very well."

Ezra shook his head. "I trust no one. Now, what was that about an escaped prisoner?"

In a few brief sentences, Enzo summarized what little he knew about the fugitive from the Gray Collective. The lines in Ezra's face deepened as he listened.

"Our patron worries about this AW Project. If successful, it could significantly change the balance of power between the Technocracy and the Nine Traditions. We can't allow that to happen. The more resources they waste battling each other the better. Every trace of the experiment must be destroyed. This escapee must be killed."

"Can you do anything?" asked Enzo. "The bikers are probably already on their way."

"Even my abilities have limits," Ezra admitted. "Still, I will strengthen their resolve. They won't retreat."

The gray-haired man laughed harshly. "The gang will locate and slaughter the fugitive. Or they'll die trying."

Chapter Sixteen

Seventeen was struggling into his festival outfit when someone knocked on the door to his room. "Who's there?" he called, pulling a black tunic shirt over his head. "Be with you in a minute. I'm getting dressed."

The door opened and Sam Haine, followed by Albert, entered. The three of them filled the small chamber. "Having fun, boy," asked Sam, "getting all fancied up for this damned-fool shindig?"

"These clothes aren't exactly what I would have picked myself," Seventeen admitted as he fumbled with the wide silver clasp of a black leather belt. "I think the prison uniform was a lot more comfortable. And it was definitely much more practical."

Sam chuckled. He wore an old-fashioned white

suit, white shirt, red bow tie, and a Panama hat. With his handle-bar mustache, thick eyebrows, and twinkling blue eyes, he resembled a famous old writer whose name escaped Seventeen at the moment. In one hand, he held a long wood cane, in the other, a glowing cigar. Oddly enough, it emitted no smoke or smell.

"I love a good Havana," said the old man, noting the direction of Seventeen's gaze, "but it bothers too many of these healthy, no-bad-habits, New Age types who've joined the Verbena lately. So I do a few tricks with my cee-gars to conform to the proper regulations. Damned if I ain't grown accommodating in my old age."

Albert snorted in derision. The African wore a multicolored dashiki that stretched from his neck down to his sandals. His bare arms and face were painted with mystic sigils. For a gentle soul, the giant black man looked quite threatening.

"Sam refuses to admit he craves attention from the younger generation," said Albert. "He hates to be ignored. If he was half the curmudgeon he claims to be, no one would speak to him. My friend growls a lot, but it is mostly for show."

"Watch it, you ugly sack of skin and bones," said Haine, waving his cane at the black man. "You go around revealin' too many of my secrets and people will start thinking I'm tiring out. We can't have that happen. Too many people need me around to remind them what this damned Ascension War is all about."

Robert Weinberg

Sam directed his cane at Seventeen. "Free choice is the issue, son. Clear and simple. The Technocracy wants to make the world safe for the Sleepers by taking away all the decision making. Safe and secure for all, but no thinking. Be a damned dull place if those characters ever take over. You can see their influence already; the Technocrats are growing more powerful all the time. Trying to ban this and that, censor books, tell us what we can listen to or what we can and can't see. It's a pretty grim picture. Life without imagination or vision. But that's the way they like it."

Sam took a deep puff on his cigar. "That's the real reason we fight, son. Don't let anyone tell you otherwise. If the Technocracy triumphs, humanity loses."

The old man shook his head. "Damned if I don't ramble on like some politician. You finished putting on that fancy outfit, boy? Time for us to mingle with the movers and shakers in attendance here at the celebration. Hopefully, somebody in the crowd will recognize you. Or know this Alvin Reynolds you're searchin' for."

"I'm ready," declared Seventeen, fastening the last buckle on his outfit. He was dressed entirely in black and silver. He wore long black slacks, knee high boots, a black velvet tunic with silver clasps at the neck, a long black cape, and black leather gloves. The tunic was a little tight across the shoulders but otherwise everything fit perfectly. One of the advantages of magickal garments was that they adjusted themselves without bothersome tailoring. "Though I feel like a fool in these clothes."

"You look very distinguished," said Albert. "The designers of the Casey Cabal did a fine job picking out your clothes. Tradition spellworkers enjoy flaunting their differences. They prefer garish outfits. I assure you that compared to many we will encounter this night, you are quite conservatively dressed."

Sam Haine laughed. "We make a fine trio," he declared, his gaze traveling back and forth between Albert and Seventeen. "Black, white, and every damned color in-between. Enough jawing. Let's get outside. The ceremony starts at midnight, and there's a bunch of people I want Seventeen to meet before then."

Nearly fifty people were crowded in the glade where Seventeen had spent the afternoon with Jenni. Two immense bonfires burned, one at each end of the glade, the bright blaze projecting strange shadows on the surrounding trees. Several young women, clad in long white robes, were serving cups of punch made in a gigantic cast-iron cauldron. Seventeen glimpsed Jenni among their ranks. She looked up for an instant, as if sensing his gaze, and waved cheerfully. Smiling, he managed a quick wave in return before Sam Haine dragged him off to meet another batch of dignitaries.

Robert Weinberg

The white-haired man knew everyone. While several of the more conservatively dressed guests seemed less than pleased upon encountering the Changing Man, they were all unfailingly polite. Sam Haine, Seventeen soon realized, was notorious among spellcasters: everyone either hated or loved him.

"Seventeen," said Sam, almost an hour later, "meet Conrad Wyeth. He belongs to the Order of Hermes. Master Wyeth has expressed an interest in your problem. He thinks he might be able to help you regain your memory."

Wyeth, stylishly dressed in an Armani suit, nodded. Nearly as tall as Seventeen, the man projected the air of someone confident of his own powers. With his neatly clipped gray hair and goatee, he exuded self-importance. Standing next to him, Sam Haine looked like a country bumpkin.

"I feel certain that given enough time I can break down the mental blocks placed in your mind by the Technomancers," said Wyeth. The tall man spoke in clipped, precise tones, as if addressing a crowded lecture hall. "With your permission, I'd like to try. As both a willworker and a psychologist, I find the notion challenging. You'd regain your memory and I'd gain valuable experience."

"How long would the process take?" asked Seventeen.

"Assuming your captors were experts at memory deprivation," said Wyeth, "I suspect it might require several weeks of hard work to completely destroy the barricades."

"You're sure the boy still has his memory?" asked Sam. "Couldn't those damned Progenitors have just wiped his mind clean?"

Wyeth shook his head. "If they did, he'd have the knowledge and intelligence of a new-born babe. Obviously, that's not the case. They could force-feed him information, but there's no method yet devised to teach a man how to use his motor reflexes without long hours of training. Anyone who moves with the natural grace exhibited by Mr. Seventeen retains his core memory. It has merely been sealed off from his conscious mind."

"Unfortunately," said Seventeen, "I don't have several weeks." His hands tightened into fists, remembering the weird, embryonic form floating in the growth tank. "The Technomancers responsible for my condition are planning a major assault on the Nine Traditions. If they aren't stopped, and quickly, none of us may have much time left."

The Hermetic mage frowned. "Under ordinary circumstances, I'd merely assume you were a lunatic with delusions of persecution. However, I've known the Changing Man for decades. While I often find him infuriating, he's no fool. Since Sam Haine believes you, I can do no less."

Wyeth smiled, a big toothy grin quite out of place with the rest of his features. "Besides, I hate those bastards in the Technocracy. With them involved,

I'm willing to break a few rules. Tell me your story. From the beginning. Sam gave me a few highlights, nothing more. If you want my help, I need to know what I'm facing."

Before Seventeen could say a word, the twin fires in the clearing roared with sudden fury. A woman's voice, clear and sharp as a knife, rang out. "The time is near. Prepare to welcome the Goddess."

"Damned foolishness," muttered Sam Haine, chomping on his cigar. "Summer solstice ritual's about to begin. Lots of mumbo-jumbo and all that stuff. Dancin', singin' nonsense. As if real magick requires anything more than the will and the way."

"Oh well," said Wyeth to Seventeen. "Hold your story for a bit. No use trying to talk when the crowd joins in the activities. Why battle the noise? There's no rush. We have the whole night to talk."

The psychologist's words rang hollow in Seventeen's ears. Feeling distinctly uncomfortable, he looked around. Everyone in the clearing was standing still, waiting for the high priestess of the Goddess to begin the invocation to the Wyck. All eyes were focused on the center of the grove, where the tall blond woman, dressed in a flowing white robe, stood beside the sacred spring, a long ceremonial dagger in her right hand. A large ram lay bound at her feet. The Verbena might hold a certain appeal for New Age mysticks, but they were not a leftover fringe group from the Peace Movement. Their Tradition was an ancient one, shaped by a violent history. Shapechanging and animal sacrifice were accepted elements of their beliefs.

"On this sacred night," said the high priestess, "let us open our minds to the greatness of the Cosmic Mind that holds us all in its embrace. The power of the Goddess fills this glade. Prepare yourselves to receive her blessing."

A feeling of contentment swept through Seventeen as the combined wills of all the spellworkers in the area blanketed the region. His spirit soared, yet he felt terribly uneasy. Something was wrong.

Looking around, Seventeen soon discovered that he wasn't the only one who sensed impending danger. His gaze met and held that of a young Asian woman twenty feet away. Dressed in a loose-fitting pair of pants and a sky blue jacket, she appeared equally uneasy. Her dark eyes widening, she nodded as their eyes locked, as if acknowledging an unspoken communication. Then, moving with a fluid, magickal grace, the mysterious beauty reached over her shoulder and drew forth a sword that pulsed with mystick energy. At that instant all hell broke loose.

A gigantic hand slapped Seventeen in the back, sending him sprawling to the ground. The clearing erupted in a roar of automatic weapons fire. Guns bellowed and sub-machine guns chattered a deadly song. The attack was sudden and unexpected and came from all sides.

Robert Weinberg

Struggling against waves of pain, Seventeen rolled over. Someone had shot him between the shoulders at close range. An ordinary man would have been unconscious, perhaps dead. But Seventeen was not an ordinary man; he possessed gifts even he himself did not fully comprehend. Closing his mind to the pain, he forced himself to sit up. His miraculous healing powers were hard at work. The bullet was already gone from his body and the wound was closing, as muscle and skin swiftly regenerated.

Everywhere there was chaos. Throughout the grove, men and women were screaming, some with pain, others in anger. More than a dozen willworkers had gone down in the first, totally unanticipated volley. Others, surrounded by glowing protective auras, were striking back at the hidden enemy. Seventeen's flesh tingled as bolts of magickal force hurtled into the night. Lightning flashed and the air crackled with static electricity. Yet, surprisingly, the spellcasters each worked separately, not as a whole. Their attacks were haphazard, uncoordinated. They seemed bewildered by the precision and violence of the assault.

"It's those goddamned Men in Black," sputtered Sam Haine in Seventeen's ear. The old man crouched low to the ground, cigar still clenched between his teeth. Albert was nowhere to be seen. Seventeen nodded, immediately sensing what the

Changing Man meant. Working together, the NWO agents generated a panic field that caused people to act irrationally. There had to be dozens of them out there to cause the mass confusion in the glade.

"We better..." began Seventeen, then had no chance to finish his reply. Their submachine guns blazing hot lead, three identical attackers, dressed in black suits and wearing black hats and astonishingly enough, black sunglasses, burst out of the trees a dozen yards away. The bullets from their weapons sliced a direct line toward Seventeen. A second more in that position and his body would have been riddled by gunfire. He moved—but not in a direction the attackers expected.

The ex-prisoner attacked. Leaping forward, he cleared the trail of bullets in one gigantic motion, his blood pumping with rage. There was no question in his mind that he was the reason for the Technocracy's attack on the cabal. The ruling triad of the Gray Collective wanted him dead and were pulling out all stops to ensure his demise. Seventeen was tired of running and hiding and pretending. It was time to strike back.

His left fist smashed into the face of the lead gunman with the force of a jackhammer. The Man in Black collapsed and lay unmoving. Seventeen hardly noticed. Sweeping out his arm, he clotheslined the second attacker and flung him with great force into the third man. Bones cracked like dried wood when they collided. Seventeen knew all the killing moves and he was strong enough to make them work.

At his feet, the three bodies sizzled. Glancing down, Seventeen recoiled in disgust. His attackers were melting. Progenitor clones self-destructed when they died. Still burning with anger, he looked around in search of more enemies to destroy. Sam Haine was gone, but Seventeen wasn't worried. The old man was a survivor. It would take a lot more than a bunch of Men in Black to harm the Changing Man.

"Kill him!" commanded a harsh voice from the nearby forest. "A field promotion to the one who brings that Deviant down!"

Instantly, Seventeen dropped to the earth as a dozen guns bellowed, sending a lead curtain flying overhead. The ground was slightly sloped, offering him a small amount of protection. Stray bullets whined overhead, forcing him to remain pinned. Seventeen's muscles tensed, preparing for another wave of attackers. It was his bare hands against the Men in Black and their guns. In his arrogance, he thought the odds were pretty close to even.

He never had a chance to find out. A shriek of surprise and pain sounded from the woods, and then ended as abruptly as it had begun. Then a second man screamed. Again, the noise was cut off in an instant. An unknown force was eliminating the Technocracy killers one by one. The gunfire ceased as the Men in Black suddenly found themselves battling an enemy in their midst. Raising his head from the ground, Seventeen caught a flash of light blue and a glimmer of steel. The mysterious Asian woman was making her presence known in deadly fashion.

Scurrying on his hands and knees, Seventeen rushed into the forest. When he gained his feet, he was bewildered to find himself alone. The woods were empty. His attackers had disappeared, evidently retreating to regroup. Nor was his mysterious rescuer in evidence. Shaking his head in disbelief, Seventeen walked back into the grove. Other than the corpses littering the ground, the area by the trees was empty. The sounds of battle centered around the middle of the clearing.

There, the surviving Tradition mages had gathered in a large circle, a mystic force field protecting them from the gunfire of the Men in Black. Finally working in tandem, the willworkers were slowly fighting back against the nearly two dozen black-suited individuals who surrounded them, guns and submachine guns blazing. Magick battled magick, with the two forces evenly matched.

Searching the crowd with his eyes, Seventeen spotted Jenni Smith among the circle of survivors. He felt a tremendous burden lift from his shoulders. Since the Men in Black had come searching for him, Seventeen felt personally responsible for the girl's predicament. There was a long bloody streak across her forehead and her expression was one of stunned disbelief. But at least she was still alive.

Seventeen took several deep breaths and readied himself to strike the Men in Black. They had come hunting him. Drawing their attention with a surprise rush from the rear should cause enough commotion to upset their methodical attack. He felt certain that he could take out five or six of the killers before they were able to focus their attention on him. By then, aided by the distraction, the Tradition mages should be able to mop up the rest. It wasn't a great strategy, but it was the best plan Seventeen could come up with.

Before he could take a step, huge engines roared like thunder from the dirt path that led to the glade. Bright headlights blazed in the clearing, momentarily blinding everyone. Mages of both the Technocracy and the Traditions suddenly froze, stunned by the sense of encroaching evil.

Howling insanely, twenty bikers on motorcycles hurtled into the clearing, their gigantic Harleys sending chunks of grass and earth flying in every direction. In the space of a few heartbeats, like Indians circling a wagon train, the cycle gang surrounded the Men in Black and the Tradition mages. No one moved or said a word.

Armed with steel crowbars, metal chains, and switchblade knives, the gang was obviously hunting trouble. Though their black leather jackets proudly proclaimed them "Knights of Pain," Seventeen knew the new arrivals were much more than a gang of rogue bikers. They were new players in a game whose stakes were still a mystery.

"There's two ways we can play this fuckin' hand," shouted a gigantic tattooed man, his chest bare except for a criss-cross of steel chains. Evidently, he was the leader of the gang. Hordes of red and blue lizards covered every inch of his skin. In one massive hand, he held a machete. He waved the blade over his head. "You give us the fuckin' fugitive and we back off and let you people settle your fuckin' differences. Or we blow you all to hell. Like I said, two choices. The only thing I care about is the motherfucker you're hiding. Don't make me wait. I ain't real patient."

For an instant, no one said a word. Then, as if obeying an unseen signal, the Men in Black whirled, raised their guns, and started firing at the bikers. Seventeen swore in shock. The bullets had no effect on the gang.

"Fuck diplomacy!" bellowed the tattooed giant. "Kill 'em all!"

Motorcycle engines bellowed their approval as Knights stepped hard on their gas pedals. Howling insanely, the bikers slammed their cycles forward, smashing into the outer members of the crowd. They attacked with an animallike ferocity. Shotgun shells bounced off them as if their skin were made of steel. Filled with a mad lust for blood, the gang members fought without grace or style. Instead, they ripped and tore and crushed anyone in their way. Agents of the dark, they sought only to destroy.

The Tradition mages forgotten, the Men in Black fought a battle they could not win. Their guns useless, the clones and their human allies were powerless against the fury of the lunatic bikers. They dropped helplessly before the savage onslaught of the monstrous horde. Behind them, the Tradition spellweavers raised their hands into the air, summoning the ancient mystick forces of the glade.

"Smash through to the bastards!" roared the leader of the gang, exhorting his followers on to greater violence. His tattoos glowed, the lizards crawling like living things across his flesh. "Quick, before the fuckers complete their spell!"

"I have you now," declared a voice from behind Seventeen. It was the same man who had yelled instructions to the Men in Black a few minutes earlier. Caught totally off guard, Seventeen whirled. A short, thin man with bland features and watery blue eyes stood less than ten feet away. In both hands he held a long nozzle attached to a tube that lead to a tank across his back. "Burn time, sucker."

There was no time for Seventeen to react. The thin man's finger was already squeezing the trigger of the flame-thrower. But he never completed the action.

The Road to Hell

Materializing out of thin air a step behind the attacker, a tall, gaunt black woman reached out with clawlike hands and seized the man's arm at the shoulder. With a frightful noise of rending flesh and bone, the woman ripped the limb from his body and tossed it to the ground. The thin man shrieked in agony as blood jetted from the wound in a hot red stream.

The woman laughed, her lips twisted in a wide grin of uncontrolled passion. Her victim dropped to his knees, his life blood gushing onto the soil. Turning his head, the dying man looked to catch a glimpse of his killer. Still laughing, she stepped forward and placed a wide hand on his abdomen. Fingers like steel claws squeezed tight. Cloth and skin shredded like tissue paper. Shrieking with pleasure, the woman ripped long strands of the man's intestines from his body and wrapped them around his face. His body a steaming ruin, the man collapsed to the ground, his dead eyes filled with a look of absolute horror. At the same instant, as mysteriously as she had appeared, Seventeen's demonic rescuer was gone. The entire incident had taken only a few seconds.

Stunned, Seventeen stood frozen in place. Life and death had become a meaningless jumble during the past few minutes. It was if he were living in a dream where reality and unreality merged together. Trying to push what he had just seen to the back of his mind, Seventeen turned. Confused and dazed, he knew that he must act immediately or else his friends would be in terrible danger from the Knights of Pain.

He need not have worried. The bikers were no longer on the offensive. Faces pale with worry, they crouched on their bikes, edging from the circle of Tradition mages. A huge dark cloud hovered over the glade, blocking out the moon. At its center, two balls of red fire glowed like gigantic eyes. Thunder rumbled. The air in the mystic grove rippled with psychic energy. Great forces were stirring.

Behind their transparent wall of force, the faces of the Tradition willworkers were serene. Drawing upon the power of the life-energy of the sacred spring, they had summoned the elemental forces of nature for aid. For all of their evil, the biker gang was no match for the spirits of the earth.

"Fuck it all," screamed the leader of the gang. His body no longer glowed. The lizards no longer moved. His voice was thick with fear. "Scatter!"

Motors growled as the bikers fled for their lives. Beneath them, the ground shook, as if the land itself was rising to prevent their escape. Winds howled, sweeping with chilled fingers across the glade. A jagged bolt of lightning crashed, just missing one of the Bikers. Disciples of the Goddess, the Verbena had turned to the soil for aid against their unnatural enemies. And the earth had struck back.

Seventeen, crouched low to the ground, watched the biker exodus with wide eyes. Not all of the Knights escaped the wrath of the grove. As the horde of gang members slashed between the ancient trees that surrounded the spring, long branches whipped out of the darkness and snared several of them around the neck. Bones snapped like sticks of chalk as the riders were hauled up into the air; their empty bikes crashed into the sides of ancient trees. None of the bodies returned to the ground. Of the twenty attackers, Seventeen counted seven smashed motorcycles. Thirteen of the Knights of Pain, including their tattooed leader, had escaped.

In the woods, a car engine growled. Only one. The noise receded swiftly. Seconds later, a series of explosions shook the night.

"Sounds like a few of those Men in Black escaped," declared Sam Haine, appearing like a shadow at Seventeen's side. "That was them leaving. Rest of the bunch were killed by the bikers. Not that we'll get anything out of it. Cars belongin' to the NWO have built-in self-destruct mechanisms. Technocracy don't like folks looking inside their toy autos. Who knows what secrets they hold?"

"Are you all right, Seventeen?" asked Albert. The giant's dashiki was ripped and torn in several places but otherwise he appeared unharmed.

Overhead, the dark cloud was already dissipating.

Robert Weinberg

The wall of air surrounding the Tradition mages had dissolved as if it had never existed. The white light of the moon reflected off the water of the magic spring. Once more, the sacred glade was peaceful and serene. Except for the corpses spread across the lawn.

"I'm okay," said Seventeen, feeling a bit woozy. He recognized the symptoms and their cause immediately. "Other than that I'm feeling terribly hungry again. My body needs fuel."

"Seventeen," cried Jenni Smith, running over, her eyes wide with concern. The young girl grabbed him around the waist and hugged him tight. "I knew for sure the Men in Black were hunting you. Then, when those bikers arrived..."

Suddenly, Jenni stiffened. Trembling, she let go of Seventeen and backed away, her arm pointing beyond him, at the mutilated corpse of the man with the flame-thrower. Her voice shaking with fear, she asked, "Who's that? What happened to him?"

"He tried to kill me," answered Seventeen, without considering the implications of his words.

"So you ripped him to shreds," gasped Jenni, horrified. "And stuffed his guts down his throat! Oh my god, oh my god!"

The girl shrieked, her screams filling the clearing. Immediately, half a dozen of the survivors of the fight came running over to see what was wrong. Jenni, her face contorted with horror, stared at Seventeen like he was some savage beast.

The Road to Hell

"He's not one of us," she babbled wildly to the crowd surrounding her. "Look at what he did to that man over there! Those bikers didn't come here to destroy him. They came to rescue him!"

Seventeen shook his head in astonishment. He felt woozy from lack of nourishment. His mind was not as sharp as it should be. "You're crazy," he muttered. "I didn't kill him. He was going to murder me when this tall, gaunt woman appeared out of nowhere and tore him apart."

"Gaunt woman?" said Jenni. "Where? There's no woman in our ranks who would rip a man's guts out." Her voice grew cold and filled with anger. "You're the only one here strong enough to do something like that."

"Wait a minute," said Conrad Wyeth. The psychologist no longer looked very stylish. His suit coat was gone and his gray hair stood on end, as if he had been jolted by a bolt of electricity. Still, his voice was as firm and confident as ever. "You can't condemn a man on mere suspicion. Sam Haine brought this stranger among us. Surely you're not suggesting the Changing Man would knowingly aid a killer?"

"Sam's a good man," said a voice from the gathering crowd, "but he's made mistakes in his time. Defending yourself against attack is one thing. But ripping a man to pieces and shoving his guts into his face, that's Nephandi work."

"Even the Changing Man doesn't know that

much about the newcomer," said another. "Who's to say he's not a Nephandi spy? The motorcycle gang never attacked us before. Maybe he led them to our sacred grove."

Several others joined in the accusations. Without conscious thought, Seventeen curled his hands into fists. He didn't want to fight these people, but he could sense their anger rising.

"You are all fools," came a woman's voice, calm and measured, from the fringe of the forest. The Japanese warrior woman emerged from the trees. Behind her stood a middle-aged man with a black beard and golden skin. Though he said nothing, his eyes radiated great strength. "This man is innocent of any wrongdoing. I witnessed the entire incident. It happened exactly as he described."

"Who are you?" asked Jenni Smith belligerently. "And why should we believe the words of another stranger?"

"My name is Shadow of the Dawn," said the newcomer, sounding slightly amused by the question. "I am a Dragon Claw of the Akashic Brotherhood."

Her hands moving faster than the eye could follow, the warrior unsheathed her long and short swords. Arms outstretched in front of her body, she held the twin blades crossed unwavering in the moonlight. The mystic weapons glowed with inner fire. "By my swords, I swear that what I say is truth. Is there anyone here who doubts my word?"

"I'm not stupid enough to question the sword oath of a Dragon Claw," said Sam Haine. His gaze swept the crowd. "The rest of you dumber than me?" His question met with silence. The old man shook his head. "I didn't think so."

The Changing Man glared at Jenni Smith. "Enough barking at shadows for one night. We've got dead brethren to bury. Seventeen needs rest, as do we all. Leave him be. There'll be time enough tomorrow to look for answers."

The crowd dissolved as quickly as it had gathered. Jenni Smith was the last to depart. She stared at Seventeen for a long moment, conflicting emotions racing across her features. There were tears in her eyes. Finally, she opened her mouth to say something, then closed it without a word. Turning, she hurried away without a backward glance.

Seventeen shook his head. He would never understand women.

"That's one very confused young lady," said Sam Haine to Seventeen. "I'm not sure how you bumped into Jenni Smith, son, but she's always been considered a little odd by the other members of the Casey cabal. Doesn't really have any close friends. Keeps mostly to herself. Be wary of the girl, Seventeen. She was in an awful hurry to accuse you."

"But," said Seventeen, "she told me that you sent her to see me. We spent the afternoon together, talking. Jenni seemed to know all about me."

Robert Weinberg

"Albert," said Sam Haine, a pained expression on his face, "see if you can locate that young lady. Though I'm willing to bet she's nowhere to be found." He clenched his hands in disgust. "The clever little spy had the audacity to use my name? I hate to be made a fool. Oh well. We'll see Ms. Smith again, I'm sure. For some reason, she has her eye on you, boy—and I intend to discover what that reason is. And who she represents. Later, you can tell me everything you two discussed."

Pulling his cigar out of an inner pocket, Sam Haine clamped his teeth hard on one end. Magically, the tip of the Havana began to smolder.

"Nice knives," remarked the Changing Man as he edged around the young woman who called herself Shadow of the Dawn. Three steps further brought him up to her companion.

"You look familiar," he said. "Have we met before?"

"I'm afraid not," the man replied, his deep voice resonating with inner strength. "I've been out of touch with magick makers for many years. Though the name of Sam Haine, the Changing Man, is known to me. I am called Kallikos."

"Damn me if I haven't seen your face before," said Sam Haine. He frowned, concentrating, then shook his head in annoyance. "It'll come."

The Changing Man glanced at Shadow of the Dawn, who was carefully sheathing her swords. "You traveling with the girl?"

"That I am," said Kallikos. "Shadow seeks her destiny. I am her mentor."

"Lucky for me you two were here tonight," said Seventeen. He smiled at the young woman, not sure how to act in the company of a member of the Akashic Brotherhood. She smiled back. While Shadow was not beautiful, her features intrigued him.

"Luck," said Kallikos slowly, "had nothing to do with it."

"Aha," said Sam Haine. He looked over his shoulder at Seventeen. "You hear that, son? Friend Kallikos and his ward came looking specifically for you this evening. Evidently they sensed you would be at this celebration. Maybe they even realized you might need some help. Pretty damned amazing, I'd say."

Seventeen said nothing. Things were happening so fast that he could not keep track of what was going on. He was at the center of maelstrom in which all the other participants seemed to know more about him than he did.

"You're a Time Master?" Sam Haine asked Kallikos.

"One of little note," said Kallikos. He shrugged his shoulders as if dismissing the remark as unimportant. "I serve my visions as best as I am able."

Sam Haine snorted in amusement. He turned and stared at Seventeen. "Son, I don't know why you're so damned important. But, considering you've attracted the attention of at least three Conventions of the Technocracy, the Nephandi, and a Time Master, this mess must be pretty significant. I gotta feelin' major trouble's brewin'."

"More than you realize," said Kallikos enigmatically. "More than anyone can imagine."

Chapter Seventeen

Klair licked his lips. Something was terribly wrong. He was in the vast hall of *The Computer*, but the details were all wrong. The floor was cold steel, not warm copper. He sat on a metal chair, fully dressed, his biomechanisms complete. The vast Artificial Intelligence, hundreds of feet high and equally wide, covered with thousands of lights and relays and other nonessential parts, was nowhere in evidence. Instead, he faced a shiny metallic desk made of an unknown, silvery material, behind which sat a holographic figure the size and shape of a man.

"Comptroller Klair," said the being. It spoke with a smooth, silky voice, inhuman only in its unnatural calmness. "Thank you for coming on such short notice. Your cooperation is noted in my records. I assure you that such help will not go unremembered."

Dumbfounded, Klair nodded, not sure what to say. From the remarks made by the holographic creature, he could only assume it was the new representation of *The Computer*. A tall, handsome man, with dynamic features, broad shoulders, and a powerful build, it appeared almost human. Dressed in a plain gray coverall, the hologram looked vaguely familiar.

Equally disturbing was the attitude of the representation. It no longer sounded like a meld of machine and man. The tones and words were conciliatory—almost friendly. To Klair, it seemed as if the AI were trying to act human.

"I-I live to serve the purpose of my Convention," said Klair, deciding a small half-truth was best for the moment. He was loyal to the Technocracy, but his own interests came first. "I expect no reward. My work is payment enough. Unity is my only goal."

"Of course," said the hologram. It smiled, a relaxed, natural smile. "Your dedication to my plan is commendable. However, like all flesh creations, you are more than mere steel and oil. When the present situation stabilizes here, I will see that you receive a proper reward for your service to Iteration X."

"Wh-what is happening here?" asked the Comptroller. He dared not say too much. "Why have I been summoned again? I received my orders last night. Are there other changes that need to be made to the pattern-clone? Sharon Reed wasn't pleased with the last batch of modifications I handed her but Shade forced her to cooperate. We started work on the changes today. The necessary alterations are almost complete. Obtaining her assistance with another set of plans might be impossible."

"The plans for the pattern-clone are complete," said the hologram. "Do not be alarmed. All details for its final growth are in your possession."

"Then why..." Klair began, but halted in midsentence. One of the ten-foot-tall humanoid robots came gliding into the room, walking with unnatural grace on its slender, ropelike legs. Unlike the metal figures who normally haunted Klair's dreams, this robot guardian was dented in numerous places, its silver sheen dulled as if from decades of combat. Mentally, the Comptroller shivered, wondering what sort of enemies could damage it so badly.

Klair had always felt uncomfortable staring at the unmoving Mark VI prototypes in his earlier dreams. Now, seeing it in motion, he understood why. The robot exuded an air of sheer menace. He had not noticed when the machine was stationary that there were six lasers mounted in its shoulders and chest. Nor had he ever seen the code numbers engraved around the waist of the creature. This one, the Comptroller noted, was robot 3333. For some reason, the number stuck in his memory.

The Mark VI made no sound as it marched directly up to the desk where the hologram sat. Its huge, unblinking red eye pulsed with intelligence. The robot turned for an instant to look at the Comptroller, the crimson orb glaring at him with hellish intensity. While the robot kept its arms close to its sides, Klair couldn't help gazing down at the razor-edged mandibles that served as the machine's hands. Such claws could nip off a man's head with one clip. The Mark VI had been built for one purpose, and one purpose alone. To destroy.

Reaching forward, the mechanical man touched one hand to the surface of the shiny desktop. For a bare instant, it stopped moving, as if in direct communication with another intelligence. Only then did Klair realize that the squat rectangle was in actuality *The Computer*.

The holographic figure frowned in annoyance, as if it had heard some news it didn't like. "Summon reserve units 7310 through 8547," the hologram declared. "This latest incursion into the Pattern Realm must be contained at all cost. Do whatever is necessary to repel the invaders." The voice of *The Computer* hardened like steel. "Bring me no further excuses. I want results."

With a wave of a nonexistent hand, the hologram banished the robot from the room. The Mark VI departed without a sound. Klair couldn't help but feel its solitary eye focused on him the entire time it took the robot to depart. Humans did not belong in the realm of sentient machinery: It was clear to the Comptroller that the robotic shock troops considered men interlopers in this domain. If he was not under the direction protection of the AI, Klair felt certain that his chances of survival, dream or not, would be nil.

"We are engaged in a tedious, never-ending battle against the forces of chaos," said the hologram. Its face was still calm and serene, but there was an edgy, metallic ring to its voice. "Recently, those Random Elements of the Deep Universe known as the Maeljin Incarna, the Dark Lords, have increased by a hundredfold their attacks on Autocthonia. As actual conquest of this realm is impossible for Those Beyond, I conclude with an 87% probability that their real purpose is to distract me from another project. My analysis circuits tell me that the actual conflict centers around the AW mission. The Dark Lords are anxious to gain control of the pattern-clone. This must not be allowed to happen."

Klair shook his head. "We're extremely careful about who we admit to the Gray Collective. Our tests are very thorough. I refuse to believe the Nephandus have ever penetrated our defenses. There is no way they know of our existence, much less the AW project."

"You are mistaken," said the hologram. In very

human fashion, it leaned across the desk to stare the Comptroller directly in the eyes. The projection had yellow irises. "Tonight, Mission Specialist Shade led a party of Men in Black after the experimental AW subject, Prisoner Seventeen, who recently escaped from the Gray Collective. The massive attack ended in complete failure. Most of the New World Order operatives were destroyed. Shade and only a few others escaped. According to a report from one of my spies on the scene, the intervention of an agent of the Maeljin Incarna delivered prisoner Seventeen from certain destruction at the hands of a Gray Man."

Klair's normal eye twitched nervously. "That makes no sense whatsoever," he declared. "Why would Those Beyond be interested in protecting the escaped prisoner? He means nothing to them. Those fiends exist only to destroy."

"You ask an irrelevant question," declared the hologram, reverting for an instant back to its machine persona. "The thought patterns of the Random Elements in the Deep Universe do not follow proscribed pathways. The reasons for their actions do not matter. What is important is the act itself. The intervention in tonight's raid indicates that the evil ones are well aware of the AW Project. They have somehow infiltrated your base. The Gray Collective is therefore no longer a safe haven entirely free of outside interference. That being the case, it is logical to assume that the Dark Lords mean to seize possession of the pattern-clone once it is awakened. I repeat, such a scenario cannot be allowed, even if it means eliminating the pattern-clone ourselves. Forget your plan to use the HIT Marks. They are not powerful enough to battle the servants of Those Beyond. Another solution is required."

"I'm not sure exactly what to do," said Klair, the twitch in his eye growing worse. "My assistant, X344, has handled the security for our team since we started work on the project. It always appeared to me that he was doing an excellent job."

"Iteration X cyborg X344 dreams of being one with the machine," declared the hologram, smiling again. It was as if the AI was practicing changing its facial expressions with Klair. He wondered why. "However, he possesses neither the intelligence nor the ability to form a true amalgam between the two realities. His biomechanic activities are too weak to forge the necessary bond between flesh and steel. He is not capable of stopping the Dark Lords from overrunning the Collective."

"What is required of me?" asked the Comptroller. Now, he realized intuitively, he would learn exactly why he had been summoned here. All of the conversation had been leading up to this moment. "I am loyal to the Convention. You know that. I'll do whatever is necessary to further the goals of Iteration X."

"When you awaken," said the hologram, pointing

to the center of the desk, "you will find the object you see there in your quarters."

Klair nodded, looking down. An instant before, nothing had been on the desktop. Now, a short tube perhaps five inches long and an inch in diameter rested there. The Comptroller picked up the object and examined it closely. It resembled a flashlight with lens on each end, and was made of the same shimmery metal as the desk. In Deep Universe Constructs, reality could be reshaped in a microsecond by a powerful mind. And no mind in the universe was more powerful than that of *The Computer*.

"Keep my gift with you at all times," directed the hologram. "Continue to work on the pattern-clone, completing the necessary alterations as quickly as possible. Extend to Sharon Reed your complete cooperation. Finishing this operation is more important than personal vendettas.

"If you switch to six hour instead of eight hour shifts," continued the hologram, "using smaller crews, enabling each shift more rest time, I calculate a speed-up in production that will cut two days off the final completion date. Of course, say nothing about the change in our plans to anyone, including your advisor, X344. Encourage him to pursue his own schemes against the Progenitors. Reed and her assistant are likely preparing to double-cross you upon completion of the project. The Progenitors desire the AW results entirely for themselves. It doesn't matter. Nothing will happen until the pattern-clone is brought to life."

"Then what?" asked Klair.

"When Reed begins the final countdown signaling the awakening of the pattern-clone," said the hologram, "pass X344 the tube and instruct him to twist off the two ends. Only someone of his strength will be able to accomplish this. Inside is a Deep Universe beacon which will immediately pinpoint your position and provide an anchor for a temporal bridge linking the Gray Collective and Autocthonia. A troop of my personal Mark VI guardians will be waiting. They will cross the gap between the two Constructs and take control of the collective. After capturing the AW pattern-clone and returning him to this realm, they will destroy the complex, leaving no clues to their identity. They are the most powerful fighting machines in the Tellurian; nothing can stop them."

The Comptroller refrained from mentioning that the robots seemed to be having a difficult time with the attack taking place at the moment. He was not a fool.

"They will eliminate that nuisance, Sharon Reed?" he asked, indicating his tacit approval of the plan. Klair knew it was what the machine expected him to say.

"No one living will escape the destruction," said the hologram. "Except you, of course."

"Of course," said Klair, feeling extremely

uncomfortable. He did not trust the AI. The Comptroller still firmly believed in the goals of Iteration X. His problem was with the sentient machine that unbeknownst to most members of the Technocracy controlled the Convention. He was no longer convinced that *The Computer* was concerned with humanity's Ascension. But, his sense of morality was not as strong as his survival instinct. He had no choice but to obey the AI's commands and hope that his intuitions were wrong.

"I still don't understand why Those Beyond are interested in the AW pattern-clone," he remarked, hoping that the machine would reveal more of its own plans through a slip in conversation. While totally logical, the computer was not subtle. "Their experiments in human biomodification have always centered on molding living beings into new forms. Never before have they expressed any interest in cloning experiments."

"You are familiar with the brain cell development of the AW pattern-clone?" asked the hologram. The AI sounded amused. Another emotion expressed.

"Of course," said Klair, a little stiffly. He knew everything there was to know about the life-form in the tank. He had carefully studied every printout charting the pattern-clone's growth over the past few months. "The brain structure is astonishingly complex, with many more neural routings than necessary for any human mind. Velma Wade, who handled much of the design work, assures me that such advance networking is necessary to control the body's complex internal operating systems."

The hologram nodded, still smiling. "You are aware, I am sure, from your advance briefings about the Reality Deviants of the Deep Universe, that they cannot physically manifest themselves on Earth."

"I am," said Klair, wondering where this give-and-take questioning was leading. "As creatures of the Prime Element, the Maeljin Incarna are purely thought beings. They have no real substance."

"Yet, as Random Elements whose entire existence is predicated on the destruction of static reality," continued the hologram, "the Dark Lords would like nothing better than to walk freely on the Earth, spreading corruption and decay."

"Again, I agree," said Klair. "What does this line of reasoning have to do with my inquiry?"

"Using basic logic and deductive reasoning," declared the hologram, folding its arms across its chest, "you should now be able to formulate the answer to your own query."

Klair frowned. He hated riddles and puzzles. Then, as he reviewed the conversation of the past minute, a terrible realization dawned on him.

"Though physically perfect, the AW pattern-clone's brain is a clean slate, waiting for a personality implant," he whispered. "One of the

Reality Deviants plans to seize control of the clone's mind and merge with it. In essence, the being we create would thus become the actual physical manifestation of a member of the Maeljin Incarna."

"Exactly," said the hologram. "Now you understand why the agents of Those Beyond will do whatever is necessary to seize the Gray Collective."

Klair nodded, unable to speak. He had suddenly grasped the answers to several other frightening questions. He understood why the AI had materialized in holographic form, and why it had tried to appear expressive. The machine was *practicing*.

Worse, he finally knew *The Computer*'s ultimate objective concerning the AW Project. The AI was also a thought creature, residing in the Deep, unable to manifest itself in the real world. The giant machine had exactly the same goal as the Dark Lords. It wanted access to the Earth—in a body that would make it the most powerful being in the universe.

Chapter Eighteen

Sharon Reed studied the tall, abnormally thin blonde as she approached along the catwalk. She had never seen the woman before. Though it seemed unlikely, it was possible that she was an agent of Comptroller Klair or even Terrence Shade. But, although the woman's hands were empty, Sharon regarded her with suspicion. Below them, the monster Semok stirred in his growth tank; a suicidal leap by the blonde would turn them both into an early morning snack. Sharon was not going to let that happen.

Carefully, the Research Director reached for the small bacteria vial she kept in a hidden compartment of her uniform. The deadly germs were useless unless inhaled, but grasping the tube itself helped Sharon focus her willpower. As a Technomancer, she didn't believe in magick. It was

a nonsensical term used by the fools in the Nine
Traditions. She did believe, however, that certain
superior humans were gifted with a natural ability
to alter reality. Specific objects like her vial merely
helped to improve concentration. Calling them
talismans yet was another mark of Tradition
stupidity.

Twenty feet below, the giant cephalopoid stirred.
Two immense tentacles stretched into the air,
almost reaching the narrow catwalk on which
Sharon stood. The monster sensed warm life nearby
and wanted to pull the two humans into its tank.
Semok existed only to destroy. Sharon clutched her
vial tighter. Changing the structure of the gangway
would not be difficult. If she did it precisely at the
right moment, her mysterious visitor would plunge
into the tank with her next step.

"Director," said the blond woman, chuckling
softly. "Is something the matter?"

Sharon cursed and released her hold on the
container. "Velma," she said, keeping her temper
under tight control, "since when did you become
an anorexic blonde?"

Velma Wade shrugged. "After working all day
with that monster, Nelson, on the pattern-clone's
redesigned nervous system, I felt I needed a change.
That metalhead makes my skin crawl. A tall, thin
blonde seemed right. So I shapeshifted. Why do
you ask?"

Sharon sighed heavily. Velma Wade was a

dedicated Technomancer and absolutely, unswervingly loyal to her mentor. The shapeshifter was the closest thing to a friend Sharon had. Not that the Director would hesitate for a moment to sacrifice Velma if necessary to further her ambitions. Getting angry at the woman served no useful purpose.

"Just warn me in advance of your appearance," she said, "before arranging a meeting alone with me in a place like this."

The shapeshifter nodded. "Sure. Sorry. I didn't mean to startle you."

"No matter," said Sharon. "Let's get down to business. Did you come up with any ideas for eliminating Mr. Klair and his annoying assistants?"

"I'm working on a compound right now," said Velma. She grinned. "A pleasant concoction of my own that should do the trick nicely. Klair can summon all the HIT Marks he wants. It won't make a difference. Once this stuff gets into the ventilation system, the metalheads are history. It's fast and deadly. Best of all, it only affects them. It's entirely harmless to members of any other Convention."

"What is it?" Sharon asked. She couldn't help but smile. Throughout her life, she had crushed anyone foolish enough to stand in her path. Comptroller Klair was the only exception. The Iteration X Technomancer had been a major annoyance for much too long, and Sharon relished the prospect of his upcoming demise. She hoped Velma's solution was particularly painful. "A virus that attacks metal?"

"Not quite," said Velma, "but close. Primium-based steel is resistant to all forms of bacteria developed using Life procedures. Trying to devise an agent to attack the metal is a waste. Better minds than mine have worked on that problem for decades without success. However, what I did instead was investigate the area where flesh and steel meet. The bond at those junctions is quite fragile. The joint is reinforced by a powerful liquid body cement that welds the real with the artificial. A unique compound, it is only used by members of Iteration X. Dissolve that material and most of them fall apart."

"Your compound does that?"

"Much more, actually," said Velma. "It's an incredibly viral airborne virus that first attacks the liquid cement then travels inward to the nervous system. Minutes after we release the substance into the circulation system of the citadel, all of the metalheads in the building will experience horrible spasms, as their artificial limbs and enhanced organs separate from their bodies. The process should send most of them into shock. Killing them will be a long, tiring process. But it will be nice and easy."

"We can leave the job to the sauroids," said Sharon. "Except for my special friend, Mr. Klair. I'll take care of the Comptroller personally. Maybe feed him to Semok if I am feeling compassionate. If not, Technomancer Klair will serve to answer a question I've had regarding my living carpet."

"You really despise him," said Velma.

"More than you can imagine," said Sharon. "He's so sanctimonious at times I'd like to rip..." She stopped in midsentence as the cellular phone in her back pocket beeped. Frowning with annoyance, Sharon pulled it out.

"Yes?" she answered curtly, flipping open the receiver.

"Mission Specialist Shade has returned from Earth," said the nameless switchboard operator. "He requests a meeting of the Triumvirate immediately."

"Information received," said Sharon. "I'm on my way, along with my assistant, Velma Wade."

She snapped the phone shut and put it back in her pocket. "Well," she said, "let's see how our fat friend managed with Prisoner Seventeen."

"Less well than he expected," said Velma, chuckling.

Sharon stared at her assistant. "Heard something I'm not aware of?"

Velma shook her head, an odd look crossing her face. Because her features changed every few weeks, it was almost impossible to read her expressions, although Sharon had known her for quite some time. "Sorry. I'm as much in the dark as you are. But considering how easily our escapee handled the sauroid, I can't imagine that Shade's Men in Black could have caused him much trouble."

They hadn't. The Mission Specialist's voice was colder than ice as he spoke, and it was clear from his demeanor that he was not in the mood for sarcastic remarks. None of the four Technomancers present dared to make any.

"My mission ended in disaster," said Shade. "I will be filing a full report with the Inner Council shortly, but I thought it best to inform you of the facts immediately. Our schedule needs to be revised again. This project must be completed within a week."

Sharon refrained from protesting. There was no compromise in Terrence Shade this morning. Across the table from her, Comptroller Klair also kept silent. He had obviously reached the same conclusion.

"What went wrong, Mission Specialist?" asked Velma, never afraid to speak her mind. "I assume Prisoner Seventeen was not destroyed?"

"He survived by a stroke of sheer coincidence," said Shade. "Minutes after our operation began, a band of motorcycle maniacs attacked the Chantry. From my observations of their actions, I have concluded that they served the Nephandi. My agents were caught in a deadly crossfire between the Tradition mages and these rogue factors. The Syracuse Construct coordinator was killed during the exchange, as was the Gray Man controlling the Men in Black. Without their leadership, the amalgam was destroyed. Left alone, I had no choice but to abort the mission and flee."

"Perhaps the Nephandi were also hunting Prisoner Seventeen," said Comptroller Klair. Sharon noted a slight twitch of the Comptroller's right eye. For some reason, the question made him nervous. "The two attacks may have overlapped."

"Nonsense," said Shade, shaking his head. He scowled at Klair. "The Reality Deviants know nothing of the AW Project or Prisoner Seventeen. How could they? Their intervention was just bad luck."

Klair opened his mouth to say something then closed it without a word. The Comptroller appeared to be confused. Sharon found his actions disturbing. Klair never raised hypothetical questions. If he believed the Nephandi were after Seventeen, there had to be a reason.

She was equally disturbed that Shade, who normally saw conspiracies in everything, was so quick to dismiss the biker raid as a mere coincidence. It was almost as if the Mission Specialist were trying to hide something. Mentally, she filed the thought away to be explored further.

"From your expression, I gather the lunatics didn't exterminate all the Tradition mages present?" she asked. "Prisoner Seventeen hacked to pieces by those lunatics would serve our purposes despite the losses."

Robert Weinberg

"Unfortunately, nothing like that occurred," said Shade. "My spy system reported that shortly after my strategic retreat, the Traditionalists used their combined skills to fight off the outlaws. At last report, Prisoner Seventeen was still alive. I posted a seek-and-destroy message concerning him to NWO agents throughout the country. They'll keep him on the run. But, I strongly doubt that their efforts will accomplish anything beyond slowing him down."

"That being the case," said Klair, an edge in his voice, "we must return to our original assumption that Seventeen will shortly inform the Tradition Council of our work here at the Gray Collective. The entire project is in grave danger. It is not inconceivable that the Tradition mages could trace Seventeen's path back to our domain and mount a full-scale assault on the complex."

"I am forced to agree," said Shade. "Besides, there's no question that further excuses about completing our mission will not be tolerated. During my short stay on Earth, I received a direct communication from the Inner Council. Despite the dangers, they were quite clear that they want us to proceed without delay on activation of the AW pattern-clone. We must speed up our procedures. I want this project finished in one week."

Comptroller Klair nodded his head in agreement. "It can be done," said the Iteration X leader slowly.

"If we switch from three to four shifts a day, it should significantly increase our efficiency. With more rest, our technicians will be able to work harder than before, accomplishing more in a shorter period of time. As the project nears completion, staff needs actually decrease as more and more automatic processes go into effect. Much of the final countdown will be handled by the Collective's mainframe. I do not foresee any problems meeting the new deadline."

He stared at Sharon, as if challenging her to dispute his claims. "Unless, of course, the Progenitor Research Director feels her associates aren't capable of matching Iteration X standards."

"My people will fulfill their obligations," said Sharon, knowing she had no choice but to agree. "Our goal has always been to successfully complete this project as quickly as possible. I'm glad that Mr. Klair has finally come around to our way to thinking."

"Keep your quarrels buried," snapped Shade, his voice sharp as a knife, "or they'll bury you. Klair, you have this new schedule ready?"

"I've already fed it into the mainframe computer," said the Comptroller. Klair sounded tired, downbeat. "I was merely awaiting your approval before implementing the changes. With your say-so, the program revisions will begin with the next work break."

"Put it into effect," said Shade, rising to his feet.

Robert Weinberg

Klair nodded to Ernest Nelson. Swiftly, the machine man keyboarded the necessary commands to the mainframe from his hand-held computer. Despite his minor victory, the Comptroller did not seem particularly pleased. Normally, such events left a sneer on his face that remained in place for days. Sharon had to wonder what was bothering him. For all of his faults, her nemesis was no fool: If he was distracted and concerned, it was for good reason.

"Are there any other matters of importance to be discussed?" asked Shade. "If not, I'm going to bed. I haven't slept since I left the Collective. Wake me only for emergencies."

"Rest well, Mr. Shade," said Velma sweetly, as Shade walked to the door.

Muttering curses about annoying shapeshifters, the Mission Specialist left the meeting room. Comptroller Klair, with Ernest Nelson dodging his footsteps, departed immediately after. The troubled expression on the Comptroller's face had not changed. He didn't even snarl at Velma as he left.

"Mr. Klair seems preoccupied," said Sharon's assistant once they were alone. "I wonder what's bothering him. Nelson didn't seem to be concerned about anything."

"I noticed," said Sharon. "Our Comptroller has not been himself the past few days. Something has shaken his single-minded devotion to the machines. Maybe he's finally realized the errors of his ways." She paused, then voiced a stray thought. "I'm truly tempted to ask him what's wrong and see if he replies."

"You might not like his answer," said Velma, a bland expression on her face. "Assuming Mr. Klair would actually share his innermost secrets with a Research Director of the Progenitors."

"For some reason," said Sharon, "I think he would."

Velma shrugged. "Maybe. I'm a pretty decent judge of the male personality." She grinned. "Being able to change your appearance offers all sorts of intriguing opportunities for a single young woman. But, these Iteration X hybrids barely qualify as men in my book. Mr. Shade seemed pretty upset as well. He cut off discussion of the Nephandi attack quickly enough."

Sharon nodded. "His explanation of events was sadly lacking in detail," she declared. "I wonder if anyone here will see his full report to the Inner Circle. By the way, the matter we discussed earlier regarding your latest experiment doesn't address the Mission Specialist's unique status at the Collective."

"Oh," said Velma, with a lazy smile, "I've something unique planned for Mr. Shade. Let me surprise you."

The blonde's expression turned serious. "The tension level here continues to rise as we get closer and closer to completing the AW pattern-clone.

The day he awakens, all hell will break loose. The building is going to resemble a war zone. I still think you should reconsider your original decision and tell me the code. Just in case."

"No," said Sharon. "Remember, dear Velma, what Ben Franklin said: *Two can keep a secret if one is dead.* If it becomes necessary, I'll share the auto-destruct signal with you. But, not yet. Now, forget about it. Don't ask me again."

"It's forgotten," said Velma.

"Then let's get to work," said Sharon. "We've got a lot to accomplish in less than a week. There's no time for idle talk."

"Seven days till the big event," said Velma.

For a reason she could not fully explain, the thought started Sharon shivering.

Chapter Nineteen

Madeleine Giovanni was just raising her right hand to knock when the front door of the house opened. Before her stood a middle-aged man with brown skin and a black beard. He wore a pair of plain tan slacks and a white shirt. Beneath his equally dark eyebrows were eyes that glowed with astonishing intelligence. He smiled, obviously pleased to see her. To his neighbors and in the nearby marketplace he was known as Mr. Klein, a retired school teacher. Only the highest Israeli government officials and a few associates knew that his real name was Moses Maimonides. Renowned throughout the Middle East a thousand years ago as the Second Moses, he was one of the greatest magick workers ever to walk the Earth.

"Rambam," said Madeleine, using the mage's fabled nickname. "It is good to see you again."

"The pleasure is mine, child," said Rambam. They shook hands, for neither of them was very good at expressing their emotions. Then, he stepped aside so she could enter his modest bungalow home. They spoke in English, a language in which they were both fluent. "I sensed your arrival and left my study to open the door. Since Elisha departed to study in Switzerland with Dire McCann's friend, I am alone. I miss the boy. It's very tiring with him gone. There's no one around to do the chores. Besides, the house is unnaturally quiet without him constantly asking me questions."

Madeleine smiled but said nothing. She had no doubts that Rambam missed his favorite student. And she was equally positive that the master mage was not entirely truthful about his reasons.

"I know better than to offer you any refreshment," he said with a chuckle. "Come. Let us retire to the library. Your call implied that you wanted to see me for more than social reasons. I assume you have questions to ask. If possible, I will provide some answers."

Rambam led her into his library. It was a wonderful place, a room lined entirely with bookshelves, on which were crammed, from floor to ceiling, thousands of rare volumes on many different subjects, from geography to history to mathematics to magick and its uses. Many of the texts were in Latin and Greek. One entire wall of the chamber was covered with books written by Maimonides under various pseudonyms over the centuries. His curiosity knew no bounds and his mind knew no limits. The ancient sage was the wisest man Madeleine had ever known.

Rambam took a seat behind a large wood desk, given to him by the first Prime Minister of Israel, David Ben Gurion. The mage had devoted the past half-century of his life to ensuring Israel's continued survival. More than once, his magickal powers had prevented the annihilation of the small country.

Madeleine sat on a high-backed wooden chair covered with red cushions. Months before, she had been sitting in the same place, and Rambam had offered her the gift of mortality. He was one of the few mages in the world who was capable of transforming a vampire back into a human. Though she was very much in love with Elisha, Madeleine had been forced to turn down the offer due to matters involving clan honor. Circumstances had changed dramatically in the half-year since his offer had been made, but Madeleine was still no closer to accepting Rambam's gift. In moments of deep despair, she wondered bleakly if that time would ever come.

"Elisha is well?" she asked, pushing her doubts out of her mind. Madeleine was determined to be united with her lover in mortal bliss someday. And she always achieved her aims, no matter how impossible they seemed. "I think of him often."

"How odd," said the great sage, with a gentle smile. "He said the same exact words to me the other night. Do not despair. I can assure you that he is in good health and studying hard. In a year or less, he will return. Such separations are difficult, I know. But, from what Elisha told me of your situation before he departed, even though Don Caravelli is no more, you are still not free."

"Pietro will never let me leave clan Giovanni," said Madeleine. "He needs me too much. I am his dagger and his shield. There is no one else he trusts."

She smiled. "I am very patient. For the moment, I watch and wait and obey his commands. My time will come."

"My prayers are with you," said Rambam. "Now, tell me why you came here tonight. During our phone conversation, you mentioned a mission. How does it involve me?"

"Months ago," replied Madeleine, "did Elisha pass on my warning about a traitor in your midst?"

Rambam's expression grew serious. He nodded, his eyes filled with sadness. "It came as no surprise. For over a year, I had held such suspicions. Your words merely confirmed what I already suspected."

"One of your confederates told Pietro of your offer to make me human," said Madeleine. "My sire confronted me with that accusation shortly after my adventures with Elisha in Paris. I needed all of my acting skills to persuade my grandfather that the story was a lie, fabricated by a jealous mage out to destroy me. Pietro did not reveal to me the identity of my accuser, but I felt certain it was one of your two disciples, Judith or Ezra. Thus my warning to you about them both. The other night, I finally learned the truth."

Rambam sighed. "Too late, I'm afraid. Ezra made his insanity clear several months ago in a mad rage."

Madeleine nodded. "Your *strong left hand*, if I remember the exact expression you used. What changed him?"

"Mages possess the power to shape reality," said Maimonides. "Using will alone, they can perform miracles. The stronger their will and their avatar, the greater their ability to alter the universe. Magick is a unique gift, and if used wisely, it can be a tremendous help to mankind. However, like all such powers, it can be abused. Too often, powerful mages forget that they should guide mankind, and not lead it. Instead of acting as God's servants, they start to act like gods. The ancient Greeks had a word for it—*hubris*. A godlike pride, it has brought many great mages to ruin. Including my pupil and colleague, Ezra."

"Changes in character do not happen overnight," said Madeleine. Having learned English from books, she rarely used contractions. "Did you not sense Ezra turning? Could you not have done something to stop it?"

Rambam shook his head. "Ezra was the stubborn one. He had an answer to every problem. His character was such that the transformation was a long and subtle one. It occurred over years, not weeks or months. The greatest of my pupils, he was also the most proud. There was a streak of arrogance in him that set him apart from the rest. Ezra never learned humility. He was a loner, preferring his own company to that of others."

The sage's eyes clouded. His voice grew soft. "For a short time, he found peace with another gifted mage named Rebekkah. She was a beautiful young woman and they were very happy together. Ezra was content and at peace with the world. Then, sweet, gentle Rebekkah was killed in a terrorist bombing. A random attack, without any purpose other than to kill innocents. That act pushed Ezra close to the edge of madness. He swore to avenge her death and put an end to the violence that has gripped Israel for decades. Unfortunately, bringing about such a change requires more than magick. It needs great wisdom and infinite patience. Ezra was never good at waiting.

"The task was impossible for Ezra. Years passed and he grew frustrated and bitter. Looking back, I suspect that this is when he began trafficking with the Damned and other denizens of the night. What he could not accomplish with the light, he sought to achieve with the dark. He sought ultimate power, no matter what the price. He stepped onto the road to hell in search of salvation."

"Ezra visited Pietro soon after I met with him the other night," said Madeleine. She described the carnage the insane mage had caused. "My sire repeated to me verbatim the conversation he had with Ezra. The mage claimed to be allied with a power greater than that of the Undead. Do you have any idea who he means?"

"I am afraid that he has joined forces with…" Rambam began and then suddenly was silent. The floor beneath their feet had begun to shake. Though not of any great force, the quaking set the legs of the chairs and the desk rattling. A pencil holder overturned. Rambam's eyes narrowed.

As the intensity of the tremor increased, books started to inch forward on their shelves. The floor groaned as boards shifted against the nails holding them in place. The thin carpet bunched up into knots. Madeleine was on her feet, as was Rambam. The ancient sage's expression was grim.

"This disaster is not natural," he declared, holding onto his chair to retain his balance. "Stay alert. We are about to be attacked."

Madeleine shook her head, bewildered by the sudden turn of events. An instant later she realized exactly what Rambam's warning meant when a heavy, leather-bound book leapt off the shelf and slammed into the side of her head.

A second volume caught her on her right kneecap, sending a jolt of pain shivering up her leg. Vampires were difficult to kill, but they could feel pain. Alert, Madeleine shifted her head to the side as a 19th-century mathematics text flew within inches of her nose. Another book struck her a glancing blow to the side. By now, the chamber was filled with flying hardcovers, and it was impossible to dodge them all.

Gradually, the quake intensified in fury. The floor rippled as if made of Jell-O. More and more books tumbled from the shelves, raining down on their unprotected skulls. Rambam's heavy wooden desk began to slide. That massive piece of furniture could cause serious, painful damage. The lights flickered, the bulbs glowing brightly. If they suddenly exploded, the ensuing sparks could set off an inferno that would burn the house to cinders in minutes.

"Stop!" Rambam cried. The mage raised his hands high over his head, his fingers spread in the mystick sign of the ancient Hebrew willworkers, the Kohan. His voice, though not loud, resonated throughout the chamber. "In the name of the Most High, I command you to stop!"

The quake ceased as if switched off by some master control. Rambam, his features drawn and white, nodded at Madeleine. They stood in the midst of a sea of finely bound books. A cold anger filled the mage's voice.

"Obviously, Ezra must have expected you to visit me. He prepared that small surprise to take effect when we spoke of his new mentor. Not foolish enough to think that it could be anything more than a mere annoyance, he intended it to be a warning to stay out of his affairs. His pride is insufferable. As if he could blackmail me into silence! But at least the danger is over. I have mentally checked the house. Nothing else is amiss. We can talk freely without any further surprises."

Rambam scowled as he looked down at the hundreds of volumes that covered the floor. Madeleine knew how much the scholar loved books. An attack on the library was a blow to Rambam's heart. "Ezra has allied himself with one of the Maeljin Incarna, monstrous spirit warriors who serve the corrupting power of evil in the universe," declared the mage, his voice trembling with anger. "In a vision, I have seen a dread rider on a steel horse with iron wings. This armor-clad horror carries a huge serrated sword, glowing with fire. He smells of burnt flesh. He is Lord Steel, the Duke of Hate."

"Pietro wants Ezra destroyed," said Madeleine. "In return, Ezra has sworn to kill me and all I hold dear. My grandfather thought the mage was referring to him and the rest of my clan. He is mistaken. I assume that Ezra actually meant Elisha. Is it possible for me to defeat this madman, or am I and my lover doomed?"

Robert Weinberg

"Despite his alliance with Lord Steel, Ezra is not invulnerable," said Rambam. The mage sighed. "The Maeljin Incarna are spirit creatures. They cannot exist in corporal form on the Earth. Ezra can draw magickal strength from the Duke of Hate, but he must fight his own battles. Any mortal, no matter how powerful, can be destroyed. Though defeating him will require all of your considerable skills."

Pushing books out of her path with her feet, Madeleine stepped closer to Rambam. She put her hands gently on his shoulders. "There is more to this story than you are saying," she declared, her gaze fixed on the ancient sage. "Ezra betrayed you and he threatens Elisha, your favorite pupil. Once when we spoke, you made it clear to me that Elisha is bound to you by family. Yet, you have not made a move against the traitor. What secrets are you hiding, Rambam?"

The sage's face was ash gray. Slowly, he turned and pulled his chair upright. Seating himself, he looked up at Madeleine, anguish etched in every line of his ancient brow. "There are pains that are beyond endurance. Ten months ago, a disheveled and distraught Ezra appeared to me late one night and announced that he had finally come to the realization that peace could never be attained through compromise, only by destruction. We argued and I pleaded for him to reconsider his position. I told him he had been blinded by evil masquerading as good. My words meant nothing to him. Madness filled his eyes. He laughed wildly and called me an old fool. An instant later, he vanished. I have not seen him since."

"Even though you realized one of the most powerful mages in the world had been seduced by the forces of darkness, you did nothing to stop him," said Madeleine. "I do not understand. Why not?"

Rambam's eyes were filled with tears. "You suspect Elisha is of my blood. That is correct. He is my grandson. What you have not yet realized is the identity of his father."

Madeleine was bewildered, stunned. She couldn't believe Rambam's words. "What are you saying?"

"Ezra and Judith were my finest pupils," said Rambam, his voice choked with emotion. "They also are my children. Rebekkah was another student of mine. Ezra married her and a few years later, she gave birth to a boy, Elisha. Soon after, Rebekkah was killed. Ezra, consumed with vengeance, was not capable of raising the child, so I took him into my home and he later became my student. Elisha knows nothing of his parents or his heritage."

Rambam reached out and took one of Madeleine's ice-cold hands in his. "I want to help you. Ezra must be stopped before he causes untold damage and brings chaos to the world. He must be vanquished before he destroys you and kills his son, my grandson. But, I am his father! Though he follows a path of monstrous evil, *I cannot kill my own child.*"

<u>Chapter Twenty</u>

" According to our directions," said Sam Haine,
"we should be coming up on Reynold's
Chantry House in the next few minutes. Keep
watchin' for a driveway. I suspect the estate's back
from the road a bit. Most mages don't like
advertising their presence to the locals, especially
if they're actively engaged in the Ascension War."

Carefully, Seventeen checked the side-view
mirror. The van carrying Shadow of the Dawn and
Kallikos was close behind, as it had been the entire
trip cross-country from upper New York state to
sunny Los Angeles. At six a.m., there was no traffic
on the lonely back road a few miles south of the
City of Angels. Which was just fine with
Seventeen. Two previous encounters with

Technocracy agents on the road had convinced him that empty roads were a good sign.

The white-haired man laughed. "It's bad enough when the Technomancers come to pay a visit, spoiling for a fight. Things degenerate fast if your neighbors see you tossing lightning bolts and such and their disbelief invokes Paradox." He glanced over at Seventeen, in the seat next to him, to make sure he was paying close attention. "Life gets messy, son, when those bizarre Paradox Spirits try to reshape reality back to normal. They're stronger than any Tradition mage or Technomancer, and they're twice as stubborn. Avoid them at all cost. Best way to do that is to keep your magick hidden. Or you'll be sorry."

Seventeen nodded, knowing that if he didn't indicate to Sam that he understood the advice, he'd hear it again and again. "Are you sure we shouldn't have called first?" he asked for the twentieth time since they had started their long drive three days earlier.

"Too risky," Haine replied, repeating the same answer he had given before. "The Technocracy monitors our country's communication system, son. No way to avoid their listening in on our conversations. One word from you to Reynolds over the phone lines or the Internet and they'd have all of us spotted and eliminated in minutes. Personal contact's the only sure, safe way to tell the man about his sister. And hopefully enlisting his aid in smashing that Gray Collective.

"From what our friend back at the Casey cabal told me," the Changing Man continued, "Reynolds belongs to a pretty tough bunch. Me, you and Albert, Shadow and Kallikos ain't nothing to sneeze at, son, but even we cannot take on a whole Horizon Realm. We need backup, and we need it quick."

"Why do you think Kallikos and Shadow joined up with us?" asked Seventeen, checking the mirror yet again. His sixth sense warned him of impending danger, but the roads remained clear.

"I have no idea," said Sam. "Mr. Kallikos is not a wellspring of communication. Other than that brief mention of a major disaster approaching, he's played things pretty silent. Not surprising. Those Time Masters don't like talking much." Sam chuckled. "Makes 'em appear mysterious is my theory."

Albert, stretched out in the rear of the van, snorted in dismay. "Seers are well aware of the fluid nature of time," said the giant. "They are very careful not to disturb the fragile fabric of the web."

"Maybe," said Sam, "maybe not. This Kallikos seems anxious to make sure that history turns out the way he wants, make no mistake about it. That's the real reason he's along with us. The old man's not adverse to stacking the deck in his favor. Ask Miss Shadow if you think I'm lying. Be willing to bet she'd give you an earful."

Seventeen sighed. Sam found plots in

Robert Weinberg

everything. Unfortunately, as Seventeen had discovered to his dismay, he was usually correct. "Kallikos isn't that old," said Seventeen. "He might be fifty, but no more than that."

"Take the word of an old coot, boy," said Sam. "Mr. Kallikos is a lot older than he appears. Uh oh, looks like trouble up ahead. Damned Men in Black finally must have discovered our destination."

A hundred feet ahead, four black Cadillacs blocked the road. More than a dozen of the Men in Black stood behind the cars, their guns drawn. It was the perfect position for an ambush: The highway had narrowed to two single lanes and was passing through forest. Trees and bushes lined both sides of the barren road, forming impassable walls of green.

"We could stop and turn around," said Sam, "but I got a bad feeling we'd find the road blocked a mile or two behind us too. We're caught like bugs in a rug."

"Ram them," said Seventeen angrily. "I haven't come this far to stop now. Slam their damned cars off the road."

Sam shook his head. "Not a good idea, son. The Men in Black ain't bright, especially the clones that can hardly think at all, but, the Men in Gray who command amalgams are. Whoever is in charge of this bunch probably figures we might try ramming. Maybe even set up this trap thinking that we would. I'm willing to bet one of those cars is filled with nitro. One jolt and we'd all be playing harps, if you catch my drift. Sacrificing a bunch of Men in Black for high ticket items like us would seem like a fine trade for a Man in Gray."

"What are we going to do?" asked Seventeen.

"I'm open to suggestions," said Sam. "Damned if I know." The white-haired man paused, then smiled. "But, unless my eyes are playing tricks on me, don't look like it's gonna matter. Salvation has arrived."

Focused on the two vans, the Men in Black never realized they were under attack until it was too late. Death took them unaware as six avenging angels cut them down from behind. It was less of a battle than an execution. They perished without a sound.

The attackers were a mixed bunch—a big, bulky man, resembling a football player, a slender Oriental man armed with twin swords much like those carried by Shadow of the Dawn, and four hatchet-faced, dark-skinned men with jet-black hair who appeared to be Native Americans. All wore jeans and dark blue T-shirts. The big man waved a hand in the air, as if signaling all was well, then he and his companions vanished back up the road. Seventeen was just about to ask Sam for an explanation of the odd behavior when the four black Cadillacs exploded in spectacular fashion.

"Booby-trapped," said Sam. "Just like the cars at the Summer Solstice celebration. That NWO is a paranoid bunch. Don't you forget that either,

Seventeen. Those creeps see plots everywhere. They don't trust anyone. It's a trait you can use to your advantage if captured. Just tell them a bunch of lies, the wilder the better, and watch them react. It's like squirrels chasin' acorns."

"He's back," said Seventeen as he spotted the big man and his entourage walking toward them through the black smoke. "What do we do?"

"Best get out and say thanks," declared Sam Haine. "I'd be willing to venture these folks are friends with the man you're searching for."

The big man, with curly brown hair and hazel eyes, *was* the man he was looking for. In a high-pitched voice that belied his size, he introduced himself. "Alvin Reynolds," he said, holding out a massive hand with fingers the size of hot dogs.

"My Japanese friend is Kiyoshi Toda." Slender, with ageless features and deep brown eyes, the swordsman dipped his head in greeting but otherwise remained silent. Reynolds was the spokesman for the group. "I'll skip the names of my aides. You wouldn't be able to pronounce them anyway unless you speak Mayan. Welcome to the Hands of Hope Chantry. Any enemy of the Technocracy is welcome here."

"Sam Haine," said Sam, smiling. "This giant standing behind me is my friend Albert. Those two coming up from the other van are Shadow of the Dawn and Kallikos. The young fella at my side we call Seventeen. He's come a long way to find you."

Alvin Reynolds looked puzzled. "Find me? Why?"

"Your sister, Cindy, has been captured by the Technocracy and is a captive in a place they call the Gray Collective," blurted out Seventeen. "She helped me escape, but she's still imprisoned in the heart of the complex. And something monstrously evil is going to take place there very soon."

"Cindy," repeated Alvin Reynolds, drawing in a deep breath. He seemed to grow bigger, even more imposing. "At last. I knew somehow, some way, she'd get word to me. Come on. No reason to be standing out here. Let's go inside and you can tell me your whole story."

"I suspect there might have been other Men in Black behind us," said Sam.

"There were," said Alvin, nodding. "They were waiting a mile back with their Man in Gray. Not anymore."

"Efficient operation you got here, Alvin," said Sam Haine, chuckling. "Does my heart good to meet a practical man."

They spent the next hour on the patio of the huge manor house that served as the Hands of Hope Chantry, drinking juice and talking. Twenty yards of white sand separated them from the blue waters of the Pacific Ocean. Under a clear sky and bright morning sun, Seventeen repeated the story of his escape from the Gray Collective.

Alvin Reynolds sat and listened with a rapt, almost childlike expression on his face. Seventeen suspected that the mage was no fool. The few questions Alvin did ask were always quite specific and usually concerned matters for which Seventeen had no answers.

"An amazing adventure," said the Virtual Adept when Seventeen concluded. "I'm grateful for your keeping your word to my sister, Seventeen. You're a man of honor, and in these troubled times, honor is rare. I appreciate all you've done so far, but it leads me to the obvious question. What next?"

"Meaning what, son?" asked Sam Haine.

"I plan to rescue Cindy," said Reynolds. "Plus, whatever the Technocracy has planned for the pattern-clone, I suspect it's not going to benefit the Nine Traditions. It seems like a good idea to destroy it. Neither of these tasks are going to be easy. I'm hoping to get some support from the mages of Vali Shallar. But, with their help or without, I plan to invade the Gray Collective Horizon Realm and do some serious damage."

"That sounds like an invitation," said Sam Haine, chuckling. From a hidden pocket, he pulled out a cigar. He chomped down on the end, causing the tip to light. "You looking for company?"

"The more the merrier," said Reynolds. "There's enough of a fight to be divided equally, with lots to spare."

"The answers to my identity are in the Gray Collective," said Seventeen. "And, I promised your sister I would return. Though my past is blank, I feel certain that I'm a man of my word. You can count on me."

"I'm kinda anxious to learn the truth about Seventeen," said Sam Haine. "Plus, this project being cooked up by an alliance of Progenitors and Iteration X bothers me. Damned if I ain't a curious old bastard. No way I can speak for Albert, but I'll go along for the ride."

"I will too," said Albert, with a smile. "I like to keep track of Sam. He is, after all, the Changing Man. There's no one else like him in all the Tellurian."

"Shadow of the Dawn and I will accompany you," said Kallikos. "Destiny calls us. We must answer."

Reynolds shrugged his shoulders and then smiled. "Whatever you say. A Dragon's Claw and a Time Master are a welcome addition to any war party."

The burly man's voice grew serious. "One thing to remember is that since we'll be in a Technocracy Horizon Realm, our Tradition magick violates the basic natural laws of the region. The slightest use of our powers, except for *Do*, which is a physical discipline, would be unnatural in that world. Paradox spirits would swarm to us in an instant. Needless to say, it puts us at a serious disadvantage in fighting the Technomancers, who can call on all of the powers of advanced science."

Seventeen squeezed his eyes shut, then opened them. He rose to his feet, a bewildered expression on his face. "Wait a minute, please. Though I've heard Sam and other mages use the words Horizon Realm to describe the Gray Collective, I must admit I've never really known what it means. It's part of my memory that's completely blank. Having left the complex in the back of a truck, I didn't see much of the scenery. I assumed the lab was located in some mountain hideaway or hidden valley. There was a strange sensation for a second or two as the truck pulled out, but I didn't give it much thought, until now. Could somebody please explain to me what you're talking about?"

"Better than that," said Alvin Reynolds, standing up. He beckoned the others to follow. "Come with me. I'll show you."

Reynolds led them deep inside the mansion, to a room with no windows. A large-screen TV covered most of one wall, with a muted brown sofa directly across from it. The floor was a polished dark wood that Seventeen didn't recognize. It was so smooth he almost glided across the finish.

Facing the door was a seven-foot-high woven red and green tapestry. The hanging depicted a bizarre multileveled building in the midst of a jungle clearing. The art was outlined in red against the green background. Only upon further examination did Seventeen see that the weaving was much more complex than he realized. The detail was exact, down to the leaves on the trees in the forest.

"It's beautiful," murmured Shadow of the Dawn. "The work of a master craftsman."

Reynolds grinned. "More than that, it's also quite practical." Stepping forward, he pressed a hand against the top of the unusual structure in the center of the tapestry. He muttered a short sentence under his breath.

From *within* the covering, a deep, inhuman voice growled a phrase in an unknown language. Reynolds answered in the same language. The voice growled a single word.

"The guardian of the gate bids you enter," said the mage. He gestured to Sam Haine. "You first, Sam. Seventeen next, then Albert. Kallikos and Shadow of the Dawn follow, and I'll bring up the rear."

"Away we go," said Haine, winking at Seventeen. Briskly, he walked forward straight at the green tapestry—and vanished right into it.

"Go ahead," said Reynolds, noticing the startled expression on Seventeen's face. "It's nothing more than a doorway into the Horizon."

Shaking his head, Seventeen stepped forward. Reaching the tapestry, he tentatively pushed his left foot into the wall. It slide in as if passing through thin air. Drawing a deep breath, Seventeen continued forward.

The transition caused a mild ringing in his ears but otherwise had no noticeable effect. One instant he was in the mansion television room, the next he was in a large stone chamber, decorated with numerous bright wall coverings and a thick plush carpet. There was a computer in one corner and a small refrigerator in another.

Sam Haine stood looking out of a transparent outer wall. It was made of a material similar to glass but more crystalline in structure. Seventeen walked over to him, and then stood rapt, gazing at what was beyond. He did not even turn when Albert appeared in the chamber. The scenery held his undivided attention.

They stood inside a tower that looked down on a small city filled with buildings of stone and gold. Beyond the city, a jungle stretched far into the distance: a vast, brilliant green forest, with gigantic trees and brightly colored fauna. Miles away there was a series of low hills. A volcano belched smoke into the bright blue sky. And, high in the heavens, there were two suns.

The others crowded next to Seventeen. No one spoke; there was no need for words. The scene was unearthly, yet familiar. The buildings were of human design, and the flora was all recognizable earthly growth. The Indians crowding the city streets were definitely human. Yet, the setting was definitely not Earth.

"Welcome to my home," said Alvin Reynolds. "Welcome to the Horizon Realm of Vali Shallar."

Chapter Twenty-One

"We can't be on Earth," said Seventeen. "Not with two suns in the sky."

"Yes and no," said Alvin Reynolds, with a smile. "We're in a Horizon Realm. I'll let you decide exactly what that means after I explain things."

The two men sat in a small meeting room at the base of the great tower of Vali Shallar. They were scheduled to meet soon with the Rachar, the ruling cabal of mages of the Realm. Evidently bringing strangers into Vali Shallar was strictly forbidden. Reynolds wanted Seventeen to tell his story to the four members of the group. He did not say why.

Seventeen's companions had disappeared on a hastily organized trip into the jungle. Tom Ho Pak, another member of the Hand of Hope cabal, served as their guide. Reynolds hadn't explained the purpose of the mysterious venture to Seventeen. The burly mage made quick decisions but disliked having to explain his reasons. Seventeen found this behavior extremely irritating, especially since Sam Haine and Kallikos acted in exactly the same manner. Obviously, it was a trait common among powerful mages: They were so sure of themselves they saw no need to discuss their reasoning.

"The world as seen by our normal five senses is not all that exists," Reynolds began. "There is material reality and there is the psychic, immaterial world. The totality of it all we call the Tellurian. Earth, where the Sleepers dwell, is the center of the Tellurian; it is there that static reality is the strongest. As the original home of humanity, consensual reality is the main focus of the struggle between the Nine Traditions and the Technocracy, or what we call the Ascension War."

"That much I know," said Seventeen. Not patient, he was anxious to learn more before the Rachar interrupted Reynolds' explanations. "Tell me about this place."

"I'm getting there," said Reynolds, his voice calm and relaxed. The big man spoke slowly and deliberately, as if weighing each word for precisely the right meaning.

"Beyond the narrow reality of Earth lies the Gauntlet. This is a mystick barrier that separates our world from the spirit realm. Upon entering the

Gauntlet, a spellcaster's body is transformed from physical to spiritual reality. We still exist, but in a different form. Nothing to worry about. When we return to Gaia, our spirit body transforms back into our physical shape.

"The Gauntlet serves as a barrier to keep nonmages from entering the spirit realm known as the Near Umbra. It is a place that exists in the same space as our home world, but in another plane of reality. Think of it as a dimension parallel to Earth. The Near Umbra is a reflection of static reality, but is much more spiritual in nature. Much of what exists on Earth exists here as well, but in psychic form. The Garou, werewolves from our world, roam here, as do many powerful mythic beings. Wandering through the Near Umbra can be dangerous, but also exhilarating. For now, it isn't important."

"The Horizon?" said Seventeen. "Let's get to that."

Reynolds nodded. "The Horizon is another magickal barrier. It divides the Near Umbra from the Deep Umbra."

At the mention of the Deep Umbra, Seventeen shivered. A shadow of memory crossed his mind, a half-remembered vision of a demonic figure clad in glittering silver armor, riding on a steel horse with iron wings. In one hand he held an immense serrated sword, glowing with fire. Unbidden, the monster's name rose to Seventeen's lips. "Lord Steel, the Duke of Hate."

Alvin Reynolds' eyes widened in surprise. "One of the Maeljin Incarna," said the big man. "Most willworkers have never heard of the Dark Lords. As a Virtual Adept and a student of the occult, I'm familiar with the thirteen Royal Bane Spirits. How do you know of them?"

"I-I don't know," said Seventeen. "Sometimes, a word or phrase ignites a fuse in my mind and it explodes a memory buried in my subconscious. Once, before I lost my memory, I saw Lord Steel. But what it was that happened, I can't remember."

"The Bane Spirits inhabit the Deep Umbra," said Reynolds. "So do monsters without names, creatures so alien that they are incomprehensible to most mortals. It is in the Deep Umbra, far from static reality, that the Nephandi have their Chantries, places they call Labyrinths. There, too, is where those insane mages known as Marauders make their home while they plot their mad schemes of conquest. The Deep Umbra stretches outward to infinity. It is a dangerous place; exploring it is risky business. Still, there are more than a few, including a number of my closest friends, who thrive on taking such chances."

"The Horizon serves as a barrier that keeps the horrors of the Deep Umbra from Earth," said Seventeen, combining logic and a stray thought.

"That's right," said Reynolds. "However, unlike the Gauntlet, it's a unique region of its own, a sort of demarcation zone between the Near Umbra and the Deep Umbra. Using vast amounts of Quintessence drained from Nodes on Earth, mages have been able to construct artificial environments, which they call Horizon Realms. The Gray Collective from which you escaped was one. Vali Shallar is another."

"A Horizon Realm is usually entered from Earth, most often at the Nodes that supply Quintessence to the Realm. Smaller Realms need only a few Nodes to supply them with the necessary mystick energy, while larger ones like this need a number of powerful nodes. Ancient, magickal places primarily located in South America serve as the source of most of the Quintessence that fuels Vali Shallar. Hopefully, using your experiences, we'll be able to locate the primary Node that serves as a portal for the Gray Collective."

Seventeen, not sure what Reynolds meant by that, let the comment slide. "Explain to me what you mentioned earlier, about the rules of magick not working the same way in all Realms."

"Simple," said Reynolds. "Horizon Realms are small, artificial worlds, pocket universes in a sense, created by a group of mages of a certain belief. They can be Technomancers or members of the Nine Traditions. When they design the Realm, the creators try to make the refuge a perfect representation of their beliefs. They twist Quintessence in such a manner that their view of the universe is the basis for creation. Thus, in a

Horizon Realm created by the Technomancers, magick performed using scientific methods works fine and does not create Paradox. However, Verbena magick, Earth magick, would not function properly and would immediately generate tremendous amounts of Paradox, causing major problems for the user."

"I'm still pretty confused," said Seventeen.

"Think of it this way," said Alvin Reynolds, patiently. "We've built a house and filled it with modern, time-saving conveniences. If I want to cook a meal, I take a frozen dinner out of the freezer, peel off the metal foil, put it in the microwave and zap it for a few minutes. I then remove it, let it cool, and eat. It's easy for me to do.

"Consider what happens when a stranger, let's say someone who lives in the mountains and hates technology, comes to visit. He doesn't know the rules of behavior. He puts the food still in the box in the microwave. Doesn't take off the metal foil. Pushes the timer for fifteen minutes. Disaster in the kitchen. In a Tradition Horizon Realm, tradition magick works without incident. Same holds true for Technocracy *science* in a Technocratic Horizon Realm. You can get away with small stuff in either location, but that's all. Otherwise, Paradox."

"You should be a teacher," said Seventeen. "I think I understand what you're saying. Perhaps not as well as I would like, but at least, I have a grasp of the basic concepts. Now, explain to me why there are two suns in the sky."

Reynolds grinned. "That's a little more difficult," he declared. "Vali Shallar was created by Mayan Dreamspeaker mages many centuries ago. With the help of a powerful being from the Deep Umbra, they were able to form a realm similar to the ancient Mayan concept of heaven. Which includes two suns in the sky and two moons at night. The original…"

The big man grew quiet as four wizards entered the chamber. Two were Mayans, with dark skin, long black hair, and sloped foreheads. The others were slender, lithe Orientals, dressed in simple robes that identified them as members of the Akashic Brotherhood. Though they all looked to be in their mid-fifties, Reynolds had told Seventeen that none of the Rachar were less than five centuries old. They were the leaders of the Vali Shallar Horizon Realm, and their word was law.

Without ceremony, the four sat down at a long table facing Reynolds and Seventeen. They stared at Seventeen with curious, but not hostile, eyes. A hawk-faced Mayan, dressed in a green silk robe with a golden amulet around his neck, spoke first. In the ancient language of the Mayans, he directed a series of quick questions at Alvin Reynolds.

The Virtual Adept answered in the same language. His reply, though short, made several members of the Rachar smile. The Mayan with the gold ornament nodded his head as if agreeing to a request.

"Let our guest speak," the hawk-faced man declared in perfect English.

"Tell Ihuanocuatlo your story, Seventeen," said Alvin Reynolds. "Start from your escape and don't skip any important details. You can speak in plain English. All of the members of the Rachar understand the language."

Though Reynolds offered no explanation for his request, Seventeen thought it best to comply. Carefully, he retold his adventures over the past week. The Rachar listened without interrupting. Only the sharpness of their eyes indicated that they understood what he was saying.

"Thank you," said Ihuanocuatlo when Seventeen had finished his tale. "It is a compelling tale."

"But is there any proof that it is the truth?" asked one of the two Japanese members of the Rachar. "I am not calling our guest a liar, but his story is astonishing even among mages. What proof does he offer that his appearance in Vali Shallar is not part of an elaborate scheme to invade our realm? Once before, the Technocracy tried to destroy our land. This man's appearance could signal the beginning of another attempt."

"You raise a good point, Shi-Han," said Ihuanocuatlo. His dark eyes stared at Seventeen. "Other than your word, do you have any proof that the story you have told us is not merely an intricate hoax?"

Seventeen started to shake his head and then

stopped. "In a devious world full of deception and trickery, no evidence is truly conclusive. Thoughts can be altered, beliefs manipulated. But, I can demonstrate beyond most doubts that at least part of what I've told you is true. Will that suffice?"

The Akashic brother, Shi-Han, inclined his head in a slight nod.

"Give me your knife, Alvin," said Seventeen.

Licking his lips, Reynolds handed Seventeen the Case knife he carried on his belt. Holding the steel blade in one hand, Seventeen grabbed the front of his own shirt and ripped. Buttons flew to the ground as the garment tore into pieces, exposing Seventeen's chest.

"What are you going to do?" asked Reynolds, his eyes widening in surprise.

"The Progenitors at the Gray Collective did something to my flesh and blood," said Seventeen. "I think they were using me to test their data before implementing changes in their pattern-clone. Watch."

Seventeen placed the point in the center of his chest. Gritting his teeth, he jerked his hand forward an inch and with the same motion, sliced downward. Bright red blood gushed from the gaping wound.

The four Rachar stared at Seventeen in mute astonishment. Alvin Reynolds cursed as Seventeen's blood spilled onto the stone floor, his mouth gaping in shock. The Rachar said nothing, but they appeared equally amazed.

Robert Weinberg

The wound was healing. Only seconds had passed and already the bleeding had stopped. Faster than the eye could follow, Seventeen's skin was knitting together, the gash closing.

"His blood eats through the stone," said Shi-Han. It was true. The floor in front of Seventeen's feet was pockmarked with tiny holes where his blood had splattered.

"We must confer," said Ihuanocuatlo, rising to his feet. Turning to the rear door, he beckoned to the other members of his cabal. The grim-faced Indian smiled at Seventeen, his eyes twinkling in amusement. "Thank you for your amazing demonstration. Please excuse us. We will return in a few moments."

"That was damned dangerous," said Alvin Reynolds, sheathing his dagger after the four Rachar had left. "Whatever mechanism is responsible for your incredible healing powers is undoubtedly fueled by Technomancer magick. You could have summoned a horde of Paradox spirits with that display."

"It was worth the risk," said Seventeen, grinning. "Cutting myself open was the only means I had to show that I wasn't lying. Besides, slicing my body didn't require anything but nerve. Magick was only involved in my healing so quickly. I'm not sure exactly what the Progenitors did to my blood, but I have a vague memory that it was handled on a molecular level. The process combined magick and science, so I figured the chance of creating Paradox was pretty small."

"Nanotechnology," said Reynolds. "It's the cutting edge of modern genetic research. Since you survived unscathed, I can't get too upset. That was some show."

"What's this session all about, anyway?" asked Seventeen, emboldened by Reynolds openness. "Why are we being questioned by the Rachar?"

"Vali Shallar is a secret Horizon Realm," said Reynolds. "It has always been a place of legend. Aside from a handful of outsiders, its existence is known only to mages who belong to one of the several cabals centered here. Visitors are strictly forbidden except in dire emergencies, and normally their memories are wiped clean when they leave. I'm hoping that the Rachar will consider an alternative in your case."

Seventeen's hands clenched into fists. The thought of losing more of his memory was not appealing. "Knowing the situation, why did you bring us here?" he asked, trying to keep the bitterness from his voice.

"My apologies," said Reynolds. "It's a gamble I had to take. Rescuing my sister won't be easy. And, I'm convinced that whatever deviltry is brewing in the Gray Collective, it must be stopped. Or we'll all be sorry.

"Unfortunately," the big man continued, "many of the willworkers of Vali Shallar are extreme isolationists and terribly xenophobic. They hate outsiders and the changes such newcomers bring. These traditionalists would prefer to remain neutral in the Ascension War.

"Others, like me, know that if the Technocracy isn't stopped, magick as we know it will disappear. The Rachar govern the Realm, but they walk a thin line between the two beliefs. In this case, I'm praying that the ancient ones realize the importance of our mission and allow us to continue, despite the views of the isolationists."

"Well," said Seventeen, "I suspect we'll find out soon enough. Here they come."

The four members of the Rachar filed back into the chamber and took their seats. Ihuanocuatlo's face was grim and his voice weary.

"I will use English so you both can understand our decisions and why they were made," said the ancient mage. "The Rachar agree that the events described by Prisoner Seventeen are very disturbing and require action. However, the wishes of our own people, especially the Jabhi-yazer who guard our secret Realm, cannot be ignored. We thus have reached the following conclusions.

"The Hands of Hope cabal and their allies are free to mount an attack on the Gray Collective. The memories of the strangers will not be altered. However, to protect the secrecy of Vali Shallar, the minds of all engaged in this mission will be sealed, so that they will be unable to speak of the Realm if captured.

"As we feel strongly that the Progenitor experiments are a threat to the Nine Traditions," continued the Mayan, "the Rachar will provide all possible aid to the Hands of Hope in their quest. But, to placate those among us who fear discovery, we cannot allow any mages of Vali Shallar other than those of that cabal to participate in the raid."

"Good enough," said Alvin Reynolds. "I bow to the wisdom of the Rachar."

"Go then," said Ihuanocuatlo. "Your companions wait outside." The old Mayan smiled. "Evidently they have been hunting."

"Hunting?" Seventeen said to Alvin Reynolds as they left the meeting room.

"Using Tradition magick in the Gray Collective Horizon Realm would be a disaster," said Reynolds. "However, Vali Shallar has a few surprises roaming the great rain forests. There are strange places on Earth connected by Nodes to the Realm where beasts thought to be long extinct still exist. Many of the creatures have migrated to the jungles here over the centuries. While we were in with the Rachar, our companions went hunting for a rare specimen. I think we'll bring it along when we invade the Technocrats' lair. It isn't magickal so there is no Paradox involved. But its presence should create quite a stir."

"You're not talking about dinosaurs," said Seventeen, as they walked out into the bright sunshine of midmorning. Their friends were waiting by the door.

Robert Weinberg

"Too difficult to transport," said Reynolds, his tone of voice serious. "My little surprise is somewhat easier to control. And just as deadly."

"Hey, son," said Sam Haine as they joined the others, "you missed a rousing trip into the great muddy. Albert looked properly native."

"I've been in many jungles in my lifetime," declared the giant spellcaster, shaking his head in astonishment, "but never one to compare to Vali Shallar. There are plants here that no longer exist on Earth. Not to mention the amazing breeds of animals that can be found!"

"We captured a mighty warrior," said the usually quiet Shadow of the Dawn. The young woman's eyes were glowing with excitement. "He will wreak death and destruction on those who seek to enslave the Traditions."

"Your baby is all tranquilized and ready to go," said Reynolds' friend, Tom Ho Pak. A slender Korean, he was a wizard of the Order of Hermes. "What was the Rachar's decision?"

"They okayed my involvement in the mission, but without help from anyone in Vali Shallar other than the Hands of Hope," said Reynolds. "It was as much as we could've hoped for. It could have been much worse."

"So, the attack's on," said Kallikos. "Very good. When do we leave?"

"We need to transport our captive back to Earth and get the beast tranquilized and in a truck," said

Reynolds. "Then, give me an hour with Seventeen and my computer mapper. I should be able to figure out the location of the Node for the Gray Collective from which he emerged. It's going to be a long ride back cross country, but it's the only entrance we know for the Horizon Realm. Of course, getting through their gateway will be another challenge."

"You leave that problem to Sam Haine, the Changing Man," Sam said with a lazy smile. "I've got a few tricks up my sleeve you computer jockeys can't duplicate." He chuckled. "At least, not yet."

Chapter Twenty-Two

"That's it," said Velma Wade, leaning back in her chair. She patted the computer terminal with what almost seemed like fondness. "The final codes have been entered. The growth chamber cycle has been initiated. Twenty hours from this minute our pattern-clone will be fully functional. Tomorrow at eighteen hundred hours our baby comes to life."

Raising her arms over her head, Wade separated them slowly, mechanically, while chanting, "Tick, tock, tick, tock. Who knows where the time goes."

Looking up from his laptop computer, X344 glared at the Progenitor. Velma Wade grated on his nerves. She took nothing seriously. To the cyborg, whose life revolved around the concept of absolute obedience to authority, the young woman was a dangerous lunatic. X344 had special plans for Velma Wade when the time came to clear the station of Progenitor scum. She had been taunting and tormenting him for months, but the long wait was nearly over. Tomorrow, he would finally reverse the current on his tormentor. And she would become the tormented.

"My calculations indicate 19 hours, 54 minutes," said X344. "Plus or minus 16 seconds."

Wade laughed. "I bow to your superior calculating skills, Nelson," she said. "Though I suspect twenty hours is a good enough approximation for the big moment. It's not like our boy is going to sit up and start talking. His mind is empty of any intelligence. More importantly, he has no soul."

"There is no such thing as the soul," said X344, speaking instinctively. "It's merely an invention of the Traditions to keep the general populace enslaved to superstition. I know better. As a loyal member of the Technocracy, you should as well."

He snorted in disgust. "Souls, Avatars, call them what you want. They are meaningless terms. Religious nonsense for the unenlightened."

Velma Wade smiled at him and nodded. "No doubts in you, Nelson. It's the mark of a good machine man. You do Iteration X proud. No one would ever accuse Ernest Nelson, Mr. X344, of possessing a soul, that's for sure."

The blonde rose from her chair at the control

center for the steel pit where the growth tank was located. "I'm off to tell Research Director Reed the good news. I'm sure Sharon will want to celebrate with some champagne tonight." Her eyes sparkled nastily. "Why not link up with Comptroller Klair and keyboard in the information. The two of you can share a can of high-test lubricant or whatever you boys drink to get some kicks."

X344 trembled with rage. His face turned beet red, and his metallic claws clicked in frustration. He longed to squeeze the life out of the shapechanger's worthless body. But, his anger was not so great as to overwhelm his good sense. Iteration X Technomancers never let their emotions betray them. The penalty for killing a research team member was electrocution: a machine put to death by a machine. Though he hated Wade with all of his being, the cyborg dared not touch her. He knew it, and worse, so did she.

"Have a pleasant evening," said Velma Wade, licking her lips at his impotent fury. "My regards to Mr. Klair."

"Think like a machine," X344 muttered to himself as Velma sauntered off, swaying her hips suggestively. "Think like a machine. Cold, calm, emotionless. Think steel. Think steel."

Slowly, the mantra of his innermost beliefs cooled his temper. Velma Wade was a bitch, but she was a smart bitch. X344 couldn't help admiring secretly the woman's skill at manipulating his basic feelings. The Progenitor Technocrat knew the exact words she needed to break his iron control. Oftentimes, he wondered if she hadn't been schooled by the New World Order. Wade was not as secretive as Terrence Shade, but she was the Mission Specialist's equal in deceit. And X344 knew from his own spying that she was as treacherous. The shapeshifter was a very deadly enemy. But after tomorrow, she would be a very dead one.

"Think steel," he said one last time, and keyboarded his communication link with Comptroller Klair.

"What do you want, X344?" asked Klair, his voice coming in harsh but clear over the micro-transmitter fitted into the cyborg's right ear. "I'm busy with computer codings."

"Good news, Comptroller," declared X344, subvocalizing into the microphone built into his throat. In tight situations, he could use similar communications hardware to communicate with Comptroller Klair and other members of Iteration X without anyone else being the wiser. "The final programs have been initiated. The growth tank is draining. By tomorrow evening at eighteen hundred hours, the pattern-clone will be fully functional."

"Excellent," said Klair. "Meet me in my office in fifteen minutes. I'm reprogramming the security codes for the Horizon gateway. We need to talk now and make our final plans."

"I'm on my way," said Nelson.

"Oh, and do me a favor," said Klair, before breaking the connection. "Call Mission Specialist Shade and tell him the news as well. We wouldn't want our fat NWO friend to feel we've forgotten him in the excitement."

"Wade didn't bother," said X344.

"Her blunder," said Klair. "Shade will surely want to report our success to the Inner Council. I would prefer Iteration X to be mentioned as having cooperated fully with the other Conventions on this final stage of the project. No reason to sully our reputation at this late date."

"You make the decisions," said Nelson. "I just carry them out. See you shortly."

Breaking the connection with Klair, the cyborg used the Collective intercom to contact Shade. As usual, the Mission Specialist was in his combination office/sleeping quarters; as his work had nothing to do with the actual construction of the pattern-clone, he was rarely seen on the floor. He merely served as a mediator… and a spy. X344 disliked Shade but didn't hate him. The man was only doing his job, protecting the interests of all five branches of the Technocracy. His only fault was his refusal to realize that Iteration X was the only true path to salvation. Machines were the future.

"Mr. Shade," said X344, keeping his thoughts to himself, "the project is in its final stages.

Comptroller Klair instructed me to inform you of the good news. By eighteen hundred hours tomorrow, the pattern-clone will be fully functional. The AW project is nearing completion."

"What wonderful news," said Shade, his voice booming over the intercom. "At long last, success. And no signs of interference from the Reality Deviants. It seems our worries were groundless. I appreciate your call, Mr. Nelson."

"Glad to be of service, Mission Specialist," said the cyborg. "I need to break connection, as I have procedures to complete. I assume we will see you in the lab tomorrow evening?"

"I wouldn't miss this event for all the money in the world," said Shade. "I'll inform the Inner Council that the countdown has begun. They will be quite pleased, I'm sure."

"I'm sure," repeated X344, striving not to sound sarcastic. As if he cared what the leaders of the Symposium thought. "Good night, sir."

"A good night to you, Nelson," said Shade, cheerfully. "It is a very good night."

"Damn fool," muttered the cyborg under his breath after he terminated the connection. "Doesn't he realize that war's going to break out here tomorrow between Comptroller Klair and Director Reed? This place's gonna resemble a slaughterhouse before the bloodletting ends. And all the money and spy devices in the world ain't gonna buy him a safe place to hide."

Robert Weinberg

Making sure his control terminal was shut off and locked, Nelson sped off through the laboratory, heading for Klair's private office. Though the Comptroller had said fifteen minutes, X344 knew from long experience that Klair always added a few minutes onto his arrival estimates. In that fashion, the Comptroller routinely appeared early for appointments.

As he rolled up the ramp leading to the second floor, the cyborg turned over in his thoughts Shade's seeming ignorance of the upcoming confrontation. Since he was the person who most often served as referee between Klair and Reed, it seemed odd that the Mission Specialist wasn't doing more to ensure that there wouldn't be any hostilities tomorrow. Terrence Shade was many things that X344 despised, but he was definitely not naive.

It was only when he reached the entrance to Klair's office that it suddenly dawned on the cyborg that perhaps Shade was well aware of the battle brewing between the two Conventions. His lack of attention might actually be a cold, calculated effort on his part to forward the schemes of the New World Orders. *Divide and conquer.* The phrase slipped into X344's thoughts and refused to disappear.

He knocked on the entrance panel of Klair's sanctum. "Identify yourself," came the Comptroller's voice from within. As expected, he had arrived early.

"Technomancer X344, Comptroller Klair," said the cyborg, knowing that the video and audio scanners built into the door were analyzing and comparing his voice and appearance with the composite on file. Comptroller Klair was extremely careful about whom he admitted into his office. He preferred to avoid any surprises.

The door slid open as the computer verified and confirmed X344's identity. Klair was sitting behind a narrow black metal desk. His head rested between his hands, his elbows on the desktop. The Comptroller was frowning. "You're late," he said to the cyborg as his assistant rolled into the chamber.

"No," said X344, "you're early. I set an internal timer to your call. You told me fifteen minutes. As of this instant, fourteen minutes and forty-two seconds have passed."

Klair smiled faintly, though his face remained clouded with thought. "I should know better than to pick an argument over facts with a Technomancer of your talents, X344. What's bothering you? I thought you would be overjoyed to be nearly finished with this mission. At long last, no more dealings with the Progenitors. Instead, you seem distraught."

"Terrence Shade," growled the cyborg. "I always thought he was keeping the peace between our staff and the Progenitors. It never occurred to me that he was doing just the opposite. That snake's been secretly manipulating both factions, keeping us at each other's throats so that he retains total control over the project."

"Of course," said Klair, without a trace of surprise. "Did you expect anything less from a leader of the New World Order? I've been aware of Shade's divisive tactics for months. I'm certain that Sharon Reed has as well. It doesn't matter. He's merely an annoyance that will be dealt with tomorrow."

The cyborg looked around suspiciously. Normally his boss did not speak so openly of their plans. "You've swept the office for listening devices?" he asked.

"The entire Gray Collective is wired with Mr. Shade's spy equipment," said Klair. There was a certain grim satisfaction in his voice as he spoke. "Detecting them was a trivial exercise. To lull his suspicions, I left them undisturbed over the months. Today, after your call, I turned on the interference wave generator I constructed shortly after my arrival at the complex. As you well know, Iteration X never supplies one of the other Conventions with a device unless we possess a counter against it. Mr. Shade's listening network no longer functions. Nor is there anything he can do to fix it during the next twenty-four hours. He's probably quite frantic, wondering what is being planned without his knowledge. By tomorrow, he should be near to a state of total nervous collapse."

"Too fuckin' bad," said X344, grinning. "Maybe

he'll sweat off a few pounds instead of sleeping tonight. What happens to the fat man tomorrow?"

"He joins the ranks of martyrs to scientific progress," said Klair. "Along with Sharon Reed, Velma Wade, and all of the other misguided fools who pursue their erroneous paths to redemption."

The cyborg whistled. "No survivors, huh?" He had known for certain that Reed and Wade were slated for elimination. They knew too much about the basic nature of the project to be allowed to live. But even he had not expected that the entire Progenitor force at the Gray Collective would be exterminated.

"The decision was not mine to make," said Klair, shaking his head. He did not look happy. The Comptroller was not a killer. "The orders come from the highest authority."

The Comptroller hesitated, as if pondering his next words. "Once the pattern-clone is fully functional, a squad of HIT Marks will enter the Collective and exterminate anyone who does not belong to our group. I made the arrangements a month ago. You are going to be in charge of the operation."

X344's jaw dropped. "Me? Directing an entire unit of HIT Marks." He laughed with pleasure. "I can't believe it. What an opportunity!"

Klair nodded. "I thought you would be pleased. Do what you wish, but be thorough. No excessive gore, even if that means showing some restraint with Velma Wade. I want this job done quickly and efficiently. After all, we are part machine. Logic, not emotions, must guide our actions."

"Whatever you say, sir," said X344. He wasn't going to argue technicalities with Klair. Velma Wade would die in the most painful manner imaginable. Afterward, there would be little the Comptroller could do about it. And, the cyborg felt certain that Klair wouldn't be terribly upset with his actions, especially if Sharon Reed suffered as well.

"What is the exact plan?" he asked, clearing his mind of all thoughts of revenge. "Where are the HIT Marks and how do we get them into the lab at the proper time?"

"That," said Klair, "is why I summoned you here." The Comptroller reached into an inner pocket of his jacket and pulled out a short tube perhaps five inches long and an inch in diameter. The device reminded X344 of a flashlight, though it was obviously some unrecognizable instrument. It had a crystal lens on each end and was made of an unrecognizable metal that glowed silver.

"This unique instrument is your responsibility," said Klair, passing the object over his desk to the cyborg. "Don't let it out of your sight for an instant. It's vital to what happens tomorrow."

"What is it?" the cyborg asked as he examined the object with the full scanning powers of his augmented vision. Try as he might, he could not detect a seam or wield in the tubing.

The Road to Hell

"A Deep Universe beacon," said Klair. "Once operational, it will pinpoint our exact position in the Horizon Realm and act as an anchor for a temporal bridge between the Gray Collective and Earth, allowing the HIT Marks immediate access to the laboratory. As soon as they arrive, you're in charge."

"I won't fail Iteration X," said X344, pride welling up deep within his breast. He was honored to have been selected for such an important task, though, in his opinion, he was the obvious choice for the assignment. Klair might have the brains, but he didn't possess the necessary ruthlessness. Only an operative with field experience like X344 had the strength and tenacity to handle such assignments. "How do I activate the beacon?"

"Twist off the two ends," said Klair. His voice trembled slightly with excitement. "Only someone with your incredible physical strength can do it."

Klair paused, as if trying to recall one final detail. Finally, after more than a minute, he continued. "After you finish opening the tube, X344, I'd toss it as far away from you as possible. *Do that immediately*. This device is still in the experimental stages. I suspect being extra careful would be a very good idea. An *extremely* good idea."

"I'm not worried," said the cyborg, shifting the tube from claw to claw. "But I'm not a fool either. Opening a passage from a Horizon Realm to Earth must require a lot of psychic energy. No way do I plan to contribute any of mine to the endeavor."

Robert Weinberg

"Very good," said Klair, his usually harsh voice softening for a moment. "We've been through a lot together, my friend. I'd hate to lose you now at the moment of our greatest triumph."

The cyborg laughed. "I'm not so easy to kill, Comptroller. The factory accident that mutilated my hands and feet would have finished an ordinary man, but not me. Instead, I became even better: part man, part machine. I've got the will to survive. Nothing around that can put an end to X344. Besides," he declared, "I want to see the look on Velma Wade's face when she realizes her airborne virus ain't working."

Klair smiled. "The fools. Those naive, stupid fools. Did they really think they could escape our electronic espionage drones by hiding in the basement? Genetic rats? What foolishness. I gather from your remark that you've taken the proper precautions?"

"The moment she introduces the virus into the air, our purifiers kick into high gear," said the cyborg. "We're safe. The only thing we gotta be careful about is that thing they're growing in the tank. Whatever it is sounds dangerous."

"We can handle it," said Klair, smugly. "Their science is nothing compared to ours. Tomorrow will be a great day for Iteration X."

"It sure as hell is gonna be one filled with surprises," said X344.

Klair, a strange expression on his face, nodded.

The Road to Hell

Chapter Twenty-Three

Terrence Shade laughed. A routine systems alarm had sounded a few seconds earlier, indicating problems with the devices.

Running a quick scan of the network revealed that all of the devices in the Gray Collective had ceased operation eighteen seconds earlier. It was quite amusing. He felt certain that the sudden blackout was a direct result of the announced final countdown of the AW Project. No doubt Charles Klair was the man responsible for the termination. The Comptroller was a brilliant scientist, a superior Technomancer, and a man of no imagination or cunning.

If Shade had been the one in charge of sabotaging the monitoring devices, he would have merely rerouted the signals so that the sights and sounds picked up by the monitors came in just garbled enough that they could not be deciphered. General systems errors in Technocracy Horizon Realms were rare but they did sometimes occur. Total breakdowns never did. The best espionage created doubts, not certainties.

"Klair lacks subtlety," Shade murmured softly. Until the alarm had gone off, he had been sitting in a plush easy chair, rereading his favorite book, Machiavelli's *The Prince*. No matter how many times he perused the volume, Shade always found it invigorating and informative. It was much more entertaining than fiction. And much more useful.

"His counterbalance, Sharon Reed, lacks patience," he concluded, walking back to his chair and closing the volume. There would be time for reading later. Now, he had a few final preparations of his own to put into effect. Lazily, he stretched his arms over his head. Despite the shutdown of his spy systems, Shade was in an excellent mood. His work was nearly finished.

In Shade's opinion, Reed and Klair made a wonderful team. They had complimentary personalities, driven not by love but by hatred. Their intense rivalry pushed them to extremes. Thus, they finished their work much more quickly than would two friends or allies. Using the two of them on this project was a stroke of genius. At least Shade considered that to be the case. One trait he did not lack, and he was the first to admit it, was modesty. He had been the Associate who had specifically requested each of them for the AW Project. Others might claim credit, but Terrence Shade was the person directly responsible for the Gray Collective's success.

Though not his first triumph, it was definitely Shade's greatest. If he had been a religious man, he would have said it was his destiny.

All his life, he had been a manipulator. It was in his blood, in his genes according to Progenitor credo. The New World Order had been the first to recognize his talent, recruiting him while he was still in high school. They had taught him how to utilize his gifts, educated him in the subtle intricacies of mind control, and installed in him the knowledge that the ends always justified the means. In return, he had paid the Convention back many times over.

Shade had quickly risen to the position of Mission Specialist for the Convention, developing major projects under the supervision of the NWO Board of Directors and reporting directly to the Symposium. Recently, there had even been some talk of elevating him to membership in the Inner Council. It was all just rumors, most of which originated with Shade himself. He saw no reason not to promote his own interests. Becoming one of the leaders of the Technocracy would please Shade a great deal. More importantly, it would please his secret mentor and advisor.

Shade's whole body shook with inner merriment. The Technicians of the Technocracy were all so naive, so trusting. The fools actually thought he was loyal to their idealistic, paternalistic beliefs. He knew better. Loyalty, conformity, and allegiance were catch-words for the Masses. Terrence Shade believed in nothing other than his own self-interest. Power to realize his slightest whim was his ultimate goal. And he was willing to pay the ultimate price to achieve it.

He walked over to the small alcove in his suite that contained his desk, wall shelving and telephone system. Seating himself at his desk, he picked up the receiver and dialed a complicated string of numbers. The communications unit provided Shade a direct link with the New World Order headquarters located on Earth. It was over these guarded lines that he made his reports about the progress on the AW Project. Not that those messages had the least semblance of truth. His exchanges with the Symposium and their supposed instructions to the Gray Collective were primarily his invention. They contained just enough facts to sound believable. This entire project, almost since its inception, had been directed by a power other than the Inner Council of the Technocracy. No one on Earth had any real idea of how close the secret mission was to being completed. Which was exactly what Shade intended.

The receiver rang three times. It was always

answered on the third ring. The voice on the other end was not human, but it was quite familiar to Shade. It belonged to his patron demon, the Countess of Desire, Empress Aliara of the Realm known as Malfeas.

"Well," she said, not one to engage in pleasantries or idle chatter. She knew it was Shade. No one else had a phone line that connected directly to the Deep Universe. "What is the status of the experiment?"

"The final countdown has begun," said Shade. "In approximately twenty hours, the pattern-clone will be fully functional."

"Excellent," said Aliara, a note of excitement in her sexless voice. "I am very pleased with your news, Shade. My triumph approaches. Do your fellow Technocrats suspect you of planning a double cross?"

"Probably," said the Mission Specialist, "but that is to be expected. Since this project began, the leaders of both factions have been plotting against each other. Me, they consider a minor annoyance. None of them fear the New World Order. I'm sure the Progenitors and Iteration X have targeted me for eventual elimination. Do they suspect that I might be more dangerous than I seem? That I sincerely doubt."

"They will learn otherwise shortly," said the Dark Lord. She laughed, a strange, unnatural sound. "Tomorrow, you will be rewarded with power beyond your wildest dreams. I pay my debts, Shade. The Maeljin Incarna treat their servants with the respect they deserve."

"I never doubted your intentions," said Shade, stretching the truth a few degrees. "My entire life has been spent in your service."

"The weak are attracted by the light," said Aliara. "The strong, the ones who know what they want and are willing to pay the price, serve the dark. You made the correct choice even as a child. Those who embrace the Wyrm of their own free will shall someday rule the Earth."

"For now," said Shade, "I'll settle for a small part of it. Absolute control of the New World Order after you took possession of your new body was, I believe, the agreed-upon price?"

"Your wish shall be granted as soon as I step onto Earth in physical form," said Aliara. "With my powers intact, my mind within this unique body, I will be the most powerful being in the world. Nothing will be impossible for me."

"It's nice to be on the winning side," said Shade. "Losing is so depressing. What do you want me to do tomorrow?"

"When the Gray Collective was first being formed out of primal energy," said Aliara, "I had you modify the plans slightly to put an escape hatch into the fortress leading directly into the Horizon Realm. Numerous Primium locks held it shut; it could only be opened from the inside. The

The Road to Hell

instructions for the exit were quite clear. The door
was to be used only in a dire emergency, when all
routes to Earth were destroyed and the station faced
total annihilation."

"I remember," said Shade. "The builders were not
pleased, since opening a portal into the Horizon
theoretically provided an entrance into the
Collective for dwellers of the Deep Universe. I had
to pull a few strings to get the escape hatch
approved."

"The builders were correct," said Aliara. "If the
door is left ajar, I can enter the complex in my
Umbral form. While I cannot physically manifest
myself on Earth, such restrictions do not apply to
the Horizon. That is exactly what I plan to do
tomorrow night."

"The Empress Aliara prowling the corridors of
the Gray Collective," said Shade. "How
intriguing."

"I will have that body, Shade," said Aliara. Her
inhuman voice grew shrill over the phone line.
"Other powerful beings want it. But, I will be the
one to possess it."

"I assume you want me to open this doorway?"
asked Shade.

"The locks are such that they cannot be
tampered with from outside the Realm," said
Aliara. "Otherwise, the station would have been
overrun by denizens of the Deep Umbra months
ago. More than a few of the dwellers here desire to

feast on the essence of human life, Shade. Thus, the bolts holding the portal closed must be unlocked from within. That is the final task you must accomplish to earn your reward.

"There are no complex computer codes to learn, no special spells to be spoken. The locks are old-fashioned things, made of Primium, tough and unyielding to mental force. There are seven such devices. Each is opened by a key. The keys are kept in a small guard chamber directly opposite the exit. You must enter the room, eliminate the officer in charge and obtain the keys. Once you have let me into the complex, we will relock the doors to make sure nothing else follows."

Aliara hesitated. "Monstrous life forms exist in the Deep Umbra. Allowing them access to the Horizon Realms would be a terrible mistake."

"I'll be careful," said Shade. "I wouldn't be where I am today if I wasn't extremely careful. When do you want to make your appearance in the laboratory?"

"When the countdown enters its final stages," said Aliara, "and preparations begin for the actual awakening of the pattern-clone, make your excuses and leave. All attention will be focused on the life-form. I want to be there just after it is brought to life, its mind still empty of any personality. The timing needs to be exactly right."

"I'll chart my route tonight to the escape hatch," said Shade, "and time exactly how long it will take for me to get there. If events turn ugly in the lab, I might need a few extra minutes."

"The guard at the secret exit?" asked Aliara.

"No problem," said Shade. "After all, I am a member of the ruling Triumvirate of the station. I have the right to travel anywhere in the Collective on official business. You know that when necessary, I'm quite capable of performing the most violent acts in pursuit of my goals. I won't fail."

"I have every confidence in you, Shade," said Aliara. "You are my most loyal subject. Your rewards will match your service to me. Tomorrow, we will celebrate our triumph in a sea of blood."

With that chilling prophecy, Aliara disconnected. Shade sighed. The Dark Lord was a creature of violence and corruption who thought of everything in terms of death and destruction. Shade preferred the concept of necessary adjustments to static reality. It didn't really matter, however. The results were what counted. In less than a day, he would have power beyond his wildest imaginings. For that, he would pay any price.

A small metal box, the size of a portable radio, rested on a rear shelf. It was covered with a thin coating of dust; obviously it had not been moved in months. Chuckling, Shade took the object in one fat hand. Walking over to his spy monitor, he attached the box to a node on the back of the set. He turned on his computer and typed in a short code sequence. The machine hummed in response, the picture on the video monitor flickering. A second set of code numbers followed. The hum grew higher in pitch, then disappeared.

The monitor displayed the interior of Comptroller Klair's office, within which were seated the Comptroller and his assistant, the cyborg, Ernest Nelson. He adjusted the volume control at the base of the terminal so that he could hear every word they said.

The fat man chuckled. Klair had disrupted the main spy system in the citadel, the one he was supposed to find. But he was unaware of the secondary unit, installed using machinery that was not supplied by Iteration X. As expected, the equipment was functioning perfectly. There were no secrets from the New World Order. It was always watching.

Chapter Twenty-Four

His face beaming with good cheer, Enzo Giovanni rose from his seat, rounded his desk, and grasped his cousin by the shoulders.

"Montifloro," he declared, his voice brimming with happiness. "It is good to see you after so many years!"

Enzo gazed over his cousin's shoulder and met the eyes of Ms. Hargroves, who had accompanied his guest into the office. With the slightest motion, he nodded. His secretary knew exactly what to do. Silently, she left to put his instructions into effect.

"You look as dapper as ever," said Enzo, chuckling as he fingered the expensive material of his relative's suit. "No one in our entire family dresses as well. How is Cesare? He did not come with you?"

"No," said Montifloro, obviously befuddled by the warm reception. "He is involved with the Open-Market negotiations in Europe. I am here on my own."

"Too bad," said Enzo. He indicated a high-backed, black leather chair for his cousin, then walked back around the desk to his velvet-lined throne. "The three of us together again. What a pleasure that would be!"

Montifloro looked distinctly uncomfortable. "You know why I am here?" he asked. "It is a minor matter but troublesome to those back in Venice. The clan elders worry about your lack of communication. I've been sent to monitor your progress. They require a full report on your recent activities."

Enzo shook his head. He was laughing inwardly, though his features showed only concern. "The leaders of the Giovanni, my cousin? Or Pietro, the master of the Mausoleum?"

"Of course, Pietro asked me to make the trip," said Montifloro. "As Chairman of the Board, he represents the family interests. He speaks for the clan elders."

"Does he?" replied Enzo, planting the first seeds of doubt. He needed to act with great caution. Montifloro was extremely cunning. His open approach, his apologetic attitude, was all a sham. He was here to spy, to see what dirt he could uncover. Pushing him in the right direction would be a slow, insidious process. Too much too quickly would alert him to their lies. "Sometimes, I get the impression that dear Pietro confuses his own interests with those of our clan."

Montifloro laughed. "Do I detect a twinge of jealousy, Enzo? I remember you making similar declarations years ago. Each of us believes that we could best run the affairs of clan Giovanni. Pietro has the family elders' confidence. I defer to their combined wisdom."

"You've come to check on my business dealings," said Enzo, switching subjects. The time for accusations was over. Now he needed to build confidence. "I'm not surprised. The past few months I've been so busy consolidating my position here at Everwell Chemicals that there's been no time for me keep up with my reports. However, I think you will be pleased with the results."

Enzo's voice dropped to a whisper. "Our clan stands on the brink of acquiring a controlling interest in one of the largest chemical companies in the world. Much of the work has been done in secrecy, lest the entire deal collapse. It rests solely on my shoulders. I could tell no one else the full details of the operation: Communication with home was too risky. Too many other power brokers and multinational conglomerates are after the same prize and would do anything to quash the deal."

Enzo smiled. "At least, now, that problem has been solved."

"Solved?" asked Montifloro. "How?"

"Why, *you have arrived*," said Enzo, laughing

Robert Weinberg

heartily. "Finally, someone I know I can trust is here—someone with whom I can share confidences without worry of betrayal. With you beside me, we will finally bring this mission to a satisfactory conclusion."

The intercom on Enzo's desk buzzed as Montifloro sat, stunned by the full import of his words.

"Yes?"

"Ms. Hope is here, Mr. Giovanni," said Ms. Hargroves. "She has the weekly reports. Do you want to see them now, or should I have her return later?"

"The weekly reports?" repeated Enzo, as if mulling over an important decision. This entire charade had been planned for days, ever since he had learned of Montifloro's impending arrival. Ms. Hargroves had proven to be an inspired drama coach. "Give me a second."

Enzo leaned forward on his desk. "My operations chief is here with the business reports for the past seven days. Should I have her bring them another time? Or would you be interested in reviewing them?" He chuckled, raising an eyebrow. "Ms. Hope is quite attractive, Montifloro. And she has flashing eyes and hair dark as midnight."

"No reason to bend the rules on my account, Enzo," said Montifloro. Enzo had expected no less. "Business is business. I am in no rush. Let the young lady come in."

The stunning businesswoman, dressed in a conservative black skirt and starched white blouse, bore little resemblance to the tawdry beauty Enzo had discovered a week ago. Ms. Hope walked across the room to Enzo's desk, her high heels beating a sharp staccato on the polished floor. Only the casual sway of her hips betrayed anything of her recent past. Her voice was low and sultry with the merest trace of a Spanish accent.

"Here are the reports, Mr. Giovanni. Business continues to improve. We are in for a record-breaking quarter."

Enzo nodded. "As I expected, but good news is always welcome." He gestured to Montifloro, who had risen from his chair. "Miss Hope, my cousin and trusted advisor, Montifloro Giovanni. He has been sent here to study the daily operations of Everwell Chemicals. Please extend to him your full cooperation."

"Pleased to meet you," said Hope, extending one hand to Montifloro. Her sultry voice was soft and seductive. "I'll be glad to guide you around the plant, Mr. Giovanni. Feel free to call on me for any assistance you might require."

"An offer I cannot refuse," declared Montifloro. Stylishly, he bent and kissed Ms. Hope's slender fingers. His dark eyes glistened as he stared at the young woman. Montifloro had a weakness for exotic women with long, dark hair.

Enzo smiled, knowing he had won.

Robert Weinberg

Chapter Twenty-Five

"A ccording to this map," said Seventeen, "we should be coming up on the Rollins Winery within the next few miles." He laid the document down on his lap. "You're sure this is the right place?"

"Positive," said Alvin Reynolds, grinning. "No magick required other than knowing how to use a computer trip planner and map maker."

The big man was driving the truck with the words *Everwell Chemicals* printed on the side, along with a Rochester registration number. If trucks were bringing materials to Everwell, it seemed likely that deliveries came from the corporation to the Gray Collective as well. Hopefully, the cover would provide them with just enough time to set their plans in motion.

Seventeen sat next to Reynolds in the front cab, with Sam Haine at the window. In the rear of the truck were Shadow of Night, Kallikos, and Albert, tending their prize captive from Vali Shallar. It was early evening and they were once again in New York State, a few hours south of Rochester, in the heart of wine country. The city of Naples, New York was not far distant. They were on Route 26, a state highway that cut through forest and fields, mostly devoid of human occupation. In the past few hours, they had seen only a few other cars.

"I fed all the information you gave me about your trip into my computer and had it process a search of the region," continued Reynolds. "Taking into account the direction, the highway where Sam found you, and the length of your journey, the mapping program narrowed down the possible locations to a semi-circle south of Rochester. I then initiated a search based on the assumption that the Gray Collective is most likely linked to a Technocracy Node on Earth. That meant the location had to have some relevance to their philosophy of magick. The resulting file had one entry—the Rollins Winery."

"What's so special about this place?" asked Seventeen.

"First wine-producing plant on the East Coast to use automation to label and seal their finished product," said Seventeen. "It was a major step in turning wine-making into an assembly-line product. Events like that create Quintessence and form new psychic energy sources. There's a major Node on the other side of the hill; I can sense it already. It has to be the winery."

"Yes, sir," said Sam Haine, who had been unusually quiet for the last part of the trip, "I can feel the power in my bones. This Gray Collective's sitting on a real energy well. No wonder they're able to perform such astonishing experiments."

The truck came to the crest of the hill. As there was no other traffic on the road, Reynolds slowed the vehicle down to a crawl. A few hundred feet away, at the bottom of a slight incline, was a massive brick and wood building. A gigantic billboard proclaimed it the *Rollins Winery*. A twelve-foot-high chain-link fence surrounded the plant. A short drive off the highway ended at the lone gate, fronted by a concrete blockhouse.

"Pretty elaborate security for a place where they squeeze grapes," said Sam Haine, snorting in disgust. "Bet they plug plenty of damn additives into their wine. Probably have a deal with Pentex Chemicals. Birds of a feather and all that crap."

"How are we going to get inside?" asked Seventeen. "We don't have any delivery papers. I can't imagine the guards are just going to wave us through."

"Why not?" Alvin Reynolds shrugged. "Let's see how well they can resist the combined willpower of six very determined mages."

Two middle-aged, overweight private security officers manned the blockhouse. They were busy watching a hockey game on TV when the truck pulled up to the stop. With an audible curse, the bigger of the two men ambled over to the driver's side of the cab. He was definitely not a mage.

"Whatcha doin' here?" the guard growled, staring up at Reynolds. "According to my shippin' manifests, delivery ain't due till tomorrow afternoon."

"They changed the dates," said Reynolds. He held a blank sheet of paper out to the guard. "See for yourself. Don't ask me why. I just drive these rigs."

The guard studied the white page carefully. "Yeah, I know whatcha mean. Everythin' looks to be in order. You can pass through. Use Bay 2 on the other side of the building. Only one crew on duty this time of evening. They're the ones who handle these special shipments."

"Thanks," said Reynolds, pulling back the paper. "Enjoy the game."

"Yeah," said the guard, "what's left of it."

The big man walked back to the blockhouse and pushed a button. With a clattering whine, a large section of the steel gate slid back on its tracks. Waving his thanks, Reynolds steered the big truck onto the plant grounds.

"I can't believe they'd allow ordinary men to guard this operation," said Seventeen, as Reynolds drove the transport slowly along the blacktop road that wound around the processing plant. "It doesn't make sense."

"Don't be foolish, Seventeen," said Sam Haine. "The Technocracy isn't looking to draw attention to this place, and Awakened personnel working as guards would do just that. Security's tighter here than you think. It's just not visible to the naked eye. You need to use your inner vision to sense it. Me and Albert's been neutralizing the traps." The white-haired man grinned. "We do it without much thinking. Sort of a hobby of ours, sneaking into Technocracy Constructs."

"Here's the real challenge," said Alvin Reynolds, nodding toward the open loading dock ahead. Three men smoking cigarettes sat on a six-foot-wide finger of concrete against the right wall. Next to it was a long metal ramp leading up a slight incline to a solid wall of concrete. The only door visible was a narrow one at the rear of the concrete platform.

The three men stared at the truck with neither interest nor enthusiasm. The special crew, according to the guard.

"No question the entire back wall serves as a Horizon gate," said Reynolds. "I can sense the Quintessence flow from here into the Umbra. All we need to do to enter the Gray Collective is open the portal and drive up the ramp."

"That trio are a lot less innocent than the guards

out front," said Sam. "Notice how similar they look. They're clones, probably all created in Progenitor growth tanks from the same tissue sample. Guard stock, programmed with specific skills and given shell personalities. Looking at them, I'd guess they'd be rough opponents in a fight." He laughed. "Not that I'm stupid enough to start something with genetically engineered thugs."

Turning in his seat, he rapped on the panel behind their heads. Immediately, it slid open. "What?" asked Kallikos.

"Minor problem," said Sam Haine. "Three guards waiting for us. They're Progenitor clones, probably street-fighter types. I'll go out and talk to them, confuse those boys right proper. But Shadow of the Dawn will have to finish the job. We can't have this trio around if we're going into the Horizon."

"Done," said Kallikos. "We must make speed. I sense the moment of destiny is fast approaching."

Sam closed the panel. "What the hell did he mean by that?" he wondered, frowning. "Well, no time to find out. I better go into my act. Pull this vehicle up close to the platform, son. Then watch old Sam do his stuff."

The air in the cab rippled with invisible force. Not sure what was happening, Seventeen turned to Sam. And found him gone. In his place sat Comptroller Klair.

"What the hell?" Seventeen exclaimed, his eyes wide with astonishment.

"Surprised you, son?" said Klair. His voice was exactly how Seventeen remembered it: harsh, cold, almost metallic. The Comptroller's artificial eyes glared at him with the same direct intensity. "I ran into Mr. Klair a few years ago, and I never forget a face or personality."

"But, but..." said Seventeen.

"Sam Haine, the Changing Man," said the duplicate Klair. "Life's full of surprises, son. Now, excuse me while I put the fear of the Technocratic Union in these slackers."

Opening the door of the cab, Sam Haine climbed out of the truck. On the loading dock, the three guards suddenly snapped to attention. Alvin Reynolds chuckled. "Amazing," he murmured.

"What is the meaning of this negligence?" Sam demanded in Klair's emotionless voice. "Why aren't you working? Who is in charge of this installation? I want an explanation for your behavior. Immediately."

The three clones stared at the man they thought was Comptroller Klair with wide eyes, dumbfounded. "We weren't expecting any deliveries till tomorrow," said the man in the middle, a handful of playing cards dropping from his fingers onto the cement. "The schedule..."

"Nonsense," said the imitation Klair. "This delivery was added to the schedule a week ago. Last minute supplies for the project. I came along to make sure there were no mistakes. Check your

CPU. The gateway needs to be opened immediately."

"Yes sir," said the man on the end. All three guards looked exactly the same: it was impossible to distinguish one from the other. He beckoned to a small monitor and keyboard built directly into the right wall of the loading dock. "We can't open the gate without loading in the proper password anyway."

"Well," said Sam arrogantly, "get on with it."

"Sure seems strange you appearing out of nowhere like this," said one of the trio, as the second man turned on the computer. "I checked the shipping directory yesterday. There was no delivery scheduled for today. Positively."

"Are you challenging my authority?" asked the duplicate Klair, his voice low and menacing.

"I don't make mistakes…." began the clone, then jerked his head around suddenly in surprise. Shadow of the Dawn stood behind him. Her hands shot out faster than the eye could follow. A flurry of punches knocked the guard to the ground, unconscious.

"What the hell?" said the man at the computer. A second was all he needed to sound the plant alarm. Shadow, moving faster than thought, never gave him the opportunity. The young woman yanked the guard away with all of her strength, sending him flying across the platform. He slammed with bone-breaking force into a pile of boxes heaped against the far wall. Groaning, he tried without much success to pull himself to his feet.

The third man had enough time to pull a knife from his boot. Running, Seventeen thought, watching from the cab of the truck, would have been a wiser choice. But, guards like these three were used for their aggressive natures, not their intelligence.

Shadow didn't bother to unsheathe her swords. Confronting the guard, she lashed out with one hand, knocking the blade from his grip. A fist to his jaw staggered him. A spinning jump kick sent him to the pavement, unconscious and bleeding.

"This one's out too," said the duplicate Klair, slamming a foot into the head of the man by the boxes. "That was nice and quick. Nobody died, either. Change of pace in these violent times."

"They were only performing their assigned tasks," Seventeen heard Shadow of the Dawn say as he lowered himself out of the transport cab. "Clones are rarely as tough as they appear. A true warrior does not kill without reason."

"You, my dear," said Sam Haine, who no longer looked like Charles Klair, "are noble beyond your years. I just hope it doesn't someday get you killed."

Shadow smiled. "When the situation arises, I can be ruthless."

"Hell hath no fury like a woman scorned," said Albert, emerging from the rear of the truck with

Kallikos at his side. "Our passenger is getting restless. I reduced the tranquilizer dosage. The cat will be awakening shortly."

The giant handed everyone small vials of fluid. "Spread this lotion on your skin. Tom Ho Pak gave it to me in Vali Shallar. The liquid comes from a plant that is poisonous to the beast. In all but the most extreme cases, its smell should keep you safe from the cat's attack."

"Considering the size of its teeth," said Sam Haine, smearing the lotion on his face and hands, "I think I'll still keep a good distance between me and the cat. Not that I doubt Tom's word. But I have a particular aversion to being devoured."

"We must hurry," said Kallikos as they all rubbed in the special lotion, his voice filled with urgency. "I sense that the pattern-clone will be awakened tonight. We must destroy the abomination before it is too late."

There was a strange look in Shadow of the Dawn's eyes. "A terrible evil is about to be unleashed. My destiny calls."

"Whatever you say," said Alvin Reynolds, his gaze moving from Kallikos to Shadow. "Only problem is we've got to open the gate to the Gray Collective. Guards can't do it for us in their condition."

"Probably would be obstinate fools anyway," said Sam Haine. "Never counted on their help. Seventeen's gonna do it."

Robert Weinberg

"I am?" said Seventeen in surprise.

"Sure," said Sam Haine. "I've been in plenty of Iteration X Horizon Realms. That bunch never shows any imagination. Gateway's always controlled by the same type of guardian: a computer. You enter the correct code and the passage unlocks. Simple if you know the right combination. Normally, that's privileged information. But, from what you've told me, boy, no computer, magickal or not, is safe from you."

"Quickly," said Kallikos.

A roar of animal fury shook the truck bay. "Sounds like our cat is waking up," said Reynolds. "Hook into the system, Seventeen. No truck on Earth is built to hold a monster like that inside very long. When it breaks out, we better be in the Gray Collective."

Gingerly, Seventeen placed his hands on the computer keyboard. In the week since his escape, he had not once touched a CPU. Knowing that their entire rescue mission depended on his ability to command the machine, he was suddenly nervous. If his power worked only in the Gray Collective, they were in trouble.

He need not have worried. The instant his fingers touched the keys his confidence returned. Without conscious thought, his mind melded with the computer, taking complete control of the machine. For an instant, the monitor in front of Seventeen flickered. Then it turned black.

"What's wrong?" asked Alvin Reynolds.

"Nothing," said Seventeen. "I had a nice chat with the CPU. Told it to keep this area clear for the rest of the night. I checked the status of any other willworkers in the area and discovered that none are on the grounds. And, I opened the portal."

He pointed at the wall at the end of the ramp. The concrete was gone, replaced by a wavering curtain of blackness. The entrance to the Gray Collective was waiting.

The beast in the truck roared again. "Everyone get into the cab," said Alvin Reynolds as the vehicle shook from side to side. "It'll be a tight squeeze, but we're not going far."

"Damned if this ain't exciting," said Sam Haine, as they climbed in. "Me and Albert have been involved in some pretty wild adventures, but this trip takes the cake. Gonna make some hell of a story to tell my great-great-grandchildren."

"Assuming we make it back alive to tell the tale," said Albert dryly.

"Only one way to find out," said Alvin Reynolds. Shifting the big truck into gear, he stepped on the gas. And sent the big truck hurtling into the Horizon.

Chapter Twenty-Six

"Ten minutes and counting," said Velma Wade. "All life support systems are disconnecting. Primary reflex tests will begin shortly. Everything appears to be in order."

"Keep your eye on the heart monitor," said Sharon Reed, her voice tense with excitement. "We should be getting a reading shortly."

Velma nodded, not mentioning that she had performed similar operations many times in the past. This awakening was different. The entire AW Project had come down to these final moments. A year of research, experimentation and hard work was about to pay off. Inwardly, Velma smiled. The results, however, were going to be quite different than anyone, including Sharon Reed, expected.

Recognizing the significance of the events

unfolding, Velma had changed appearance again. She was now a young woman, perhaps eighteen years old. She had long flowing hair, still blond, blue eyes and rose-tinged cheeks. Short and slender, she wore a long blue dress that matched her eyes and was decorated with large pink flowers.

"Heartbeat should commence in thirty seconds," she declared. "Stimulus is being administered as I speak."

She, Sharon Reed, Comptroller Klair, and the cyborg, Ernest Nelson, sat in metal chairs facing the main control panel for the steel pit at the center of the laboratory. Each of them had specific tasks to do, monitors and screens to check. A dozen feet away, in the center of the pit where the growth tank had once stood, was a fully automated resurrection bed. The device resembled a large metal coffin with a glass top. Inside, on an operating table, tended by a dozen different robotic hands, rested the nude pattern-clone. No longer was he connected to any tubes or bathed in growth solution. His body glowed with health and vitality. His eyes were closed, but now it appeared as if he were sleeping, waiting to awaken.

"Stimulus successful," said Velma. "We have a heartbeat. Nice and strong, as we expected. Eight minutes to full initialization."

"It's getting stuffy with all the staff in here," said Sharon, looking around at the entire Gray Collective crew. The personnel were scattered around the steel railing that surrounded the pit, watching expectantly. No one wanted to miss the awakening. "Velma, please turn the air conditioning up a notch."

"Yes, Director," said Velma, reaching for her keyboard. That phrase was the signal they had agreed upon to release the mutated virus into the circulation system. "It should be more comfortable here in a minute."

Ernest Nelson turned a suspicious gaze upon her. Velma smiled sweetly and pressed the switch. Nelson looked down at his portable monitor and nodded. Then, he turned and stared again at Velma. He smiled.

Sensing the worst, Velma tapped Sharon Reed on the shoulder. "With the number of people in the room, it might take a few minutes for the lab to cool down," she declared, making it clear that the virus plan had been nullified.

"No problem," said the Director as she pushed the button on her computer control board that released Semok from its tank. Velma glanced at the clock on her board. Five minutes to awakening. About the same amount of time it would require the mutated horror to crawl up the passageway to the laboratory. It would be an exciting moment.

"The virus has been released into the air and it has neutralized," subvocalized X344 to Comptroller Klair. "We don't have to worry about their damned germs anymore."

The Road to Hell

"Excellent," said the Comptroller. With his gaze fixed on the computer monitor in front of him, it was impossible to tell that he and his assistant were carrying on a silent conversation. "Five minutes to the actual awakening. You have the Deep Universe beacon ready?"

"I have it safe," said Nelson. "It's in the hidden compartment of my left claw. When do you want to activate it?"

"Not until the pattern-clone is brought fully on-line," said Klair. "However, we shouldn't risk waiting too long afterward. Start the device as soon as the AW starts breathing. I'm sure Reed has a fallback scheme. Plus, there is Shade to consider. I'm sure the Mission Specialist is planning somehow to gain control of the clone. For that matter, where is Mr. Shade?"

"Haven't seen him in the past five minutes," said X344. "He was hovering over me like a vulture, checking the readouts, and then he disappeared. Never said a word about where he was going."

"He'll be back," said Klair. "That's a sure bet. He won't want to miss the awakening. He'll be back."

"I'm still not sure why you want to check the locks, Mission Specialist," said the guard, a trace of suspicion in his voice. "We've never had a problem at this location before."

"We also have never completed a project of this importance," explained Terrence Shade, smiling. "I am just being extremely cautious, Mr. Lorris. In less than five minutes, the pattern-clone will take its first breath. I want to be certain—absolutely certain—that we don't have to worry about a sudden attack by creatures from the Deep Universe. With all attention focused on the main laboratory, it would be the perfect time for them to mount an assault."

The guard shrugged. "Whatever you say. As a member of the Triumvirate, you know best. But, I still think it's a waste of time."

Lorris turned and pulled a set of keys off his desk. It was the last thing he ever did. Coolly, Shade drew his .357 Magnum, placed the muzzle on the back of the guard's head, and squeezed the trigger. No one heard the shot or saw the blood splatter against the office wall.

Shade wrenched the keys from the dead man's fingers. He looked down at his watch. Four minutes till the awakening. There was barely enough time. Stepping out of the small guard room, he hurried down the hall to the massive Primium steel door that led directly into the Horizon. Unlike the entrance to the Earth, this exit had no guardian.

There were seven locks. Working with trembling fingers, Shade used the keys to open them one after another. When he finished, there was a minute left. Pressing with all his strength on the cross-bar that controlled the portal, he swung the door open.

For an instant, Shade glimpsed a sea of swirling colors, with vast waves of red and green and blue sweeping past the opening. He could sense invisible lines of force and power rippling in the psychic ocean like electricity. The patterns had a meaning, but no Technomancer had ever deciphered them and remained sane.

A figure dressed in a charcoal gray pin-striped suit, with a bright green tie and matching handkerchief, stepped through the portal and onto the steel floor of the Collective. A few inches over five feet tall, slender, nearly sexless with androgynous features, the being had hair cut short and dyed the same bright green as her tie. Her inhuman face glowed with unnatural vitality. Her eyes burned green and a faint smile curled her pale, thin lips. "Close the door, Shade," said the Empress Aliara. "Then bolt it shut. The less company, the better."

Shade did as he was told. Though he had spoken with Aliara many times in visions, he had never before encountered the Maeljin Incarna in the flesh. She radiated desire. The Mission Specialist licked his lips, his hands sweating as he closed the locks. A feverish, animal lust unlike anything he had ever experienced before held him in its unnatural grip. He wanted Aliara more than he had ever wanted any other woman.

She laughed, an alien sound. Reaching out, she touched his cheek with slender fingers. Her caress burned his skin like a hot iron. The rosy flesh of his face crackled and burned, turning black. Shade

Robert Weinberg

flinched in terrible pain. But, he was frozen in place, unable to stir, his body held captivated by the mistress of desire.

"Soon, my dear Shade," she crooned, "you will collect a reward beyond your wildest desires. First, though, I must collect my new body. Then, I will return for you."

Without another word, Aliara walked down the corridor leading to the main laboratory. With her departure, the spell holding Shade immobile disappeared as well.

The Mission Specialist screamed in agony, his hands clenching his scorched flesh. Moaning in horror, he sank to his knees. His eyes widened in shock as he realized the monstrous fate awaiting him when the Dark Lord returned. But he did not go mad. Aliara never permitted her victims to escape into insanity.

"There," said Seventeen, pointing to the loading platform a hundred feet ahead. They crossed the portal through a long dark tunnel leading into the underground transport bay. The place was deserted. "That corridor leads directly up into the lab."

"Easy enough," said Alvin Reynolds, spinning the steering wheel. "There's enough maneuvering room in here for me to back the truck up into one of the docks. Then we'll release the cat and follow."

"Hopefully the appearance of the beast will be enough of a surprise that it will throw the

Technocrats into total chaos," said Kallikos. "In the confusion, Shadow and I will destroy the pattern-clone. You, Seventeen, Sam and Albert must rescue the prisoners."

"Not much of a plan," said Sam Haine, "but sometimes the best schemes are the simplest. We'll just play it by ear and take advantage of the situations. That's the way I always operate."

Carefully, Alvin Reynolds steered the truck into the loading bay. "Everyone stay in the cab," said the big man. "I'm going up on the roof with this blaster. As soon as I blow a hole in the entrance to the lab, you press the switch that opens the cargo doors to the transport, Seventeen. Considering our passenger's mood, it won't take more than a few seconds for him to find his way there. We'll follow moments after. Everyone set."

No one said a word. Taking a deep breath, Reynolds opened the door of the truck and hauled himself up onto the roof. Seventeen rolled the window down an inch to make sure he heard the explosion. He need not have bothered. The blaster's roar bellowed through the loading area. Immediately, Seventeen punched the button that controlled the truck's rear doors.

With a shriek of bestial fury that threatened to shatter the windshield, the monster from the forests of Vali Shallar barreled out of the back of the transport. Seventeen watched the creature in the rear view mirror. Fifteen feet long, six feet high at the shoulder, weighing well over a thousand pounds, with tawny yellow fur and dark stripes, the cat resembled a gigantic Bengal tiger. But no beast so heavily muscled had walked the earth for nearly ten thousand years. Nor had any possessed enormous, bladelike fangs that extended seven inches below its lower jaws. Yellow eyes glistening, the saber-toothed tiger swung its massive head from side to side, searching for prey. Spotting the smashed door, it leapt forward, moving with the force of a steam locomotive. Opening its huge mouth wider than seemed possible, it growled its defiance to the world and then disappeared into the laboratory.

"Breathing sequence is proceeding smoothly," said Sharon Reed, nervously. In two minutes, the pattern-clone would be fully functional. At approximately the same instant, the horror she had dubbed Semok was due to break into the laboratory, spreading havoc and destruction in its wake. The sauroids had been instructed to begin their attack on the metalheads at the same time. During the confusion, she and Velma Wade had to gather a tissue sample from the clone, destroy the prototype, and flee the Gray Collective. Most likely, the rest of her research team would be killed in the mayhem, but there was nothing she could do to save them. The goals of the Convention were more important than the lives of mere Technocrats.

The Road to Hell

An unexpected flicker of a gauge caught her attention. Eyes narrowing, she stared at the panel in surprise. The indicator on that particular monitor should not be moving.

"What's going on with the brain wave scanner?" she asked, looking at her assistant. "The pattern-clone lacks any personality or intelligence."

"There must be a malfunction," said Velma. Her gaze jerked to the far door of the lab, where Semok would appear. The metal clanged as something huge slammed against it. The celaphapoid had arrived early. "Do you want me to run a quick diagnostic?"

"Not now," said Sharon, making a hurried decision. "The countdown is nearly complete. We can't delay the final initialization sequence."

"Something's very wrong," said Comptroller Klair, his harsh voice breaking into their conversation. "My scanner is picking up strong brain waves from the pattern-clone. There's no chance of a malfunction. The readings are too strong. That mind is active—and it's not an ordinary one. Some being is in possession of the clone. And it's waking up."

"Stop the initialization sequence," Sharon demanded, forcefully slamming the switches in front of her. Nothing happened.

A dozen people screamed as the steel door leading below crashed to the floor. A mass of gigantic tentacles thrust into the laboratory.

Robert Weinberg

Sharon gasped as she watched Semok pull itself into the room. The monster was bigger, more frightening than she had imagined. Its huge mandibles clicked loudly as it searched for victims to rip and tear.

"Keyboard isn't responding," said Ernest Nelson, his attention completely focused on the computer in front of him. He howled in impotent fury. "Son-of-a-bitch! We're off-line. An override program has taken over the CPU. No chance of us regaining control before the final coordinates take effect."

The cyborg rose from his chair. His face swung around and he caught sight of the monstrous creature slaughtering Technocrats a few dozen feet away. Moving with machinelike precision, he whirled on his tank treads to face Sharon. In one clawed hand he held a tube that resembled a flashlight with lenses on both ends. Face flushed with rage, he waved the object at the Director. "No way you're getting away with this, you damned traitor!"

Steel shrieked as the door leading to the loading docks exploded. Fragments of metal smashed into the startled crowd like miniature grenades. A jagged chunk slammed into Nelson's exposed back, knocking him off balance. Wheels spinning, he crashed face-first to the floor. Involuntarily, his claws jerked open, sending the mysterious tube tumbling under a laboratory table.

"What in God's name is that?" gasped Velma

Wade as a monstrous roar shook the laboratory. A gigantic form filled the smashed portal. The beast growled again, revealing tusklike teeth. Panic-stricken, the Technocrats nearest the entranceway shrieked in terror as the fanged killer charged into their midst. In seconds, blood and gore covered the walls. There was no escape. Trapped between the saber-tooth tiger and the giant celaphopoid, the helpless lab technicians were doomed.

Comptroller Klair was out of his seat, scrambling on the floor on his hands and knees, desperately searching for the tube his assistant had dropped. Sharon knew the device must be dangerous, but there was no time to worry about the schemes of Iteration X. Semok was loose in the labs. As was a prehistoric monster that had appeared out of nowhere. In fifteen seconds, the most powerful pattern-clone ever created—controlled by an unknown personality—was going to come to life. Unless she was able to stop it.

"Retract the cover of the life-support pod," she commanded Velma Wade, ignoring the orgy of destruction that filled the chamber. "Or is that off-line as well?"

"The top is retracting," said Velma Wade, her voice measured and calm. "It will be completely open in ten seconds."

"Perfect," declared Sharon, her eyes fixed on the nude body resting on the table inside the bubble. She could not, would not allow herself to be distracted by the horrors that surrounded her. "That gives me just enough time to shout the self-destruct code at the clone,"

"I'm afraid not, Director," said Velma Wade, her voice in Sharon's ear. "I can't permit you to do that."

The Research Director gasped in surprise and pain as a sliver of ice jabbed her in the back. Blood bubbling from her lips, Sharon collapsed face forward onto her computer console. As if from a thousand miles away, she heard the frightful screeching of Semok as the genetic horror killed and killed with maniacal fury. Futilely, Sharon tried to reach around and pull the knife blade from between her shoulders. There was no strength in her fingers.

Eyes glazing over, she stared up at her assistant. Velma Wade shrugged, and then smiled. "It's been fun, Director. We made a great team. But my true purpose calls."

Unable to move, Sharon watched helplessly as the blond shapechanger vaulted over the steel railing, heading straight for the life-support pod and the pattern-clone.

Flat on his stomach, X344 swept his steel claws underneath the workbench, desperately trying to grasp the Deep Universe Beacon that lay a hundredth of an inch out of reach. Pain throbbed through his head, blood blurred his vision. The fall had broken his nose, smashing it flat against his face. Choking on a combination of blood and bile, he could hardly breathe. It didn't matter. Nothing mattered but the damned tube.

"Grab it, you idiot," shrieked Comptroller Klair from the other side of the workbench. The Comptroller was directing X344's movements, telling him where to move his claw. The tube was wedged against a steel post right in the middle of a long workbench. Normally, the cyborg would have had no problems shifting the furniture out of his path. In his battered state, he was barely able to remain conscious. "Your claw is touching a tip of the beacon, you fool. Squeeze shut and you'll have it!"

Spitting blood, X344 clenched his teeth and willed his hand to close. Not knowing if he had been successful or not, he wrenched his arm from beneath the bench. He no longer had any feeling in his steel claws. The metal bolt that had struck him in the back had evidently damaged his spinal column. Standing upright was impossible. Moving his arms was becoming more difficult by the moment. His entire body felt numb. Groggily he stared at his claw. The Deep Universe beacon was clenched between his steel fingers.

"Twist the caps," yelled Klair. The noise in the laboratory was deafening. X344 had no idea what was happening. Something was growling and there was a horrible clicking, clattering noise. People were screaming in mindless fear. His head hurt and he was having trouble thinking clearly. "Think steel," he muttered, as if praying. "Think steel."

"Twist the caps, you mindless cretin!" screamed the Comptroller, from the other side of the work bench. X344 thought it odd that Klair made no effort to finish the job himself. Still, the cyborg was loyal to Iteration X. Summoning all of his strength, he twisted the two ends of the beacon at the same time. And, immediately afterward, he tossed it over the workbench to Comptroller Klair. X344 was dedicated to the Technocracy, but he was not a fool.

"NO-O-O..." shrieked the Comptroller, his voice abruptly silenced as a wall of blackness throbbed into sudden existence just beyond the bench. A molecule in width, the portal stretched ten feet high by ten feet wide. Inside of it, something silvery metallic moved, expanding swiftly to fill the opening.

Seventeen stood in the wreckage of the doorway and looked into hell. In less than a minute, the entire chamber had been transformed into a charnel house. The dead and the dying were everywhere. The walls, ceiling and floor dripped blood. Smashed bodies of men and women and sauroids covered the ground like broken puppets.

Twenty feet from the entrance, the saber tooth tiger stood growling at a monstrosity twice its size.

Seventeen shook his head in disbelief. Such creatures could not possibly exist on Earth. Then, as the horror whipped a huge tentacle around the tiger's body, Seventeen remembered he was no longer on Earth.

The tiger roared, its cry of rage shaking the building. Savagely, it leapt forward, straight at the center of the octopoid monster trying to squeeze it in half. Like a vice, huge jaws clenched on the creature's face and sheared through rubbery skin like scissors cutting through paper. The octopus shrieked, a high-pitched cry of pain that sent shivers down Seventeen's spine. The creature sounded almost human.

A half-dozen tentacles wrapped themselves around the giant tiger's body, trying to tear it away from the octopus' face. But the prehistoric beast's immense fangs were buried deep in the soft center of the celaphopoid's skull and it could not be yanked free. Back and forth across the lab, the two gigantic monsters battled, crushing anything in their path.

"Shit," swore Alvin Reynolds. The big man wasn't even watching the battle. A dozen feet to their right stood a sheet of absolute blackness. "A gateway between realms."

Piled in front of the mystick portal were the smashed forms of a handful of silvery metallic robots. A slender figure dressed in a man's suit with bright green hair stood on top of the wreckage. Her body pulsated with psychic energy. Giggling, she was engaged in tearing the head off of one of the machines. She stared into the depths of the dark curtain, as if daring more automatons to appear.

"Damned place is like a three-ringed circus," whispered Sam Haine, taking a cautious step forward. "That's Aliara, the Empress of Pain, one of the Maeljin Incarna. Bet she didn't come here to play with those tin soldiers."

He took a few slow steps forward. "Wonder what's on the other side of that passage," he said. "Bet it ain't a place to Aliara's liking."

Then, before anyone realized what he was about, Sam Haine charged the slender figure. At the last instant, she turned, as if sensing his presence. But by then it was too late. Hitting her hard in the stomach, the Changing Man sent the Dark Lord swirling into the black abyss.

For a moment, unable to regain his balance, Sam Haine teetered on the brink of the mystick portal. Then, a huge arm reached out and grabbed him by the shoulder, pulling him back from the edge. "Tell me before you attempt something like that again," murmured Albert.

Kallikos seemed utterly oblivious to the mayhem in the chamber. The Time Master scanned the area anxiously, searching for answers. "There," he said, his voice trembling with emotion. He pointed to a steel pit in the center of the laboratory. "As I saw hundreds of years ago. The cursed one has returned."

The Road to Hell

Seventeen's eyes widened in surprise. Standing on top of a steel and glass life pod were two figures. One was the pattern-clone. Much like the Maeljin Incarna, it throbbed with magick power. The clone was perfectly formed yet completely sexless. It had the most expressive, beautiful features Seventeen had ever seen. The pattern-clone had the face of an angel—or a devil.

At the artificial being's side stood Jenni Smith. Or her exact duplicate. For the brief instant he saw her, Seventeen couldn't be sure.

Sensing their presence, the pattern-clone turned its head and stared at the doorway. Spotting Kallikos, the being nodded, as if in greeting.

"Kill him," Kallikos commanded, turning to Shadow of the Dawn. "Destroy the fiend before he plunges the world into chaos."

Moving with lightning speed, Shadow of the Dawn charged across the floor, grasping her katana, Whisper, in both hands. Without a sound, she leapt high into the air a dozen steps in front of the mysterious pair. Gleaming like fire, the steel blade cut downward through the spot where the pattern-clone had stood an instant before. It was too late. Both the pattern-clone and the girl at his side had vanished.

The Horizon War had begun.

Robert Weinberg

<u>Epilogue</u>

A t the edge of the Horizon stand eight Shade Realms. They are reflections, shadows, of the Shard Realms, wild regions of untamed energies that exist in the Deep Umbra. Of the Shade Realms, the most dangerous is the Shade Realm of Forces. Here, in this Horizon Realm, is located Doissetep, the largest and most powerful of all Tradition Chantries.

Perched on the top of the highest mountain in a sea of mighty cliffs, Doissetep is an ancient place. A huge labyrinthine castle thousands of years old, its origins have been lost in the mists of history. Vast towers stretch into the black sky while hideous stone gargoyles guard its gates. Ten cabals of mages call Doissetep their home. Ascension is nothing more than a word here. Power is all that matters. Doissetep is a place of intrigue and dark deeds.

The greatest willworker of Doissetep is the leader of the Seekers of Truth cabal, the most powerful band of mages in the citadel. Named Porthos, he is over five hundred years old. A solitary figure, Porthos lives alone in the highest tower of the ancient castle. Though few realize it, he is no longer sane.

Evil dreams plague his sleep this night. Terrible events are about to happen. His world is about to change. His very existence and the existence of Doissetep itself are in danger. Porthos' features twist in anguish as his nightmares grow worse and worse. A face burns in his mind, a face he recognizes—one that he had hoped never to see again.

Screaming in horror, Porthos awakens. His dreams remain vivid in his memory. There is no denying the menace that threatens Doissetep and the very existence of the Nine Traditions. Cracked, ancient lips whisper his innermost fears.

"The many have again become one. The circle is complete. Gods help us all."

THE END

Robert Weinberg

<u>RoBeRt WeInBeRg</u>

Robert Weinberg has authored eleven novels, five nonfiction books, and numerous short stories. His work has been translated into French, German, Spanish, Italian, Japanese, Russian, and most recently, Bulgarian. A noted collector of horror and fantasy fiction, he has edited over a hundred anthologies and short story collections of such material.

At present, he is serving as Vice-President of the Horror Writers Association and teaching creative writing at Columbia College in Chicago. He has co-authored White Wolf Publishing's *Vampire Diary: The Embrace* with Mark Rein•Hagen as well as a trilogy of novels titled *Blood War, Unholy Allies*, and *The Unbeholden*.

THE HORIZON WAR TRILOGY

WILL BE
CONTINUED IN

ThE
AsCenSioN
WaRriOr

BY ROBERT WEINBERG

FORTHCOMING FROM WHITE WOLF IN
NOVEMBER 1997

Also by Robert Weinberg:

Masquerade
of the Red Death
Trilogy

For ten thousand years a race of immortal vampires has waged a secret war to control mankind. Beings of incredible supernatural power, they are driven by a thirst for human blood. They are the Kindred.

But now a new player has entered the game. Known only as the Red Death, he controls forces that make even the Kindred tremble. Who *is* this avatar of evil? And is his appearance the first sign that Gehenna, the dreaded apocalypse for both humans and vampires, is about to begin?

The only two people who can stop the Red Death are Dire McCann and Alicia Varney. Racing against time as the Red Death comes closer to achieving his goal, they desperately need to find the one historian who knows the vampire's identity.

Mage:

The Ascension Second Edition

You've read the stories—now live the adventure! Magick is not dead in the world of mages! The third game in the Storyteller Series delves into a world of mystery and awesome conflict, where modern wizards wage a battle for reality itself. **Mage: The Ascension™** provides the philosophical, magickal and political setting for our **Mage** novels and anthologies.

Magick slumbers beneath the disbelief of our modern age, but it's far from dead. In the shadows, sorcerers, mad mystics and technological wizards conspire to rule our world. The future they plan may be either darker or more wonderful than we can even imagine. Yours is the power of reality!

Against the shadowy Gothic-Punk backdrop, mages with vision, purpose and mystick power strive to force back the hand of darkness and the rigid will of the Technocracy. Sinister Nephandi, wild Marauders, implacable Technomancers and the enigmatic Umbrood oppose your every step, but the ultimate enemy in this war for worldwide Ascension is within. Do you control your power, or does it control you?